WHIPLASHED

Tony Stark came out of the tunnel and accelerated down the longest straightaway on the course. Then he saw the cars in front of him veer crazily away from something. One of the cars disappeared in a fireball. It cleared and Tony saw a man on the track, walking against the direction of the race. He was big and slabbed with muscle. From his hands dangled a pair of whips that glowed and sparked as he flicked them.

The race car in front of Tony braked and swerved. A flickering line of energy shot out and destroyed the car, splitting it just behind the cockpit. The two parts of the car, spitting vapors and flame, tumbled into the crash barrier. Now Tony really stood on the brakes, but there was no way he was going to be able to avoid the guy. He hauled on the steering wheel as the guy flicked one of the whips out toward Tony's car.

"What the f—?" Tony opened his mouth, but before much more could come out, the whip sheared through the chassis of Tony's million-dollar car like a Weed Whacker through a dandelion stem.

IRON MAN 2

ALEXANDER IRVINE

Based on the Screenplay
by Justin Theroux

GRAND CENTRAL
PUBLISHING

NEW YORK   BOSTON

Book design by Giorgetta Bell McRee

Grand Central Publishing
Hachette Book Group
237 Park Avenue
New York, NY 10017
Visit our website at www.HachetteBookGroup.com.

Grand Central Publishing is a division of Hachette Book Group, Inc.
The Grand Central Publishing name and logo is a trademark of
Hachette Book Group, Inc.

Printed in the United States of America

First Edition: April 2010

10 9 8 7 6 5 4 3 2 1

To
Stan Lee, Larry Lieber, Don Heck, Jack Kirby,
and Robert Downey, Jr.

IRON MAN 2

CHAPTER 1

The C-17 was a massive aircraft. Sixty yards long, six stories tall, empty weight 140 tons and a payload max of eighty-five more tons. It was made to ferry a hundred-plus paratroopers to a drop zone somewhere within its operational range of 2,800 miles, or to fly in armored support. Or it could be retrofitted with a mobile Iron Man laboratory containing all of the command-and-control systems necessary to maintain and repair the Mark IV in the field. Jarvis could be downloaded into its vastly improved autopilot system to make the aircraft for all intents and purposes a drone. The lab facilities were built within the gargantuan cargo area, within a stabilized frame that damped a good ninety percent of the turbulence you encountered when you moved at five-hundred-plus miles per hour through an atmosphere that was always moving. It was a good plane. Solid, reliable. Like an ocean liner in the air.

And despite all that, Tony could feel every tremor and

eddy in its frame as it approached the drop zone. His stomach turned over and he braced his gauntleted hands against the sides of the toilet bowl.

"Pepper . . . I'm dying. I'm not gonna make it," he groaned.

Her voice, remarkable for its lack of sympathy, echoed a bit in the space. "Get up," she said.

Tony spoke into the bowl. He wasn't sure what else he had to throw up, but all of the warning signs were there. "I can't go through with it," he said.

"Well, you're the one who said you were Iron Man." Pepper dragged him to his feet and guided him out of the bathroom to the staging area and mobile Iron Man HQ.

Tony looked around as the C-17 made its final approach, coming in low and slow. It started to buck around a little in the winds that swirled down the Hudson River. "Do I look weird to you?" Tony asked.

"We don't have time for this," she said.

Baiting Pepper always made him feel better. "It unnerves me to think that this is how you'd react in a crisis," he said, and like magic his stomach began to settle down.

For her part, Pepper was trying to focus on the job because if she didn't she was going to open a can of worms that neither of them wanted opened again. So, the program was to stay flippant with Tony and keep things on a professional level, allowing for a bit of banter here and there because without it Tony would think something was weird and badger her into revealing what it was. Per this program, Pepper said, "It's how I react to hangovers. Vodka and Red Bull are hardly a crisis."

She put on a headset and tried to ignore Tony in the

hopes that this would provoke him to actually get ready. It was a forlorn hope, but against all odds Tony didn't entirely disappoint her. "Turn down the flame on the shame-thrower and get me some Advil," he said, which for him was nearly an apology.

"I have Motrin," Pepper said. She wasn't quite ready to let him off the hook, and she knew herself well enough to admit that she enjoyed the banter even when Tony was at his self-centered worst.

"There is something wrong—" he began, but she cut him off.

"Nothing has ever been 'right' with you."

"About offering a man a Motrin," Tony went on as if she hadn't spoken. Motrin was for periods. Offering a man a Motrin was a hostile act. An impugning of his manhood. Tony figured this should be self-evident, but he also knew that he was on a plane with a woman and an artificial intelligence, neither of which would be particularly sympathetic.

"It's a brand name," Pepper snapped. "They're both ibuprofen!"

"We don't have time for this," he moaned, as if he hadn't started the whole thing. "Abort mission!"

"You're being a baby."

"My inner child heard that."

"Your inner child needs a good spanking," Pepper said, and regretted it even as she felt her mouth forming the syllables.

With a smirk that was the first genuine sign of life he'd shown all day, Tony said, "That's just going to make him horny."

"Shut up." Pepper opened a channel to Jarvis, who was

flying the C-17 while she and Tony went back and forth. She had no doubt that Jarvis, in his AI kind of way, had bitten back on any number of sarcastic comments.

He was all business at the moment, though. "Approaching longitudinal coordinates," he said in her headset. "T minus five seconds."

"I want an omelet," Tony complained.

Pepper turned and thrust the Iron Man helmet at him. "The ground team is in place. You need to go now."

"Arriving at drop zone," Jarvis said.

Plaintive now, Tony put on the helmet but left the faceplate open. "Do you have any crackers?"

She just looked at him. Deliberately she tapped a touch screen and the C-17's cargo bay door groaned open. Even though the plane was near its stall speed—which was lower than the top speed of any of Tony's cars—the thunder of its slipstream nearly deafened her through the headset. The plane banked to its left, angling around the edge of the drop zone. Light flared from below and searchlights stabbed the sky around the C-17. Through the roar came the thump and rumble of explosions on the ground.

"Pepper!" Tony yelled. "I know I can be selfish sometimes, and . . . I know I don't say it nearly enough, but . . . " He winked. "How's my hair?"

"You've said that before!"

"I know, but this time I mean it!"

Pepper spat in the palm of her hand and slapped him on the side of the helmet. "Great!" she shouted.

Tony looked her up and down. "I like your heels!" he said, pointing at them. "You should wear those more—"

"Go!" she screamed.

He drew himself upright for the first time that day.

"You complete me," he said solemnly. Before she could decide whether he was being sarcastic or not, he closed the faceplate, spread his rams, and tipped backward out of the plane into the rushing void.

The crowd at the Stark Expo had already been treated to dancing girls in a Victoria's Secret version of the Mark III Iron Man suit. They had seen the montage of Iron Man's greatest hits: an aerial tango with a barrage of shoulder-fired missiles, a lightning raid on a pirate ship off the Horn of Africa, a head-on collision with an air-to-air missile whose explosion coming over the Expo sound system was loud enough to register on nearby seismometers. The crowd loved it. They were primed. They were ready.

And they exploded at the sight of Iron Man falling from the sky to execute a perfect somersault at the last moment and land, arms thrust up and out like a circus ringmaster's, in the center of the stage at the Tent of Tomorrow. Inside the suit, Tony thought that since he hadn't puked on the way down, he was probably ready to face the day. He glanced down and saw that he'd hit his mark almost perfectly; a little scoot of one foot and he was exactly on the automated gantry, a slightly glitzier version of the one in his lab back in Malibu. While the cheering was still at its peak, he initialized the gantry and gave the crowd one more little show.

Robot arms, with extra lights installed for a little bit of showmanship, sprouted from the stage and formed a framework around Tony, unlocking the invisible joints on the Mark IV and lifting it away from his body. He stood, legs spread and arms extended out flat a la the famous da Vinci sketch of the Vitruvian Man. From the crowd's perspective, it would look like Iron Man had been disassembled and a tuxedoed Tony Stark constructed in his place. The whole procedure took only a few seconds, after which the gantry and all of the pieces of the suit vanished back into the stage floor without any sign of where they had been—except the bit of thermal tape Tony had used as his visual spike mark.

"It's good to be back!" he called out over the tumult, which was setting his brain on fire. He remembered when he had never gotten hangovers; seemed like just last year he'd been invincible, but now his lifestyle was catching up with him . . . or he was just getting older. Six months ago, when he'd turned himself into an armored superhero, he hadn't known what a physical toll it would take. Between the explosions, the late nights, the booze, and the recent problems with palladium, Tony Stark was not the Tony Stark he had once been.

But there was a show to give. There were important ideas to foster, there were innovations to nurture, there was a new world to bring into being. Applause and cheers and the flickering of a thousand flashbulbs washed over him. He kept his arms out and let it happen. When it started to seem self-indulgent, he let it go on a little bit more. Then he motioned for calm and started to pace on the stage.

"Ladies and gentlemen," he began. "Decades ago, my father, Howard Stark, began a grand tradition. Every ten years he would level the playing field for inventors by building a city. An idealized city. A city of the future. An Expo where for five glorious months, scientists, world leaders, and corporate CEOs could come together to pursue one goal. The goal of advancing mankind."

The Jumbotron over the crowd lit up with archival footage of the first Expo. The camera panned across visions of the future ranging from the fanciful—*Your Children's Flying Car Is Here Today!* was one slogan that drew a laugh from the crowd—to the hardheaded and practical, all against the backdrop of the New York City skyline. Crowds wandered from demonstration to demonstration, looking at everything from robot vacuum cleaners to proposals to mine helium-3 from the moon as a power source for fusion reactors.

"A place to do the impossible," Tony said. "A place to unleash ideas."

Howard Stark appeared on the Jumbotron, in his workshop sometime around 1970. Some of Tony's first memories were of his father in that shop, his lab coat streaked with unnamable fluids, his pipe always going out. . . . "Everything is achievable through technology," Howard Stark said across the years. "Better living, robust health, and for the first time in human history, the possibility of world peace!" He gave the camera a nervous smile as he walked to a scale model of that first Expo. "And everything you'll need in the future can be found right here. So from all of us at Stark Industries, I'd like to personally show you the City of the Future . . . the Stark Expo! Welcome."

Applause from the crowd swelled over Tony's father's speech. Tony himself picked up the thread. "Today I'm issuing a challenge. A challenge for anyone, any country, any company to prove their value. A chance to put up their best ideas, their best inventions . . . their best foot forward, in the hopes of leaving the world a better place than the one we came into." With a bow and a flourish, he headed for the stage exit. "That's all I've got for now. Have a good time!"

On his last words, the lights cut to black and the music picked up where it had left off, booming through the darkness as the crowd went nuts all over again. The Stark Expo, bigger and better than ever, was under way.

CHAPTER 2

In a Soviet-era housing block identical to a hundred other Soviet-era housing blocks in a forgotten part of Novogireevo, a flickering television screen showed Tony Stark's grand entrance as a Russian newscaster hit the highlights of the Stark Expo's first day. It was quite a spectacle: dancing girls, flashing lights, loud music. It looked like anything in the world other than a scientific exposition.

Ivan Vanko watched. Over the announcer's voice he heard the hiss and drip of the medical equipment keeping his father alive. The old man was dying and the hiss and drip wouldn't change that, but at least it could keep him comfortable. The hospitals had given up on him months ago and sent him home to die. Since then, a nurse checked in on Anton Vanko once a day, but Ivan had been relying on certain people he knew to keep the right drugs in the IV drips. He knew many such people. Even if he did not recognize their faces, he knew them on the street from their tattoos or from the way their eyes constantly roved over crowds, looking for threats . . . or prey.

Ivan had learned of his father's sickness during the last year of his most recent prison term. Prison authorities had let him out a few months early because the hospital was sending Anton home. So Ivan was standing deathwatch in these two dingy rooms, learning the true stories of Anton Vanko's work and Tony Stark's crimes. He absorbed as much of his father's knowledge as he could during the occasional times when the old man was strong enough to talk and teach him. He sorted through old records and plans, notebooks and loose sheaves of paper covered in diagrams and equations. Soon the deathwatch would be over and Anton Vanko would be dead. When this happened, Ivan Vanko had resolved to create a memorial to his father's stolen legacy. Plans for that memorial included Tony Stark, who in the very near future would not be parading in front of cameras and adoring crowds. Because he would be dead.

He finished warming cabbage soup on the hot plate and brought the bowl carefully to his father's bed. His father was watching the television, too. "That should be you, Ivan," he said. His voice, once a gravelly baritone, was a pinched whisper now. "That should be you."

Ivan patted the old man's hand and settled near him. "Don't get so worked up, Papa."

They sat eating soup and watched the thief Tony Stark prance through his moves on the stage. Announcers spoke breathlessly of the Stark Expo and all of the wonders it would generate. Maybe, Ivan thought. And maybe not. It could be that Tony Stark himself would not live to see the end of the Expo. Which would be a kind of wonder all its own—although not what the announcers would be envisioning as they hailed Stark's visionary qualities.

Thief, Ivan Vanko thought. The world will know this about you, Tony Stark. The thought made him restless and he got up again, pacing. He went back to the worktable and flipped around in some of his father's papers. There was so much to learn.

"I'm sorry," his father said. Ivan knew he must be thinking the same thing that Ivan was thinking, but his father was a gentler man. Too gentle. What was the American expression? To swim with the sharks? Anton Vanko had never been a man who could swim with sharks.

Ivan, on the other hand, had seen the worst that Russian prisons had to offer. He was the shark that other men feared to swim with.

"All I can give you is my knowledge," his father said.

And that would be enough. Ivan shuffled through boxes of his father's papers and brought out a cardboard tube. On the peeling label he read the English words: Stark Industries. It was time for Ivan to claim his heritage, and for Tony Stark to learn the bitter truth about his own.

Was it scientific work, done in the days before scientists fully understood the dangers of their materials, that was killing his father? Or had the long decades of neglect and anonymity, of righteous jealousy, finally proved to be too much? Either way, Ivan knew the difference between understanding a cause and assigning blame.

Whatever the cause of his father's death in a medical sense, blame could be laid squarely at the feet of Howard and Tony Stark. The proof was in the tube he held, and in the knowledge his father had created and committed to paper.

Ivan turned with the tube, popping the old metal stopper off one end. He tipped the tube and shook it, spilling a sheaf of blueprints into his hand. These would be his legacy. Anton Vanko had traveled the world and come back to Moscow, poor and forgotten in his old age. His son Ivan would take up the mantle of his father's knowledge and his father's invention, and he would claim for the Vanko name the renown it deserved.

Tony Stark was on television and on the covers of magazines. Anton Vanko and his son Ivan were in a two-room flat with cold water and acres of snow-swept concrete outside, plagued by gangs who only left Ivan alone because they could read his tattoos and knew that there was softer prey to be had elsewhere.

Nobody would believe that in this two-room Novogireevo apartment were two of the great geniuses of the twentieth century. And why would they not believe it? Because the story had been suppressed, obscured. Because Anton Vanko was dying anonymously despite the debt owed him by Howard Stark. These things had to be avenged. The true story had to be told.

The wall over Ivan's worktable was a collage of clippings from coverage of Tony Stark and Iron Man. Tony posing in the suit for a magazine, holding the helmet under his arm like he was a quarterback for an American football team; Iron Man caught on a cell-phone camera through the window of a jet with engine trouble; stock photos of Tony accompanying profiles of Stark Industries' new direction now that the company had abandoned weapons manufacturing. The world's media could not get enough of Tony Stark, who looked down over Ivan's table with a smirk under the headline I AM IRON MAN in any number of languages.

Iron Man. He would learn, Ivan Vanko thought, that the world is full of things that can destroy iron.

Ivan set the tube on his worktable and started to look over the blueprints. He was about to ask his father a question when the medical machines emitted a prolonged warning beep. Ivan turned. On the heart monitor, a flat line. He dropped the blueprints and went to his father's bedside as the machine chirped its useless warning. He touched his father's face and bent his head to the old man's chest, listening for a heartbeat, but he wasn't sure he would have been able to hear it over the machines, and Anton Vanko's heart had been so weak that its beat was barely noticeable by touch. Ivan took the spoon from his father's bowl of soup and turned it over so its convex surface faced his father's nose. He held it there for a count of thirty. No vapor appeared. Anton Vanko was not breathing.

So, Ivan thought. He nodded and set the spoon down. For a few minutes the only sounds in the room were the warning beep and the answering squawk from Irina the cockatoo, perched on a stand near the window. His father had been dying for quite some time now; he had prepared himself and was oddly without grief at the moment. By any standard Ivan was not an emotional man in ordinary circumstances; he had learned the hard lessons of self-control in prison and discovered that they had value beyond the walls as well. All of his emotional resources he had poured into his relationship with his father in this, Anton Vanko's last year; other than that, Ivan had no attachment to any living being save Irina. He grew freer the fewer attachments he had, and more powerful the freer he became. The exception, again, was his father.

I am an orphan, thought Ivan Vanko. Every man must sooner or later be an orphan, unless he breaks his father's heart by dying first. It was the way of things. Perhaps it was the only true gateway to manhood, this passage through a father's death, and perhaps Ivan had been approaching the gate for so long that as he passed through it did not affect him as it would another man. Grief would still come, in its own time. Ivan knew this. There would be the details of bureaucracy, the settling of affairs, and at some point during the filling out of forms and arranging of services, grief would return.

Or, Ivan thought, I can let all of that burn. I can bury my father. I will not be here long. Soon enough I will be ready to confront Stark, and then I will leave Russia and never come back. What good will filling out forms and settling estates have done me then?

A weight lifted from Ivan's shoulders. He renounced not death, but the bureaucracy of death. He declared his independence from the nation that would have him devote his time to paperwork when there was revenge to be had. Standing in the middle of the room where his father had died, Ivan Vanko stretched out his arms and felt the vitality of his mind and body. Inspired by the death of his father, he would create. Sorrow would be the engine and the fuel.

He unplugged all of the medical machines and stood looking at them for a moment. They would be useful for parts, perhaps. As his work progressed, he would have a better idea. Ivan returned to the worktable and spread the blueprints out in the spill of lamplight. The English words ARC REACTOR filled him with a sense of purpose. It would be a great thing to show these blueprints to Tony Stark, Ivan thought. The only thing greater would be to kill him. Ivan planned to do both, or the nearest thing to it. If Stark would never see the blueprints themselves, he would see their results.

This was going to be the sweetest of ironies. Knowledge of the arc reactor technology had saved Tony Stark's life. A great arc reactor had powered his main factory in California until two years before, when it had exploded and destroyed much of the facility under circumstances that were still unclear, which to Ivan Vanko meant that the truth had been suppressed. Tony Stark believed the arc reactor was his. For the look on his face when he realized how wrong he was—for this alone, Ivan Vanko would have given his life. But he did not think it would come to that because Tony Stark was arrogant and prideful, and would never think to credit an adversary with an intellect equal to his own.

Until it was too late.

Soon, for Tony Stark, it would be too late. Ivan Vanko would do the work his father had been prevented from doing. He would have his revenge on Stark, and the world would know the name Vanko.

CHAPTER 3

Tony's chauffeur, trainer, man Friday and all-around good buddy Happy Hogan was there to meet Tony as he came offstage. "How'd it go?" Hap asked.

Tony shrugged. "I've done better."

"This way, sir." Happy pointed and they headed immediately through the wings to the backstage meeting and media area.

Dotted through the crowd of hangers-on and well-wishers were a smattering of real live innovators. Tony caught sight of software pioneer Larry Ellison, who raised an open hand. "Great speech, man," he said. Tony gave him the high five he wanted, and even managed to crack a smile for the cameras. He signed a replica Iron Man mask for a little kid, scribbled out a few other autographs, then gave Hap a quick look when a gaggle of college-aged women clustered around him wanting pictures with him.

"Not now, ladies," Happy said, and hustled Tony on down the corridor toward the backstage doors.

"Let's get out of here," Tony said.

Looking around to see if anyone had noticed Tony faltering, Hap said, "You okay, man?"

"Aces," Tony said. Truth was, he felt more like aces and eights, the dead man's hand. Between the hangover and the general ongoing trouble with the RT's palladium power source, Tony Stark felt pretty much like death warmed over. He'd started to notice odd discolorations around the arc reactor housing in his chest. Odd tendrils of a sickly purple color radiated out from it. They didn't hurt to the touch, but even though Tony wasn't a doctor—well, he did have an engineering PhD, but he wasn't a doctor doctor—he knew that odd purple lines weren't supposed to appear under a person's skin. Put that together with the unpredictable bouts of weakness and the sudden tendency of the palladium fuel cells to attract a foul-smelling greenish sludge, and the impression that emerged was one of a problem in need of immediate attention.

Tony had Jarvis working on it, but he needed to be working on it too. Jarvis was smart, but he lacked the human ability to irrationally jump from idea to idea until the solution appeared against all odds and despite the human mind's inability to stick to rational chains of logic. In other words, Jarvis lacked intuition. Tony believed that this RT-slash-palladium problem wasn't going to be solved without a large dose of intuition. Ergo, Tony needed to be there.

Instead he was opening the Expo, which he also needed to do but which was maybe not quite as urgent or life-altering. Still, he had needed to do it; he had done it; now he was going to go do other things that needed doing, like designing a new RT power source that wouldn't poison him. A plan.

Happy shoved the backstage door open and a fresh wave of shouts and flashes washed over them. Tony rose to the occasion, shrugging Hap off and playing to the crowd as they maneuvered toward the car. Through his camera-ready grin, Tony said to Hap, "This is the secret exit?"

Happy's answer was to trigger the remote that opened the roof of Tony's most recent favorite set of wheels: an Audi R8 Spyder. Ah, Tony thought. The Spyder, with all of the R8's drivability, the added zip of a 580-horsepower twin-turbo V10 engine borrowed from the RS6, and a soft top to boot—because there were times when you needed to put the top down on the Pacific Coast Highway rolling down from Malibu to Los Angeles. This R8, which Tony had owned for less than three months, was, he had decided, the finest thing ever to come out of Audi's Neckarsulm nerve center. German engineering would save him from the madding crowds through the improvident sacrifice of hydrocarbons.

Also he wanted a drink. The shakes and the more brutal effects of the day's hangover were wearing off. It was time to live again.

He grabbed the key from Happy. "I'm driving," he said. He loved the Spyder so much he was considering getting the electric version. This would make him one of the few people on the planet who owned both a fully electric car and an antique hot rod that got three miles per gallon. I am large, Tony thought. I contain multitudes.

As he was getting settled in the driver's seat, a ravishing brunette appeared next to the Spyder. "Tony," she said.

"There you are!" Tony said, although he had no idea who she was or how she'd gotten through the security perimeter. "I've been looking for you!" He had found that, in cases of hot women appearing and seeming to know him, this course of action usually worked better than the sheepish but more honest have-we-met routine. Typically he would remember their previous interactions as the conversation went along, and until then, he could shovel the BS as well as anyone. It was what worked for him.

So of course she threw him a curveball by saying, "Pleased to meet you, Mr. Stark," and thereby proving herself to be the exact opposite of the typical groupie-wannabe who came up pretending to know him so she could get to know him. By approaching the situation in a straightforward and honest manner, she utterly destabilized all of Tony's protocols, defenses, and strategies where women were concerned.

"Meet me?" Tony repeated. The footing of the conversation changed and he switched automatically into smooth-talking Tony mode. She was worth knowing, that was for damn sure. "Wait, I'm sorry . . . we don't know each other? That ends now. Let's start with names, Miss . . . ?"

"Marshal," she said.

Still vamping, Tony nodded. If he didn't know her, how had she just walked up to him like this? Didn't he have security people who were supposed to stop strangers? Or maybe he'd told them not to impede the progress of gorgeous brunettes. "Irish. I get it. Tempers and depression," Tony said. "Promise me you won't get sad when we fight. On to first names. I'm Tony, Ms. Marshal, and you are . . . "

"U.S.," she said, and slapped an envelope onto his chest.

Tony didn't raise his hands to take it, but it didn't matter. If she'd put it in contact with his person, he was served. "Uh-oh," he said.

"You are hereby ordered to appear before the Senate Armed Services Committee tomorrow morning at nine a.m.," she said. She let go of the envelope and turned around.

"Who put you up to this?" Tony called after her. "Senator Dodd? Boehner?" Both were his enemies, although for reasons that were as different as the two mens' politics. "And using you!" Tony went on, unable to help admiring her as she walked away. "That was a nice touch. Big style points there."

He turned to look at Happy, who was reading over the subpoena. "Do I have to do that?"

"This?" Happy said. He looked up at Tony with what seemed to Tony to be an inordinately smug grin as he crumpled the subpoena up and threw it in the back seat. "Yeah. I think you do."

Nine tomorrow morning in Washington, Tony thought. A fate worse than death. He could fly, he could drive. Either way he was going to have to find Pepper, who right then was still up in the air with Jarvis. One show after another. That was the life of Tony Stark. And nobody was going to have any sympathy for him, that was for sure.

Might as well fly to Washington, Tony decided. What he really wanted to do was fly down in the Mark IV and come in for a hot landing through the roof of the main hearing chamber. He tried to think of ways that he might be able to justify such an action, but even his most contorted chains of logic didn't do the trick. So he'd just have to drive out to the airport instead and coax Pepper down out of the sky.

That night Tony distracted himself at the hotel by tinkering with some of the less refined features of the Mark IV. The big design innovation from the Mark III, in his opinion as the suit's designer—okay, co-designer with Jarvis, if you wanted to get technical, but since he'd designed Jarvis too Tony figured there must be some kind of transitive property of creation that meant he had designed the whole suit—the big design innovation was the use of nonmetallic polymers and carbon-nanotube meshes in a number of the suit's components instead of the titanium alloy that was the building block of the Mark III's armor. Put together with a subroutine running the gantry and a reservoir of raw material, essentially these design changes meant that Tony could build parts of the suit at will any time he needed to put it on.

He hadn't done it this way yet because he hadn't tested the process to his satisfaction, but he knew it would work. If he could refine the process the way he planned to, he would be able to create the suit on demand as long as he was carrying around an extra RT to fuel the molecular engineering processes necessary for the creation of complex polymers and pure carbon nanotubes from ambient materials.

All he had to work with in the hotel was a suitcase-carried virtual desktop, complete with a downloaded version of Jarvis. "Jarvis," he said. "What if I could make the suit using the same process I used to make that Tech-Ball thingy?"

"What indeed?" Jarvis asked. "There would be some reductions in certain qualities due to a materials change, but in all likelihood you could create a suit that was highly resistant to heat, plasma, and electrical energy attacks, if perhaps slightly less resistant to attacks based on the delivery of kinetic energy."

"Not good enough," Tony said. "I want it all. Did I bring a Tech-Ball?"

"In the breast pocket of your suit jacket, sir. Which I believe you discarded over the back of the chair you are sitting in."

Tony retrieved the Tech-Ball without commenting on Jarvis' snark. He'd built it in, and he would just have to deal with it. Although he did think that the snark had somehow interacted with Jarvis' ability to channel its own emergent pathways of consciousness in a suspicious way. Jarvis got snarkier faster than he developed any of his other qualities, which led Tony to believe that somehow either snark or the impulse toward snark was intimately tied to intelligence.

Or, Pepper might have commented, intimately tied to the particular intelligence of Jarvis' creator, and thus reflected in the structure of Jarvis.

In any case, Jarvis was right about the location of the Tech-Ball. Tony spun it around in his palm, thinking that he was going to have to figure out a better name for it, especially if he was going to develop and market it. Also he would need to figure out just what the hell Joe and Jane Six-Pack would do with a Tech-Ball. What did your average human in an information economy need with a small sphere that could alter the properties of its matter on command?

When Tony had come up with the Tech-Ball on a brief, inspired research excursion during the initial design phase of the Mark IV armor, he had thought at first that it would change the world. Then he had realized that it was so astonishingly cool that he had no real idea what to do with it. Then he had decided that it was so astonishingly cool that he wanted to keep it for himself.

This was not, as his late father might have commented, in keeping with the spirit of the Stark Expo, however. Tony knew this. He planned to debut the Tech-Ball at some point during the Expo, and get some of the world's brainiest people working on the development of possible applications for it.

None of that would happen tonight. The only things that were going to happen tonight were: a bit more tinkering with the materials issues surrounding the potential new version of the Mark IV; the occasional indulgence in an alcoholic beverage of high quality and exorbitant price; a brief conversation with Pepper to make sure that he didn't walk into the Senate hearing the next morning without knowing something crucial that he should have known. Pepper, more even than Jarvis, was an external brain for Tony. She was also, of course, an enormously capable executive assistant, the most trustworthy and admirable person he knew, and in many ways the one person in the world who kept Tony Stark something like sane.

He couldn't tell her any of that, though. At least not too often. What he could do tonight, Tony thought as he poured himself a drink, was get her in here and find out what those conniving senators had in store for him.

Although what the hell, this was Atlantic City. What was the point of stopping here on the way to DC if he wasn't going to take advantage of what the boardwalk had to offer?

Tony left the drink on the table and his phone in his pocket. Off to blow off some steam, he thought.

CHAPTER 4

It was not the first time Tony had testified before the
Senate, but he had a feeling it was going to be the least
pleasant. He was at a table more or less by himself. In the
first row of seats behind him, a line of uniforms and gray
crew cuts interrupted only by the presence of Pepper, who
periodically bounced up to whisper something cajoling or
cautionary into his ear. Behind that first row was a gallery
of citizens who had waited in line to see the show. Tony
wasn't sure what to make of a person who would wait in
line to watch a Senate hearing; he was all for civic engagement . . . well, no. Who was he kidding? He couldn't
care less about civic engagement. These people were here
to see him roasted by the slings and arrows of barbarian
senators. Tony loved to mix a metaphor when no one was
listening.

The trick here, he thought, was going to be to put his
head down, let everything roll over him, and rope-a-dope

his way to freedom. For it to work, he would have to get the crowd on his side. This might not be easy, since in the grip of a savage hangover such as the one Tony was at that moment experiencing, the human mind was not always at its nimble and the human tongue was prone to damaging slips. So he would have to simultaneously wow the masses with his improvisational abilities and keep a lid on those abilities so they didn't go too far.

As of right that moment, perhaps twenty minutes into the hearing, Tony thought it was working. He was getting laughs, and more importantly, the faces on the senatorial dais were getting more and more . . . well . . . stern.

His primary antagonist was a certain Senator Stern, of nondescript politics except for a notable skill at grandstanding. Tony decided to be nice to him. Mostly. He fiddled with the Tech-Ball he'd made the other day, putting part of his brain to work envisioning world-changing uses to which it might be put.

"I'm sorry we're not seeing eye-to-eye here, Mr. Stark, but according to these contracts you agreed to provide the U.S. taxpayer with—" He flipped through a file and read. " 'All current and as yet undiscovered weapons systems.' Now do you or do you not, at present, possess a very specialized weapon—"

"I do not," Tony said firmly. Out of the corner of his eye he saw someone enter the hearing chamber. The face was familiar but he couldn't place it right away.

"You are not in possession of said weapon?"

"It depends on how we define the word 'weapon,' " Tony said. From a certain perspective, he nearly added, the Tech-Ball could be a weapon. Clearly its intended function had little to do with combat, but you could hit someone with it. Did that make it a weapon?

"The Iron Man weapon," Stern said.

"My device does not fit that description."

"And how would you describe your device?" Stern's tone of practiced weariness grated on Tony. If they wanted a show and they were going to perform roles, he thought the least he could do for the assembled masses—not to mention those poor suckers who happened to be watching on TV—was shake things up with a little improv.

"I would describe it by defining it as what it is," he said.

"Which is?"

"A high-tech prosthesis." Laughter echoed down from the gallery. Tony glanced over at Pepper and saw that she had buried her face in her hands. This was his clearest signal yet that he had the rest of the crowd eating out of his hand, or would very shortly.

Stern started to get his senatorial dander up. "The Iron Man suit is the most powerful weapon on the face of the Earth," he said. "Yet you use it to sell tickets to your theme park."

"My father conceived of the Stark Expo to transcend the need for war by addressing its sole cause: the coveting of resources," Tony said. He stuck the Tech-Ball in his pocket so it would stop distracting him, but the idea of using it to conduct energy stuck with him and the next thing out of his mouth was, "Primarily energy. If your priority in this hearing was truly the safety—"

"Our priority is for you to turn the Iron Man suit over to the military."

"I am Iron Man," Tony said. "The suit and I are one. To turn over the Iron Man suit would be to turn over myself.

And that would be indentured servitude or prostitution, depending on what state you're in."

Stern played along after a glance at the gallery told him he would have to. "I enjoy a good laugh," he said. "This, however, is no laughing matter. I am no expert in—"

"Prostitution? Of course not. You're a senator." This got a bigger laugh than the prosthesis crack. Out of the corner of his eye, Tony saw Pepper glaring daggers at him. *I know, I know,* he thought. *I should reel myself in and act appropriately. But how can any of these people take this seriously?*

"On weapons, Mr. Stark. Fortunately we have someone here to testify who is. I'd like to call upon Justin Hammer, our current primary defense contractor." Stern leaned back to murmur at one of his senatorial colleagues as Justin Hammer strode down the aisle. He was like a museum specimen of American Gladhander, subspecies Ivyleaguensis. His tie was a little loose, his pants a little tight, his hair a little long over the forehead and a little too willing to flip boyishly around as he nodded at acquaintances on his way to be sworn in.

This was Tony's successor at the top of the arms-industry food chain. In Tony's opinion, he looked like he ought to be selling Saturns. Or Oldsmobiles.

As Hammer passed Tony's table, Tony murmured, "Sloppy seconds," just loud enough for Hammer to hear.

"Blow me," Hammer said without breaking stride.

Tony turned his focus back to the committee. "Let the minutes reflect," he said, enunciating clearly into the microphone, "that I observe Mr. Hammer entering the chamber and am wondering if and when an expert will also be in attendance."

Senator Stern's gavel banged over another outburst of laughter. If Hammer was bothered, though, he didn't show it. "I may well not be an expert. But you know who was?" he asked, playing to the gallery but addressing the question to Tony. "Your dad. Howard Stark. A father to us all, and to the military-industrial age. And just to be clear: he was no flower child. He was a lion. He knew that technology was the sword, not the shield that protects this great nation. A sword that when rattled can calm threats from foreign lands and slay dangers before they arrive on our shores."

Tony let Hammer talk. He was congenitally disposed to grandstanding, which was fine. The bit about Tony's father, now, that was different. Something would have to be done about that. Tony fiddled with the Tech-Ball, manipulating its shape and the consistency of its material. What a nifty little toy it was. One of these days he was going to figure out a way to make money with it.

Hammer went on. "Anthony Stark has created a sword with untold possibilities, and yet he insists it's a shield! He asks us to trust him as we cower behind it!" With a head shake angled exactly toward the main network camera feed, Hammer went on more slowly. "I love peace. But we live in a world of grave threats. Threats that Mr. Stark will not always be able to foresee."

Tony rolled his eyes. Anthony? Nobody had called him Anthony since maybe the first day of kindergarten, which he'd only gone to because other kids did.

"God forbid a similar technology is created by a country far less moral than our own," Hammer said. "Believe me, ladies and gentlemen, when I say that Mr. Stark keeps the secrets of that suit at the peril of our citizens." From the breast pocket of his suit, Hammer took an Iron Man action figure. "I found this in my sister's car," he said with great gravity. "It belongs to my nephew, Timmy. He believes in Iron Man."

All of this so far had been played to the cameras, but now Hammer turned directly to Tony, turning the entire hearing room into a stage for just the two of them. "Please don't let him down, Tony."

Okay, Tony thought. This has maybe gone on long enough. He slipped his new PDA from a fancy bit of holo-enabled glass he and Jarvis had put together the week before. It was a rectangle of fiber optics, pure computing power that looked like a piece of Plexiglas.

Senator Stern didn't bother to conceal his satisfaction at Hammer's theatrics. "Thank you, Mr. Hammer. The committee would now like to invite Lieutenant Colonel James T. Rhodes into the Chamber." He looked toward the green room door, where Rhodey was entering in full dress uniform, looking uncomfortable and out of place. Unlike the brass sitting in the front row, Rhodey didn't like being in front of people and he didn't like dealing with politicians. This would probably mean that his career was topped out at bird colonel, but he was fine with that. He'd told Tony on a number of occasions that if a promotion to general ever came up, he would turn it down. Rhodey wanted to stay active and in the field as much as possible.

Tony met him in the aisle and shook hands. It was a bit stiff, but Tony was glad to see Rhodey there. If there was any living human Tony knew he could count on to do the right thing, that person was James Rhodes.

On the other hand, it would have been nice to know

about it ahead of time. "I didn't expect this," Tony murmured to Rhodey as Rhodey passed.

"Look," Rhodey said, "it's me. I'm here. Deal with it."

"I have before me," Stern said after Rhodey had been sworn in, "a report on the Iron Man compiled by Colonel Rhodes. Colonel, can you please read into the minutes page fifty-four, paragraph four?"

"Certainly, Senator," Rhodey said. "May I first point out that I was not briefed on this hearing, nor prepared to testify—"

"Duly noted," Stern said without looking up from his notes. "Please continue."

Ever the good soldier, Rhodey swallowed the snub and went on. "This paragraph out of context does not reflect the summary of my findings."

"Did you or did you not write, quote, 'Iron Man presents a potential threat to the security of both the nation and her interests'?"

By way of answering, Rhodey continued and completed the quote. " 'As he does not operate within any definable branch of government.' I, however, went on to recommend that the benefits far outweigh the liabilities—"

"Thank you, Colonel Rhodes," Stern said.

Undeterred, Rhodey finished his sentence. "—And that it would be in our best interest to fold Mr. Stark into the existing chain of command."

God love you, Rhodey, Tony thought.

"I'm not a joiner," he said, "but I would consider Secretary of Defense. Provided the hours could be—"

"This isn't a job interview," Stern said. Apparently, Tony thought, the senator suffered from some kind of interruption-related disability. "Colonel Rhodes," Stern went on, "please read page fifty-six of your report."

Rhodey glanced at the indicated page and brought the copy of the report to a bank of monitors, which lit up as he approached, each displaying a blurry satellite image. He sat and took a laser pointer from a ribbon-encrusted breast pocket. "Intelligence suggests that the devices seen in these photos are in fact all attempts at making manned copies of Mr. Stark's suit." He indicated points on each of the monitors where a squinting and imaginative observer might have been able to infer the presence of something like an armored suit.

Enough, Tony thought. He fired up the mini virtual desktop on his PDA and set to work getting some visual evidence that would actually prove something . . . even if it wasn't what Stern and his colleagues had set out to prove.

"This has been corroborated by our allies and local intelligence on the ground," Rhodey was saying, "indicating that they are quite possibly, at this moment, functional."

Tony stood and touched an icon on his PDA. "Let's see what's really going on here," he said as he slaved the bank of monitors to a subroutine of Jarvis that ran natively on the PDA. "If . . . I . . . may," he said, vamping as a series of classified videos—some of them existing only on intranets behind security walls that the Department of Defense would never get through—loaded and began to play. At top left, a North Korean proving ground was hosting a test flight of a skeletal suit whose occupant looked deeply uncertain about his role in the proceedings. Something like a repulsor, mounted on a directional jet in the suit's back, fired, lifting suit and pilot into the air. He lifted one arm and fired off a series of mini-rockets from a magazine mounted on one forearm.

"You're right," Tony said, "North Korea is well on its . . . "

Suit and pilot disappeared in a flash of light that overwhelmed the camera. When the image resolved again, the smoking remains of the suit were being hosed down by firefighters.

"Nope," Tony said. "Whew. That was a relief."

The same or similar results played out on the other monitors. "Let's see how Russia is doing . . . oh dear," Tony went on. "Japan! Japan has to be closer—ohh, I guess not. India? Not so much. Germans are good engineers. Yowch. That's gonna leave a mark." Then he froze all of the looping videos except one, and expanded that one until it took up the entire bank of monitors. "Wait," he said. "The United States is in the game. Look, it's Justin Hammer."

Looking over his shoulder at the camera crews filming the hearing, Tony added, "Hey guys, you might want to push in on Hammer for this."

What unfolded on the single remaining video was a comic disaster. Hammer himself stood off to one side of the frame as a crew strapped a volunteer into an armored exoskeleton. It had clearly been constructed with the Iron Man suit in mind, but Tony could tell by looking at it that the weight distributions were all wrong for the location of the propulsion systems. Hammer stood back and winked at the camera.

The real-life Justin Hammer in the Senate chamber looked like he had a mouthful of spoiled milk. On the monitor bank, Hammer's prototype suit lifted off into the air over the proving ground, which was a sand pit out behind Hammer Industries' main manufacturing facility. There was a nice landscape shot of the hills behind it as the prototype's exhaust carved a perfect loop-de-loop against the blue sky. The prototype fired off a number of small rockets. As they detonated on the ground, Hammer whooped and said something self-congratulatory toward the camera. The loop-de-loop turned into a spiral at exactly that moment, and the thrusters cut out as with the operator moving parallel to the ground. By itself, this would have been unfortunate; when pieces of the prototype started to fall off things turned comic as the operator tumbled out of the air with a trailing yell. He landed in a sitting position, kicking up a huge plume of sand. Hammer could be heard yelling to cut the video.

Tony froze the playback on the moment when the operator hit the ground. He glanced back at the crowd and saw winces and grimaces as everyone present experienced sympathetic pains in their tailbones.

"I would like to point out," Hammer said, "that that test pilot survived and only suffered minor spinal bruising. He is currently white-water rafting with his family."

Senator Stern pointed his gavel at Tony. "By making a mockery of this hearing you are shortchanging the American people!" he said with all the high dudgeon he could muster. Which was quite a bit; Stern had served three terms and developed his dudgeon until it was the envy of even his senatorial colleagues.

"Agreed," Tony said. "Camera one, go tight on me and give me a slow creep on the senator. It's time for a little transparency."

"My patience is waning," Stern warned, but now it was Tony's turn to interrupt.

"You want full disclosure?" he asked. "I don't trust you. I'm sorry. You're creepy. I may be a little nutty. I may go off half-cocked sometimes, but—strangely—I am inherently trustworthy, and have been for the better part of six months." Tony turned to face the camera, which was still tight on him, broadcasting his image to whoever happened to be watching Senate hearings at the moment. "Look at me. Now look at him. Now look at him looking at me."

Stern's face appeared on the monitors. "I think we've heard enough," the senator spluttered.

"The good news is," Tony said, recapturing the camera's attention, "I'm your nuclear deterrent. The goal of the suit is not to use it. And it's working. You're welcome. I have successfully privatized world peace. Not that I'm above throwing on the suit and breaking up an international bar fight here and there. But that's just putting my finger in a dike. No offense, Senator Buxton; I don't mean to belittle the ongoing issues you've had with your levee systems. The point is—"

Gavel poised, Stern said, "There had better be one."

"You want my property," Tony said. "You can't have it. I try to play ball with these ass-clowns and be their dirty little secret. Something goes boink overseas, I get the three-a.m. booty call. Usually from the Pentagon. Or, often from one of the faces you see before you."

He was starting to wonder how much more time he was going to have, as unrest spread through the gallery and Stern said something about producing proof. One of the keys to an effective speech was knowing when to end it. "My bond is with the American people, whom

I will always keep safe," Tony said. "And I will serve
the people of this great nation at the pleasure of . . . myself." He gestured for the camera to come in tight on
him again. "And if there's one thing I have proven to the
world at large by any metric, it's that you can count on
me to pleasure myself."

And there was the gavel, hammering down as Stern
said "Adjourned!" and rose to stalk off the committee dais. Tony hopped down from the lectern he'd taken
over, flashed peace signs, blew kisses, the whole works.
He caught Justin Hammer's eye and added a final line
straight into the camera, just because he was Tony Stark
and he could.

"I don't know if I'm a sword or a shield," he said. "But
I do know that Hammer is a tool."

On that line, coverage of the hearing ended and the
Senate chamber erupted. Reporters ran to file reports,
Senate aides ran to make meetings and spin the reporters, various hangers-on milled around figuring out what
to do next. Tony winked at Senator Stern. "I don't get why
you're after me like this," he said. "I did you a big favor.
I successfully privatized world peace. What more do you
want from me?"

But Stern wasn't playing along. "Fuck you, buddy," he
said. "We're done here." Flanked by flunkies, he stalked
out of the chamber. Hmm, Tony thought. Time to redirect
campaign contributions.

If he'd been watching the monitors, he would have seen
one of them catch Justin Hammer heading up the main
aisle toward the exits. He might have even seen Hammer
snap his prop Iron Man action figure in two.

CHAPTER 5

Fool, thought Ivan Vanko. He was working and watching television. Two televisions, as a matter of fact. And he was carrying on an occasional conversation with Irina the cockatoo, who was named after the pianist Irina Zaritz-kaya, whose performances of Chopin Ivan's father had found very affecting. On one television, Tony Stark was making a mockery of his country's democratic processes and the buffoons entrusted to oversee them. Ivan could appreciate this impulse. He too considered himself opposed to the mechanisms of the state. But Stark represented something even worse than state power. Stark was the unchecked power of money to get what it wanted regardless of law or morality. Tony Stark could build the most powerful weapon on the planet and then declare it was not a weapon, and because he was a rich man the senators would not treat him the way they would a poor man who made such claims. The poor man would have left the Senate chamber in manacles.

Of course, in America the poor man could not build the most powerful weapon in the world. For that you needed money.

In Russia, you also needed money if what you wanted was the most powerful weapon in the world. But in Russia, hardship taught ingenuity. Ivan Vanko had plans but very little money. So he relied on ingenuity. That was what he had on the tabletop in front of him. Stark had known deprivation only once, in a cave when his life depended on his ingenuity. He had survived, and like people all over the world, Ivan Vanko had followed the story eagerly. The narrative of Tony Stark's transformation from callous weapons merchant to armor-suited idealist was irresistible.

The stories we tell ourselves, Ivan Vanko thought, have much to teach us. He was nearly finished. All that remained was the alloy mix, melted and poured in exactly the right amount at exactly the right time. The last time he had attempted this, the building superintendent's wife had complained for weeks about the smell. She was an old woman who did not know the language spoken by the ink on Ivan Vanko's skin. It was interesting to be spoken to as if he were an ordinary person, one more man to be shrilled at by an old woman.

Her husband had quietly apologized and left a bottle of vodka on Ivan's doorstep the next day. Ivan had returned it. He needed no apologies from old women.

He would, however, be willing to hear an apology from Tony Stark, perhaps in the last moments of Stark's life when the true and monumental nature of his crimes had become clear to him.

On another television, an old episode of *Nu Pogodi*

played silently. Yes, Ivan thought. *Nu, pogodi*—you just wait. He had always loved the wolf and wanted him to catch the hare. But Ivan Vanko was no fool; he knew this could never happen. The wolf was a hapless villain, forever pursuing ridiculous schemes and forever doomed by the luck of the hare.

The coffeehouse intellectuals might have said that Ivan identified with the wolf because to him, Tony Stark was the hare. But Ivan was not a coffeehouse intellectual; there were few of those in Novogireevo. What this neighborhood had was anonymous commercial buildings, apartment buildings seemingly designed on a unifying principle of soul-deadening monotony, and roving gangs whose favorite pastime was killing people who didn't look Russian.

And it had Ivan Vanko . . . who, unlike the wolf of *Nu Pogodi*, had a plan that was going to work.

It was the first episode on the television right then. This was still one of Ivan's favorites. The wolf and hare were not yet fully formed characters the way they would be in later episodes. Or perhaps the truth was that the hare was not. The wolf was who he was, beautifully and essentially, from the first frame of the first cartoon, when he picks a cigarette up off the ground and inhales as if all of life's joys paled in comparison to this bit of good fortune. Then he sees the hare and the hunt is on.

Ivan was not the wolf. Primarily this was because he understood that life's joys were partial and bittersweet, hardly reducible to a moment's pleasure in a rescued sidewalk cigarette butt.

Certain things, however—certain beliefs and certain actions—could attain a kind of perfection. He forgot the wolf, forgot the hare, and poured liquid metal. The heat washed over his face, the sweat stung his eyes. Ivan reveled in the heat and light and in the white-hot burn of his belief.

After the pour, Ivan watched the thin alloy ring cool, losing its glow and becoming a tarnished silver color. He had the casing already machined and waiting, the wiring linked and spliced into a delivery conduit, and the interior of the arc space was polished and lined with a superconductive film. A Russian, Vasily Petrov, had first described the arc discharge in 1802; the world had been using his work since then. Ivan intended to claim the arc reactor for Mother Russia as well. Typically his feelings of nationalism were muted by his experiences in prison and with the apparatus of the Russian state; when he thought of the rest of the world, however—and especially when he thought of Tony Stark—he was a Russian first.

It was a Russian tradition to make do in the face of adversity. Ivan would do this. He was building an arc reactor in the living room of a dilapidated flat with pirated electricity and no tool more sophisticated than a tabletop lathe. It could be done—Stark had famously done it in an Afghan cave—and Ivan was going to do it. Let Stark see that he was not the only man capable of genius.

The alloy ring had cooled. Ivan glanced over at Nu Pogodi. The wolf was drawing a bead on the water-skiing hare with a speargun. Perfect timing, Ivan thought. It was time to take the next step.

Four hours later, Ivan's eyes watered and his neck ached from hunching over the fine soldering and smithing work required in the construction of a functioning miniature arc reactor. Until that exact moment, only two had existed in the world. Now there was a third, tiny and perfect, glowing on his worktable as if possessing secret knowledge. This was a moment his father would have loved. Ivan wanted to share it with someone, so he reached out one hand toward Irina's perch and waited for her to climb onto his knuckles.

"Isn't it beautiful, Irina?" He put a seed between his lips and leaned close to her. Irina cocked her head from side to side, then plucked it from his mouth. Ivan watched her manipulate it, marveling at what she could do with just a beak and a tongue. If she had hands, he thought, Irina might make arc reactors too.

But she did not. Ivan Vanko did, so he had made an arc reactor. He was the second man in history to do so. It would forever gall him that Stark was the first, that Stark had suppressed Anton Vanko's pioneering work and then taken sole credit for further developments. Ivan did not know the details of what had happened six months before when the Stark Industries building in Los Angeles had been destroyed. Rumors had flown of a giant robot, of terrorist infiltration, of a second Iron Man. The truth was known to very few people, and Ivan was not one of them. Nor did he care to be; he was satisfied to know that the building's arc reactor had exploded, seeing that as a warning shot fired by the universe across the smug and corrupt bow of Tony Stark and the company that bore his name.

How he wished he could have seen it.

The tiny arc reactor on his table could explode with enough power to level much of Ivan's apartment building. How much larger would an overload explosion have been in a full-sized reactor? Ivan, like every other literate human on the planet, had seen pictures of the arc reactor that powered Stark's California facility. He could imagine that the release of energy must have been enough to change local weather patterns. Ah, to have been there.

He would have to console himself with being there when Tony Stark the man was destroyed.

"Do you really love me for who I am?" he asked Irina. "Or do you tolerate me because I fill your stomach?"

He thought he knew the answer, and it was fine with him. Not all mutually beneficial arrangements needed to be emotional. He put Irina back. She groomed one of her wings and Ivan returned his attention to his newest creation.

The arc reactor fit perfectly in the palm of Ivan's hand. He plugged it into the ancient desktop computer he used for math he couldn't do in his head and ran a diagnostic program he had written. All of the arc reactor's processes were happening exactly as they were supposed to, within the parameters he had sought.

"This is a great day, Papa," Ivan said. "Today there is a new future in the world."

And tomorrow there would be meetings with strangers. Ivan mistrusted strangers, but he knew of the Ten Rings. He had seen men in prison wearing that symbol on their bodies. Those men, whatever else anyone knew about them, were granted deference and respect by even the most hardened gangsters—and guards—in Kopeisk Prison or any of the other prisons that were the worst of the worst. Ivan had seen several of those, and heard stories from the rest. Along the way he had seen those men with the ten rings tattooed on the sides of their necks and known that they were part of something larger than an ordinary gang or criminal syndicate.

So when he needed to put his plans into motion, he had haunted the train stations looking for the tattoo of ten rings. Then a conversation had begun and he had been told to look for a certain Mongolian who could often be seen placing bets on chess games at the Phoenix Chess Club, near the First State Ball Bearing plant.

Two weeks ago, when it became clear that his father did not have long to live, Ivan had found the Mongolian. The day after tomorrow, he was due to meet the Mongolian again. Then he would know whether the Ten Rings would help him, and what they would be willing to do. Along the way he had learned a little about the organization, but just enough to realize that there was much more he did not know—and that he was better off that way. The Ten Rings apparently were the kind of organization that either killed you or absorbed you once you knew a certain amount about them and how they worked. Ivan had no desire to be killed and less desire to be absorbed. He was his own man, with his own goals and his own methods. If the Ten Rings could help him, he would find their help useful. If not, he would find his own way.

"Papa," Ivan said. "This new future. I will take hold of it. It will be ours, yours and mine. A Vanko future."

The arc reactor glowed. Irina cackled. Outside, the sun was setting and it was beginning to snow. Ivan began to piece together the next part of his plan.

CHAPTER 6

During the course of her professional relationship with Tony Stark, Pepper had many times considered the philosophical proposition that no good deed goes unpunished. And now, on Tony's new scramjet (a loaner courtesy of SpaceX and Elon Musk), which was accelerating fast enough that all of them were pressed lightly back into their seats, she considered it again.

Her crime—or, put another way, her good deed for which she was being punished—was inviting Rhodey to catch a ride on Tony's plane back to California. Since Rhodey was stationed at Edwards Air Force Base, northeast of Los Angeles, and since he and Tony had been friends for quite a number of years, and since this friendship was currently strained, Pepper had reasoned that there were several good and complementary reasons for extending the invitation. And even knowing Tony's occasional propensity to act like a twelve-year-old, she had not anticipated the current situation. Right now he was so steamed that he wasn't talking to either her or Rhodey. He was barely being civil to the flight attendants, who usually inspired him at least to flirt.

She sat in the acceleration couch between her boss and one of her boss's best friends. One of them would not talk to the other; both were feeling betrayed; Pepper was wishing she had pursued a long-forgotten dream to be an actuary. "This is ridiculous," she said. "Are you for real? Are you not going to talk for the entire flight?"

Looking at her, Tony pointed at Rhodey, who still owed him an apology for ambushing him at the hearing. "What's he doing here? Why isn't he on Hammer's plane?"

"I was invited," Rhodey said.

"Of course he was invited," Pepper said. "Rhodey is always welcome."

"Not by the owner of the plane," Tony said.

"Tony—"

"That's bad jetiquette," Tony said. "Guests are not allowed to invite other guests."

Rhodey tried again. "Tony—"

"I'm not a guest," Pepper said. A warning tone crept into her voice.

"Can you tell him I'm not talking to him?"

"Then listen," Rhodey said. "What's wrong with you? Do you know that showing classified footage on national television is—"

"Tantamount to stabbing your best friend in the back at a Senate hearing?" Tony interrupted. "How about a heads-up next time?"

This was where, if either of them had been rational, one of them would have pointed out (and the other acknowledged) the possibility that Rhodey hadn't had any more notice about his appearance than Tony did, and that Tony had in fact not said anything to Rhodey about a subpoena, which put Tony on delicate ground when it came to vilifying Rhodey for not saying exactly the same thing.

But that both of them were long past the point at which they could be rational was Pepper's impression, and Rhodey confirmed it. "What, do you want me to Twitter you about classified intel and your subpoena to appear before the United States Senate?" he asked.

This was what a good counselor would have called escalation. "Talk through her," Tony said, pointing at Pepper despite having just talked directly to Rhodey and responded directly to something Rhodey had said to him. She wondered what a counselor would call that. Some kind of evasion, no doubt. Tony excelled at evasions of all kinds.

Including evasions of certain realities that existed between him and one Virginia Potts.

That thought put Pepper over some threshold of whose existence she had only been dimly aware. No, she thought. No no no. Enough. She bent forward, fighting the jet's acceleration—God, it was fast—and dug through her purse. "Forget it. I'm putting on my iPod."

"No," Tony said. "Let's talk schedule."

"Now?"

Rhodey looked on in amazement. "How do you put up with this?"

"Don't get me started," Pepper said.

"Talk though her," Tony said. "Not to her."

Dropping her iPod back in her purse, Pepper took out a notepad. "Fine. Since you brought it up. Can we schedule the call with the Secretary General of the UN? It's embarrassing that we missed—"

"Birthday party," Tony said.

"Absolutely," Rhodey said. "Let's move that to the top of the list. Tony must party."

Pepper took a deep breath. She wondered how long it would take her to hit the ground if she jumped out of the plane at that exact moment. "I recommend that in keeping with the times, we do something small, elegant," she began, determinedly assuming the role of party planner.

"What, you want me to do Ashtanga yoga at a retreat in Ojai?" Tony said.

Pepper changed the subject. It was either that or comment on the excruciating financial double-entendres, and she didn't think she could survive that. "Monaco," she said. "I think we should cancel."

The Monaco Historic Grand Prix was one of Tony's favorite biennial rituals. Pepper knew what he would say before he opened his mouth, but that was part of being Tony Stark's executive dogsbody girl-Friday. You said the things you had to say, he did whatever he wanted to, and you were in a position to give him a finger-wagging I-told-you-so when his hardheadedness blew up in his face.

"Absolutely not," Tony said, exactly as Pepper had anticipated. "I was invited to race my car. And I never turn down an invitation."

Which Pepper knew, of course. She had seen the financials on the car. Stark Motor Racing had spent a ton of money restoring the historic race car that had once taken up space in Howard Stark's garage and now sat in Tony's, next to all of the other expensive toys he owned.

"Great," Rhodey said, with enormous false enthusiasm. "Oh. Wait. No, that would be a terrible idea."

"What?" Tony looked suspicious.

"Hanging out with you is bad for our friendship," Rhodey said. "And it sure as hell is bad for business."

Tony looked away toward one of the windows, out of which Pepper could see the sky darkening to something like black. They were high, high, up, and angled so from one side of the plane you were looking straight out into what appeared to be space. "You like working with him," Tony said. "I can tell."

Rhodey shrugged. Pepper recognized the way he saw a small advantage and immediately committed all resources to maximizing it. That was classic military doctrine. "You want your military contract back, I can arrange it," he said, knowing that Tony did not want that but also knowing that Tony wanted the access and adoration and security that came with long-term Pentagon contracts. Rhodey also knew, and Pepper saw him working, the plain but unspoken truth that Tony Stark wanted Rhodey to think well of him and approve of his choice to abandon weapons manufacturing for something that was at least superficially less destructive.

Tony was in some ways a delicate flower. Pepper had learned to keep him watered and positioned so the sun hit him in the right ways. She thought that Rhodey knew some of those ways too. She also wished that Tony was not quite so high maintenance, but maybe that was just the price of working with genius. If she had gone on to become an actuary, she doubted that she would ever have had experiences like the ones Stark Industries—and Tony personally—had given her.

"I can't believe you're going to Monaco with him," Tony said. "Monaco's our place."

It was true that Tony and Rhodey had gone to previous Monaco Historic Grand Prix races. It was also true that neither of them had ever thought that those races had any special significance until they had been positioned that way by Tony's immediate snit on the topic. You couldn't reward this kind of behavior, Pepper thought. Tony got manipulative when he thought people were looking elsewhere for support and money and contacts and validation. That manipulation was no basis for a relationship that might involve billions of dollars in defense contracts—not to mention the security of the (broadly construed) free world.

Rhodey appeared to have gone through the same thought process Pepper had just articulated to herself. Suppressing a smile, he repeated, "It's business. The world didn't stop just because you stopped making weapons. You left a vacuum. Hammer filled it."

Sometimes Pepper wasn't sure how much of their banter happened because Tony reacted in certain ways to Rhodey's militaristic rectitude, and how much resulted because the two of them were actually the same person, each finding a slightly varied way to react to identical stimuli. For example, Pepper thought, either one of these two men might seize on the occurrence of *Hammer* and *vacuum* in the same sentence, and put it together with the ongoing macho tension in their relationship, and make a comment that united the connotations of the word *hammer* with connotations of the word *vacuum*.

Also, it was not beyond either Rhodey or Tony to create the situation in which those associations could be commented on, just to provoke the other party. Pepper thought she was probably seeing both processes happen at once, and Tony confirmed her suspicions when he took the most obviously adolescent tack in response to Rhodey's comment.

"So you're telling me you're proud of the fact that Hammer filled your vacuum?" Tony said.

Even though she'd been expecting it, this godawful line demanded drastic action on Pepper's part. She dropped the notepad back in her purse. "Have you ladies ever thought about therapy?"

Leaning onto the table, Rhodey got serious. "They're not going to drop this, Tony. You want a heads-up? This is the stark reality. Next time they come for you, it's not gonna be in suits playing nice. It's gonna be in tanks rolling up your driveway."

"I hear you," Tony said. There was a pause as the suborbital jet heeled over and began its descent.

The three of them had very different perspectives on the conversation. Tony wanted what Tony wanted, because Tony Stark was privileged and brilliant and rich and used to having his desires catered to. Rhodey wanted what was best for the United States, as he saw things, because he had sworn an oath to uphold and defend, et cetera et cetera, and to him the Iron Man suit was the culmination of a long tradition of U.S. military superiority driven by technological innovation. The roots of this disagreement went back to the immediate aftermath of Tony's renunciation of arms manufacture, right when he'd come back from Afghanistan. Rhodey had been furious then and only softened his opposition once he'd seen the Mark IV in action. Then, like any other colonel who worked in weapons development for the Department of Defense, he'd been so thrilled with the existence of the Mark IV that he could hardly contain himself. Tony was privately of the opinion that much of Rhodey's hard-line attitude about Tony's actions came from simple jealousy. Rhodey wanted a suit. It was that simple.

Pepper wanted both of them to understand that they were in the end working for the same thing and that their insistence on petty differences symbolized by uniforms and federal contracting protocols exacerbated the problems that both of them said they wanted to eliminate.

Not that it had ever done her any good, or would do her any good, to say that out loud. She sighed loudly because that was a signal both Tony and Rhodey understood. Then she sat back in her chair with her recovered iPod and an expression of frustrated and superior disdain. These were the weapons she had to work with, so she made them work. She looked over at Tony, hoping he had noticed how far awry the conversation had gone, but he was staring out the window at the clean curve of the Earth visible from the fuselage window of the private suborbital scramjet.

The first time Tony had seen the earth from this altitude, he'd been in the Mark II as it was icing up and nearly killing him. At the time he hadn't really been in the right frame of mind to take in the view. Since then, when he'd gotten the suborb into service, he took every chance he could to look down on a view that—until six months ago—only astronauts had ever seen.

It wasn't quite space, depending on who you talked to, but they were high enough that NASA would have awarded them astronaut wings. Fifty miles was the space agency's cutoff. Tony had designed this Stark scramjet prototype to peak right around fifty-five. The orbital burn was usually about five minutes, and they would be in free-fall for about twenty before a fifteen-minute descent. New York to Los Angeles in forty minutes. Tony liked it. He liked it a lot.

He also liked looking down and seeing the curve of the earth, the aura of the atmosphere tapering into the clean empty black of space, the sinuous outlines of continent and river and weather front. Seen from an altitude of fifty miles plus, the Earth was a transcendently beautiful place. It was enough to give Tony some inner peace and provoke in him the faintest vestige of Kumbaya Syndrome. Despite which, he wasn't quite ready to forgive Rhodey—who, Tony noticed, was staring out the window with pure childlike joy and wonder on his face. He was an Air Force lifer who had never been to space. This was a big moment for him.

"Next time," Tony said, "you're flying commercial."

CHAPTER 7

As a snowy April evening deepened around him, Ivan waited near a railroad crossing in an industrial area known for chemical smells and dumped bodies. He was about to find out if he could trust his silent partners in the plan, whether they were going to be wolves or hares.

Headlights pinned him. He looked over and saw a police car. Ivan grinned. He wasn't a tourist or a Chechen to be shaken down. He was a hard man, harder than they would know even if they could see the story of his life written on his body in homemade prison ink. He had a spiderweb for each of his first four murders; he had the cross because the system persecuted him and the cathedral with many towers because he had been to prison more than once. He had the stars on his knees because he would never kneel. He had eyes on the back of his neck. And no one had ever put a tattoo on Ivan Vanko that he didn't want.

He stared the police down. After a moment they moved

on. When they had gone, Ivan turned to find an Asian along the tracks waiting for him. The Mongolian was here. Ivan approached him and waited for the sign. The Mongolian looked around, then peeled back the collar of his coat to reveal the Ten Rings tattooed on the side of his neck. The gesture was unnecessary; Ivan remembered the Mongolian and the Mongolian remembered him. The ritual was important, though. By showing Ivan his tattoo, the Mongolian drew Ivan in. Now they both knew that Ivan knew that he was dealing with the Ten Rings intentionally, and that whatever consequences followed from that intention, they were Ivan's to bear and Ivan's alone.

Since his last meeting with the Mongolian at the Phoenix chess club, Ivan had asked some old prison acquaintances what they knew about the Ten Rings. In sum, their reactions had fallen into two groups: they didn't know who the Ten Rings were and/or they didn't want to know who the Ten Rings were. And these were the worst of the worst, the men feared by the guards in Russian prisons. Those who would venture an opinion suggested that the origin of the Ten Rings was in Afghanistan, or maybe it was Chechnya—but here was a Mongolian, walking without fear in a part of Moscow where Asians were at risk of their lives. Did this mean that the true origin of the Ten Rings was in China?

If so, that put a new spin on their influence within Russia. The dragon and the bear had a long and difficult history even when they were nominally allies. Ivan had the briefest of misgivings. What if by enlisting the help of the Ten Rings, he was contributing to the infiltration of Russia by Chinese interests?

Just as quickly, this attack of conscience was gone.

Funny, Ivan thought, how Russia can do her worst to a man and a man will still love her. He put away his misgivings. Wherever the Ten Rings had originated, they were a force now. They could get things done that Ivan wanted done.

And they apparently shared Ivan Vanko's antipathy toward Tony Stark.

Ivan flashed a lot of cash. The Mongolian reached for it and Ivan jerked it back, playing keepaway just because he could. Then he stopped. He was not afraid of the Ten Rings, but he didn't want to antagonize them, either. He held out the money and waited.

The Mongolian produced a badge on a lanyard. MONACO HISTORIC GRAND PRIX, it said. Below the logo of that historic race was a picture of Ivan Vanko and a series of codes that entitled him to unrestricted access. He could cruise the paddock with the moguls and movie stars, he could walk along the track before the race began, he could go anywhere. Monaco on race day would be his.

And so, in front of a worldwide television audience, would Tony Stark.

Ivan could have chosen any of a thousand different ways to express his creativity. The weaponsmith was an artist just as the blacksmith or silversmith. Ivan's chosen form was a meter and a half long, made of articulated tungsten carbide vertebrae. He had machined each vertebra himself and socketed them together onto a woven tungsten carbide cable. Each vertebra featured a sharp, hooked tooth, slowly decreasing in size from several centimeters long at one end to half a centimeter at the tip. A handle, insulated and wired to the power supply, extended another fifteen centimeters. He could have chosen any weapon to destroy Stark, but in the end what Ivan wanted was the whip. He wanted to give Stark a thousand lashes, to carve his armor and his body into sparking bloody slag. He wanted Stark to die a slave's death after living a master's life.

Deactivated, the whip lay on his worktable. Ivan wound copper wire around the vertebrae, weaving it along the cable and through holes like the nerve openings in a spinal column. Tungsten carbide had an extraordinarily high melting point and just enough paramagnetism to hold its structural integrity in an intense electromagnetic field. Copper provided unparalleled conductivity—and copper was readily available, there to be stripped from any abandoned building. Ivan had melted and respun some of the wire himself to get exactly the gauge he wanted. He had wound perhaps a kilometer of hair-thin wire onto this whip. If he had designed the weapon correctly, the copper would reach a temperature of approximately 2,700 degrees Celsius when it was powered up, melting instantly into a kind of plasma that would be held in place by the paramagnetic field the current would create along the tungsten carbide cable.

Essentially Ivan Vanko would possess a whip of white-hot molten metal. Not even Stark's armor would survive it for long. Nothing could.

Ivan finished wiring the whip. He shrugged into a harness he had built of leather-wrapped tungsten and placed the miniature arc reactor in a housing set over his sternum. This was a little joke for Stark. Ivan also enjoyed the look of it; wearing it he felt like a man with a reactor powering his body and his mind. He was a superman, rising from the slums of Novogireevo and bringing the might of suppressed Russian fury to bear on the glitzy thievery of Stark.

He ran the cable from the RT down his arm to the handle of the whip, attaching it at shoulder, bicep, and radius. Before he plugged it in, Ivan put on a glove; even with the insulation, he did not expect to be able to hold the whip bare-handed. The glove extended well up his forearm and would protect from accidental grazes of the whip.

Taking the whip in hand, Ivan stepped away from the table to a clear space in the middle of the floor. Sense memory told him that he was standing at what had been his father's bedside. This was appropriate. He plugged the power cable into the whip.

It sparked to life with a noise like a car-sized van de Graaff generator, a hum that shook the bones and a crackle that Ivan could feel pressing on his eardrums. He gave himself over to it, holding the whip out and staring at its brilliant white light, letting its shape burn onto his retinas. He flicked it out and bits of plasma jumped from the tip, searing holes where they landed. Irina squawked and fluttered her wings, scooting to the end of her perch farthest from the light and noise.

It was time to test it, Ivan thought, even though he knew it would work. He could tell from the power thrumming through his arm, and from the waste heat he could feel even through the heavy glove. He held a piece of the sun, woven and turned into an extension of his arm.

Glancing around the room, he caught sight of the television replaying highlights of Tony Stark's Senate hearing. Oh, lovely timing, Ivan thought. He flicked the whip out away from his body and then pivoted to bring it down in a sweeping arc. The sound of it contacting the television was like lightning striking inside Ivan's head. His ears rang and his eyes watered from the flash. An involuntary grin spread across his face as he blinked away the tears and looked on what he had done.

The television, which had been showing Stark, and before that *Nu Pogodi*, now lay in two roughly equal halves, the ancient screen and tube exploded into sprays of glittering fragments. A small fire burned in the depths of the casing. Ivan had not felt a thing, no sense of resistance or even impact. His grin broadened. He looked over his handiwork and flipped the whip in a tight loop as if spinning a lasso. The tip sparked against the floor, leaving a gouge in the rug and the linoleum floor underneath. He touched a stud on the inside of his wrist and the whip shut off.

Now that he was operational, it was time to get back out into the world and set things in motion. There was one more whip to build—after all, he had two hands—but first he had someone to meet.

CHAPTER 8

After the Senate hearing (which was either a triumph or a debacle, depending on who you asked), Tony holed up in the lab for a couple of days with Jarvis trying to solve that pesky problem with the palladium. On the third morning of this project, he decided to make a fresh start. The first thing to do was clean the desktop. Away went the quarterly reports, the logs of experiments done as proofs of concept on Iron Man–related materials and command-and-control innovations, the exploded views of the Spyder's engine (which Tony thought could maybe be tuned to get a little more jump than the five hundred and eighty horses it came with), the various prototypes of new and different miniature arc reactors that might deliver greater energy and use less fuel.

All of it had to be gone because the palladium issue was reaching a critical point. "Initiating palladium replacement test. Number four eight six," Jarvis said.

"At least we're making progress," Tony said dryly.

For once, Jarvis' sense of humor failed him. "Out of a possible ten thousand, four hundred and ninety," the AI said.

Tony sighed. Maybe Jarvis was trying out a new humor matrix and it wasn't working. "Try dysprosium and cerium," he said, and watched the virtual display compile a new molecule in place of the palladium fuel catalyst. "Run that model."

On the virtual desktop, different molecular structures appeared as Jarvis created a thousand possible ways to put dysprosium and cerium together into a fuel that would run an RT without killing the operator. Three quickly emerged as possibilities. Jarvis labeled them A, B, and C, and ran them together through a massively accelerated simulation, putting them through a thousand hours of use in less than a minute. "A is unstable," Jarvis noted.

"Then scrap it," Tony said. "Never mind, I'll do it." He grabbed A, crumpled it up, and punted it into a nearby virtual trash can. For a minute he let himself stare at the periodic table as if revelation would present itself among the noble gases or the lanthanoids. Then he snapped himself out of it. Jarvis would keep simulating on his own for a minute while Tony made sure that his earthly vessel continued to function.

"Dummy!" he called out. "You're on phlebotomy detail. You! Blend me up some of those ghastly-tasting nutrients." The two robots embarked on their tasks and Tony refocused his attention on the periodic table. "Jarvis. Let's try dysprosium and hydrogen." He wasn't sure if hydrogen was going to get the kind of energy release that he needed, or if it could be electrically active enough to arc without some kind of fusion process being integrated into the RT, but what the hell. It was worth blowing some of Jarvis' processing power to find out.

Dummy returned with a pipette and the blood scanner. Tony stuck out an arm and watched as the robot pricked his finger and inserted the pipette into the scanner. "Dummy, nice job," he said. He looked over toward the lab sink, part of which had kitchen utensils and appliances mixed in with autoclaves and centrifuges. You had dumped a number of substances into a blender and was currently monitoring the blender's progress. "You, learn something," Tony said. "It's called bedside manner."

As if on cue, the blender exploded and a fountain of dark green and undoubtedly nutritious slop splattered across the countertop. Tony surveyed the scene. Robots, he thought.

He left Dummy holding the blood scanner and went over to the sink. "That's okay. It's not easy being You, is it?" he said to You. He took the pitcher with the remains of the shake off the blender and drank the green stuff off as quickly as he could, ignoring the taste. There would be cleaning to do. Tony wondered if he could trust You to do it without destroying all of the green goo-covered instruments.

It could wait, he decided. Pepper was going to show up pretty soon for her daily briefing and harangue, and Tony had plans for this that superseded even the solution to the palladium problem. At least for the moment.

"Now," he said to You when he'd choked down the shake. "Go get that thing I asked you to get, and if you break it I'm going to give you an Epsom salt bath and turn you into a wine rack."

You rolled away and Tony came back to the virtual

desktop. "Rise in palladium levels," Jarvis said. "Biological toxicity now at twenty-two percent."

Bad news. Tony looked at his reflection in the mirror. Bad news there, too. He looked like hell. If he didn't find a better power source for the RT, palladium poisoning was going to render all of his other problems moot.

In the mirror, he traced the purple lines spreading from the center of his chest. They were thicker and longer, and looked like some of them were sprouting smaller lines that wandered off to meet each other, creating a webbed effect. It crossed Tony's mind that he should maybe see a doctor. He wasn't going to be any good to anyone, senators or supermodels, if he was dead.

He heard someone on the stairs and looked over his shoulder to see Pepper tapping her code into the access panel and coming in the lab door. Tony got rid of the used palladium ingot and picked up the Tech-Ball, flipping it around nonchalantly as he turned to meet her. He'd gotten the idea for it from watching Bakugan cartoons, and right now he had it flipping open into various shapes that reminded him of the way a beetle's wings appeared from under a hard carapace. A flying Tech-Ball. That would be cool, he thought. His heart did a little flip as the RT started delivering more power now that its source was less corrupted.

"What were you thinking?" Pepper snapped without preamble as soon as she was through the door.

This took Tony aback just a bit, but of course he couldn't let her know that. "Just now?" he said. "If a Fruit Loop was the size of a washing machine, would I be able to take a bite out of it?"

Pepper ignored this. "Did you just donate our entire modern art collection to the Boy Scouts of America?"

Tony had in fact done this. At least he had ordered it done, and he thought that his orders had been carried out. But because he was in a literal mood, he decided not to commit to an answer about which he could not be one hundred percent certain.

"I'm not sure," Tony said. "I didn't physically check the crates."

"We curated that collection for over ten years!" Pepper said. She was purely baffled, he could tell. So was he, actually. Why had he done that again? He had never been a Boy Scout, had no particular love for scouting or the outdoors. . . . "It's worth more than six hundred and eight million dollars!" added Pepper.

Tony shrugged. This was not a persuasive line of argument. "Of my money."

"It's tax-deductible," Pepper said. "Why didn't you check with me?"

"Can I do it? See, I'm checking with you." Tony, who paid more in taxes every year than most Fortune 500 companies made in profits, let the Tech-Ball bounce off the desktop. It created a virtual model of itself that mirrored its real-world actions. Then he turned it into a series of polyhedrons just by way of killing time while Pepper fumed. Sphere became tetrahedron became cube became dodecahedron, icosahedron, tetrahemihexahedron, . . . he wondered how many sides he could make it create before the human eye would be unable to distinguish the polyhedron from a circle. Thousands? How many thousands?

"Check with me *before* you do it," Pepper said.

"God, you're so materialistic! Is it okay, then?"

Pepper gave up. "Yes, it's okay."

Tony nodded. "Good. Think fast."

As he spoke, he tossed the Tech-Ball to her. Reflexively she reached up to catch it—but instead of slapping into the palm of her hand, the Tech-Ball turned itself inside out, wrapping itself around her hand like a cocoon made of highly advanced and proprietary Stark Industries polymer composites.

"I don't want to play ball with you," Pepper said after a moment.

Tony was already back at the virtual desktop. He made and filed a brief note about possible law-enforcement applications for the Tech-Ball, then forgot about it. "There is nothing but this," he said.

"No!" Pepper started to tick things off on her fingers. She stopped, waiting. The Tech-Ball turned itself back into a ball. Stowing it in her purse, she said, "There are a hundred other things to talk about. Which category would you like to start with—Stark Industries?"

"Not yet," Tony said. He cleared the desktop again, storing what he would need later but throwing most of the random notes and sketches away. Also he got rid of the most recent set of potential fuel cell models. They weren't going to work. He needed something that would. He set Jarvis on another path involving mildly radioactive heavy metal alloys.

"Iron Man," Pepper said.

Tony shook his head. "Love it, but pass." What was there to talk about? Iron Man was Iron Man.

"Finances?"

"Okay," Tony said, "but we'll double back." How I do love this game, Tony thought. Things sure would be different when he couldn't play it anymore. Actually he was looking forward to not talking finances anymore. He had so much money he couldn't imagine how he might spend it even if he lived to be a hundred, and Stark Industries was well capitalized enough that it could survive just about anything. Money had never been a worry of Tony's, and it sure wasn't now.

"Expo?" Pepper asked.

Ah. That's more like it, Tony thought. He nodded. "Shoot."

"Elon Musk wants—"

"Love him," Tony interrupted. "Done."

"You haven't even heard what—"

"I don't care," Tony said. For the man who had lent him a prototype scramjet, all of the resources of Tony Stark and Stark Industries would be mobilized without question. "Make it happen. Let's get through this. Quicker. Make executive decisions, Miss Potts. That's what I have you around for."

She rolled her eyes but played along. Perfect, Tony thought. "Wind farm initiative, plastic tree plantation, solar retrofitting . . . "

"Whoa . . . " Tony held up a hand. Too much. When he'd said quicker, he hadn't meant that quick.

Pepper ignored him. "Sustainable housing," she said. Then she took a breath to go on.

Tony threw up his arms. "Wait! Who is running the company?"

Giving him her best chastising gaze, Pepper said, "You're certainly not."

"Are you suggesting I don't have my company's best interests at heart?"

"I'm suggesting that whatever you have at heart, the company's best interests don't always stay in your head."

"Ah. Well. Whose head do they stay in?" He needled her a little. "Yours? You were about to say yours, weren't you? Admit it. You think you would do a better job running the company than I do."

Pepper started to say something, cut herself off, then stood up straight, looked him in the eye, and said, "Yes. Yes, I do."

Aha, Tony thought. She walked right into it. He glanced into the next room to see what You was up to. Was the timing right? Looked like it might be.

"Then you should," he said.

"What?" Pepper looked wary.

"Run the company. I'm making you CEO," Tony announced.

She paused. Her face ran though six or eight almost-expressions, each mastered and masked before it could be completely realized. When she spoke, Pepper's voice was level and absolutely serious. "Don't joke about this if you're not serious," she said.

"That doesn't make any sense," Tony said as You trundled into the lab with a bucket of champagne and two flutes. Tony poured. "If you're going to represent this corporation," he said as he handed her one of the flutes, "I suggest you be a little more careful in the way you choose your words. I hereby, irrevocably, appoint you chairman and CEO of Stark Industries. Do you accept?" He held his flute out as he spoke.

"You . . . you are serious," Pepper said. She started to shine, the way only Pepper could. "I . . . I think. I, yes. Yes!" She held her flute out. "I will! I accept! I do!"

They toasted and drank, meeting each other's eye. "Congratulations, Ms. Potts," Tony said, and killed off his flute. He meant it.

Unlike many of Tony's actions, this one appeared impulsive but was in actuality thoroughly considered. The Senate hearings had been the last straw. As CEO of Stark Industries, Tony (and Iron Man) was a lightning rod; as an employee, valued for his technical insight but not counted on for oracular pronouncements or shareholder reassurance, he could be invisible. Well, not invisible. Less visible. Which was what he wanted. By giving up control of his company, he would regain control of his life.

That was the plan, anyway. And Tony could not think of a more capable person to run his father's company than Virginia Potts, upon whom he had bestowed the nickname Pepper and upon whom he was now bestowing the title Chief Executive Officer.

Pepper drank off her champagne as well. "Will that be all, Mr. Stark?" she asked, indulging in a bit of playfully excessive formality in her last act as his executive assistant.

Their faces were very close. How had that happened? And how was it that now, when Pepper was the boss, she was so much more . . . well . . . ?

No, Tony thought. Bad idea. It's been a bad idea every other time we almost did it, and it's a bad idea now. He held her gaze a moment longer, then said, "That will be all."

She handed him her flute and thought furiously. "I have so much to do," she said. Turning on her heel, Pepper left him there with his dim-witted robots and impending palladium doom. Well, Tony thought. Better get back to work. The boss will be watching.

CHAPTER 9

Tony could only work for so long, even on a problem as pressing as the RT's power supply murdering him by degrees, so he decided to take out some of his frustrations by sparring with Happy in a boxing ring he'd had put into the house for exactly this purpose. It was regulation size, complete with springy floor and padded posts. The upside of having a boxing ring in his house, and a driver who was a former Golden Gloves champion, was that while the palladium was poisoning him, Tony was getting some great exercise and looking—if he didn't mind saying so himself—terrific. The downside of this was that Tony didn't really know how to box, so Happy tended to pound the hell out of him and lecture Tony while he did it. Tony had private suspicions that Happy was making the lessons harder than they needed to be, so he could take an extra shot at the boss once in a while. Revenge, maybe, for some of the situations Tony had gotten Happy into. If that was true, Tony couldn't blame him; but it didn't make the sparring any easier.

"Cover," Happy said after sticking a jab into Tony's nose. "Don't drop. Hands up. Jab-jab-hook-uppercut, jab."

Eyes watering from the jab, Tony threw the combination. Happy flicked the punches aside and said, "You're dropping your hook. I got a clear line to your button. Again." Tony threw the same combination and apparently made the same mistake, since as he was loading up the hook Happy snapped another jab over his guard and into his mouth. Harder than the last one.

He heard the front doorbell ring, or maybe that was a ringing in his ears. When his vision had cleared, Pepper had come into the gym. Tony shook his head and tried to act unaffected by the punch; he wasn't sure how much she had seen. "The notary is here. I need you to sign the transfer paperwork," she said, not giving anything away.

"Later," Tony said. "I'm on Happy's time." Now that he'd made the decision and gotten the transfer of power started, he didn't much care how long it took because Pepper was already doing all the work. He started snapping a series of punches into Happy's gloves, working up a rhythm, then added an MMA-style elbow just for punctuation.

"What's with the elbow?" Happy said.

"It's time to expand my arsenal," Tony said, and threw another one. "Ju jitsu, muay thai . . . "

"We're boxing here," Happy said. "Get your gloves up and fight like a . . . "

Something distracted him and as Tony watched, Happy's face melted into a caricature of the man who has just seen something that will change his life forever. " . . . man?"

Tony turned, following Happy's line of sight, as an outrageous knockout walked into the room: wavy spill of dark hair, curves like the track at Monaco, lips that the expression *bee-stung* had been invented to describe. Tony and Happy both stopped sparring.

Happy tapped him in the back of the head. "Eyes up."

"Tony," Pepper said, with just the barest hint of humor. "It's the only time you'll have to sign over your company. I promise."

Then the goddess spoke. "Please initial the boxes," she said to Pepper. "Each form is in triplicate. I've marked each place for signature."

"Absolutely," Pepper said. Looking down at the forms, she said, "Tony. Come on." Then she glanced up at the notary and noticed that her attention was focused in the direction of the boxing ring. "Where do you need the fingerprint?" she said.

"Oh," the goddess said. "Right next to your signature." She turned her attention away from the ring to the business at hand. "Ms. Potts . . . I just want you to know that it's so inspiring to see the career path you're taking."

"Apparently this is what fifteen years of wrangling with Tony Stark gets you," Pepper said wryly. "I will not miss it. Tony!" she called.

"Bring it here!" Tony answered from the ring.

Pepper rolled her eyes so the notary could see the expression. "Sorry," she said.

With a winsome shrug, the notary followed her to the ring. "I don't mind."

At the edge of the ring, she slid her notary book out

onto the canvas and then climbed in after it. Tony, pre-
dictably, changed his mind the minute she got there. "I'll
be right back," he said, handing the goddess his mitts.
"Happy, give her a lesson."

He bounced out of the ring. Happy looked the notary
up and down, not sure how to proceed. "Uh," he said.
Ever box before?"

"No," she said. "I just do some martial arts."

"Who is she?" Tony said as he got close to Pepper.

"She works for us in Legal," Pepper answered as she
signed more paperwork. "So she's potentially a very expensive sexual harassment suit if you continue to ogle her."

Tony considered this. "I need a new assistant, boss,"
he said.

Pepper nodded. "I have three potentials for you to sit
down with."

"I don't have time to sit down," Tony said. "I need
someone now. I feel like it's her." He looked back at the
ring, where the notary and Happy faced each other.

"Come on," Happy said. "Show me something."

"No, it's okay." The notary glanced back over toward
Pepper and Tony. "I'll just wait for Mr. Stark."

Happy feinted at her. "Just one move. Something cool."

Tony divided his attention between the ring and the
search he was doing on the heads-up display in the corner
of the room now that he had wrung the goddess' name out
of Pepper. "Natalie Rushman . . . Wow," he said as her
resume came up. "She is overqualified."

"Agreed. You're making my point for me," Pepper said.

"Very impressive woman," Tony went on. "Look at
these stats!" He scrolled on. "Fluent in French, Italian,
Russian . . . Latin? Nobody speaks Latin."

Pepper cleared her throat. "I do."

"And did you model in Tokyo?"

"Tony," Pepper said. "I know what you're doing."

"Really? Then you got me beat."

Pepper decided she'd had enough. "Miss Rushman!" she called out. "Let's get this done, shall we?"

Natalie came out of the ring, flipping Tony's practice mitts to Happy with an apologetic shrug. When she got to the once and future heads of Stark Industries, she looked through the transfer paperwork to see where it stood. "Okay," she said when she'd gotten it all arranged. To Tony she said, "I just need your impression."

"I think you'd be great in the sack and distracting on the job," Tony said. "As opposed to Pepper, who's great on the job and would be distracting in the sack."

Natalie's gaze flicked over to Pepper. She looked back at Tony and held up an ink pad. "Really," she said. "I meant your fingerprint."

Holding her gaze, Tony inked his thumb and put the prints on a number of sheets that she held out for him in succession. After the last one was done, as Natalie shuffled the papers back together, he said, "The company's all yours, Pep."

"Will that be all, Mr. Stark?" Natalie asked.

"Nope," Tony said.

"Yes," Pepper said sternly. "It will. Goodbye, Ms. Rushman." As Natalie walked away, Pepper looked at Tony. Seeing the look on his face, she said, "No."

CHAPTER 10

"Ugh," Tony said. "I hate driving in Monaco on race day. Can we go any faster?"

Happy shook his head. "Seriously, boss, it's just going at the pace it wants to. Seconds away."

"We could have avoided this altogether," Pepper said. She thought they had more important things to do than attending a Monaco Historic Grand Prix, and she didn't care who knew it. The race had started out in 1998 as a way for fans of open-wheel racing to have some fun with the cars of yesteryear. It was an amazing event that featured a weekend of racing every other year in May. The race itself was divided into classes. It was exactly the kind of thing Howard Stark would have done if it had existed while he was alive, and so of course Tony had to follow in these particular footsteps his father had never had a chance to leave.

"Not a chance," Tony said. He leaned forward and told Happy to lean on the horn.

"It won't do any good," Happy said. This was manifestly true to all three of them because they all knew that Tony's limousine was part of a motorcade parading past the grandstand toward the Hôtel de Paris. It was also manifestly true to all of them that when Tony wanted his way about a juvenile whim, he usually got it. So when Tony said, "Do it," Happy did. He leaned on the horn, long and hard, drawing angry looks from the police escort in front of them.

Then he said, "We're here, sir. Looks like they're expecting us."

Leaving Happy to deal with parking the car, he and Pepper hopped out to the cheers of thousands of race fans. Tony soaked it all in. He had big plans for this day. It didn't matter that Pepper was being a sourpuss, or that palladium toxicity was slowly killing him, or that the melon slices had been overripe at breakfast that morning. Tony was determined to enjoy this day like it was his last one on Earth. Classic fast cars, fancy company, beautiful women . . . the advancement of humanity through technology could wait until tomorrow. There was nothing like the Monaco Historic Grand Prix.

He turned around to find Pepper and saw her basking in the admiration of the paparazzi gauntlet in front of the Hôtel de Paris. "Okay, missy, that's enough," he said, taking her arm and guiding her toward the lobby doors. She looked terrific and Tony couldn't blame the photogs for their attention. Or Pepper for lapping it up. She wasn't used to attention, and now that she was stepping out of Tony's shadow (or Tony was stepping out of the way to let light fall on her), she was going to be getting a lot of it.

Inside the hotel, they headed in the direction of the

Bar Américain. Before they had crossed the lobby, Natalie Rushman appeared, poured into a cocktail dress for whose existence Tony was profoundly grateful. "Mr. Stark!" she called out.

Pepper's giddy smile vanished. She rounded on Tony. "When did this happen?"

"I thought you liked her," Tony said.

"You are so predictable," Pepper growled.

Tony nodded toward a last photographer who had trailed them into the hotel. "Smile or don't," he said through his own smile. "Right now you look like a frightened pony. Your nostrils are flaring."

In the aftermath of the flashbulb, Natalie got close enough to chase away the photographer. "C'est bon," she said, and fixed Tony's tie. "How was your flight?" she asked.

"Wonderful," Tony said. "What's on the agenda?"

They moved into the bar, Pepper standing a little apart from Tony and Natalie. A waiter materialized at the exact moment they sat down. "Bonjour," he said, laying drink napkins in front of each of them. "Je peux t'offrir un verve?"

Every year Pepper spent hours with a French phrasebook before they went to Monaco, and every year she tried without success to actually speak the language. This year was no different. "Oui," she said. "Pour moi, un tasse . . . uh . . . un ananas . . . ahh . . . "

Without moving any muscle in his face, the waiter emitted a barely audible tsk. "Mmm, maybe you speak English," he said. "Is better."

"Excusez-moi," Natalie cut in. "Je peux l'adier."

"Oh, vous etes Monegasque!" The waiter beamed and focused his attention entirely on Natalie. Tony could see

Pepper starting to boil over. He thought about taking action, but today was a day of fun, and what could be more fun than watching the tension between two women with differing claims on him? He sat back.

"Non, non, non," Natalie said. "Je suis Américain."

"Non-possibile," the waiter protested.

Natalie looked at Pepper. "You want pineapple juice, yes?"

"Yeah," Pepper said.

"La femme voudrais un jus d'ananas," Natalie said, turning back to the waiter. "Pesser fraiche s'il vous plait. Avec un petit eau minerale."

"Oui. A tout de suite."

"Wait," Pepper said. "Fresh pineapple juice, please. If it comes in a can—"

Natalie was nodding. "That's what I just said."

"With a splash of—"

"Soda. Yeah."

Forced to be gracious, Pepper choked out a *merci* as Natalie turned to Tony. "And for Mr. Stark, a Tom Collins, correct?"

"Perfect!" Tony said.

"Et un Tom Collins pour l'homme," Natalie finished, sending the waiter on his way. "Dinner is at 9:30," she said, pointing out their table.

Tony said, "I'll be there at eleven."

"Of course," she said without missing a beat. "Happy will be picking you up at ten-thirty."

One of Tony's favorite tech entrepreneurs and fellow old-race-car zealots, Elon Musk, appeared out of the crowd. Pepper nodded at him. "Mr. Musk."

"Congratulations on the promotion," Musk said.

"Elon, good to see you!" Tony said. "These Merlin engines are fantastic."

Accepting the compliment, Musk said, "I have a good idea for an electric jet."

Cocking a finger at him as he and Pepper walked away toward the bar, Natalie trailing somewhere behind them, Tony called, "I like it."

He and Pepper got close to the bar. "You look tense," he said to her. "I'm going to have Natalie book you a massage."

"I don't need Natalie to do anything for me," Pepper snapped.

"Ms. Potts, green is not an attractive color on you."

Pepper rolled her eyes. She was angry at herself for being so obvious. "Please."

The conversation might have taken an inopportune turn then, had it not been for the entrance of Justin Hammer, who, in full-on false bonhomie mode, boomed out "Tony!" as he approached the table.

"Good God, could it be? It is! My least favorite person on Earth!" Tony said. He looked over at Pepper and added, "What's he doing here?"

"You're not the only rich guy with fancy cars," Hammer said. He inclined his head at Pepper and said, "I just wanted to pop over and congratulate Ms. Potts on her promotion. Mind if I join you at your table?"

"Mind if I get a restraining order first?" Tony answered.

A plasticine blond appeared next to Hammer, who took her by the arm. "Christine," he greeted her. To the table he added, "I believe you know Ms. Everhart."

"Roughly," Tony said. He waited for a reaction from Hammer but didn't get one. Ah—Hammer didn't know about the little interlude he and Ms. Everhart had shared. The possibilities for torment were endless.

"Mr. Stark. Lovely to see you again," Christine said.

"By the way," Hammer said to her, "this is the big story right here! New CEO of Stark Industries. Congrats!"

Christine shook hands with a trying-not-to-beam Pepper. "Yes," she said. "My editor was hoping I could get a few words with you."

"You should," Hammer encouraged. "Christine is doing a piece on me. I thought I'd throw her a bone."

"She did quite a spread on Tony last year," Pepper said, and the smile melted off Christine's face. "It was impressive." After making sure her subtext was clear, Pepper peeled off from the group. "We'll speak later," she said as she left. "I need to wash."

A brief silence after Pepper's departure nearly got oppressive, but Christine rallied. "Now that I have you two here," she said brightly. "So. Is this the first time you've seen each other since the Senate hearing?"

"So," Tony mimicked her. "I hear your contract was canceled, Justin?"

Sensing blood in the water, Christine produced a digital recorder and held it discreetly in front of her. "You heard wrong," Hammer said. "It's just on hold."

"As in permanent hold?" Tony went in for the kill. "They're doing a casualty report."

Hammer dismissed this with a wave. The two of them started walking back toward the table. "I'm actually hoping to have something to present at your Expo," Hammer said.

"Great," Tony said. "We're doing another one in 2033. If you ever invent something that works, I'll save you a spot." He walked off and left the two of them there. There were better things to do on race day than hang around with people like Justin Hammer.

Not the only rich guy with a fancy car, Tony thought. Like I wouldn't know Hammer would have a car here. This was the thing about people who only wanted to talk about themselves. It never occurred to them that people might already know all of the things they were going to say. On the screens mounted along the walls of the Bar Américain was the pre-race countdown. The noise from the crowd in the bar ratcheted up. Cars were starting to appear on the circuit, and the start of the race was only moments away. Tony would have loved to watch, but he had a little business to take care of first.

The bathrooms in the Hôtel de Paris were big enough that Tony felt comfortable having a quick conversation with Jarvis. He slipped a wireless earbud into his right ear and entered the stall farthest from the door. Drawing a drop of blood with a pipette, he held it up for the sensors on his PDA to analyze. "Palladium levels stable," Jarvis said almost immediately.

Tony sighed. "For the moment." Then he straightened up. It was Race Day! In Monaco! Time to get on with enjoying it.

Hammer was trying not to think about Tony Stark because it made him angry. He didn't want to come across as angry in front of Christine Everhart. Not only did he want her to write a positive profile, he wanted her to keep him company after the race. So he put the best face on everything, starting with himself and including Tony.

"What does the future hold for Hammer Industries?" Christine asked. They were at a table off to the side of the bar, with her recorder and notepad between them and a few various famewhores and hangers-on circulating around.

Hammer made a show of considering his answer even though he'd been rehearsing it for weeks. "My goal has always been minimizing loss of human life. Some people want to keep the best technology out of the reach of our soldiers. I want to put it into their hands. I want to protect the people."

"So that footage that Tony Stark showed at the

Senate . . . " she prompted. She got a gleam in her eye as she said it, and Hammer knew two things about her then. One, he would never be able to trust her. Two, she would be dynamite in the sack if he ever got her there.

"Listen," he said. "I love Tony Stark. We love each other. We're not competitors. Tony stepping out of the picture has created tremendous opportunities for Hammer Industries. Unfortunately, Tony is his own worst enemy. Tony's only competition is Tony." He caught himself, realizing how many times he'd just said Tony's name and how little he was talking about himself and Hammer Industries. "Actually, scratch that," he went on. "Let's not make this day about Tony. Let's make this about Hammer."

He tapped on her notebook, in which she had just stopped writing. Her handwriting wasn't quite legible to him, especially not upside down. "Read me back what you took down about Hammer Industries," he said. "Is that cool? I just want to make sure . . . "

She had tuned him out, he saw with a flash of embarrassed anger. Instead she was looking up at one of the televisions that lined the walls. The Monaco Historic Grand Prix announcers—the French-language ones, anyway—had suddenly started talking much more excitedly.

Christine got up and walked away from him to get a better look at the screens. Unused to being walked away from, and not liking the sensation at all, Hammer turned to see what was so interesting.

"You have got to be kidding me," Hammer said.

Closer to the lobby side of the Bar Américain, Pepper was suffering through an excruciating conversation with Natalie, whose earnestness was not to be believed. "If there's anything I'm doing wrong," Natalie was saying, "I hope you'll tell me. I'm so relieved to have a woman with your intellect to consult with should I need it . . . " Okay, she's smart and conscientious and (I can admit it) gorgeous, Pepper thought; but if she's this naive I'm going to have to kill her to save the company. And myself.

I am sort of the company now, she thought. I am front and center, the face of Stark Industries. Or if that hasn't happened yet, it will as Tony steps farther back and people get more used to me handling everything that he used to.

Well, no, she corrected herself. Much of what they thought he used to handle, Pepper had in fact taken care of for the past several years. This had become even more true after the death of Obadiah Stane. Tony hadn't been in any shape to assume the day-to-day running of the company, the board meetings and the reporting requirements and the delicate tangos with regulators and subcontractors and local governments. So Pepper had started doing it. She was good at it. She would be better at it now that Tony was doing the kinds of things he was good at instead of making a half-hearted effort to do the things he kind of thought he should do. Tony in the lab tinkering was infinitely preferable to Tony in the executive suite. Let him build Tech-Balls and next-generation Iron Man suits, and let Stark Industries profit and grow from the accidental insights thrown off and patented during the course of Tony following his obsessions.

As long as those obsessions didn't get him killed. Pepper still got a cold knot in the pit of her stomach when she remembered the first time she'd seen him in the suit, and seen the scorch marks and those puckered holes that could only have been caused by bullets . . .

She cut off that train of thought, the way she always cut it off. She and Tony had an understanding. It was probably all they would ever have.

Natalie's phone rang. Glancing at it, Pepper noticed something odd. The number on the screen read 0-00-000-000-0000.

"Just to know you're there, and that you've done all this a million times before," Natalie went on as if the phone didn't exist.

"You going to get that?"

Natalie covered the phone with her hand. "Oh, it's just my dad. I'll call him back."

Your dad calls from a scrambled number? Pepper wanted to ask. But this wasn't the time. "I don't mind," she said. In fact she wanted Natalie to answer because Pepper had been ever so slightly suspicious of Natalie Rushman since the moment she had let slip that loaded comment in Tony's gym, which had led to her demolition of Happy Hogan. There was something too perfectly put together about this girl, with her languages and her martial arts and her modeling and her legal talents.

Pepper nodded at the phone.

Natalie looked like she *did* mind, but she said, "Oh. Okay. Hi, Dad," she said into the phone. "It's going great . . . Mr. Stark just landed, so we're having a great time already. Yes. Of course . . . I love you too." She hung up.

"I'd prefer it if you didn't tell people about Mr. Stark's itinerary," Pepper said.

"I know, but my dad's a huge fan—"

"That's not a request."

Pepper started working on her BlackBerry. Even while she was off on one of Tony's jaunts, she had a company to run. But almost immediately, Natalie said, "Ms. Potts?" And she tugged at Pepper's sleeve.

That was the last straw. Pepper looked up, about to chew her a new one. Then she saw what was on the nearest TV screen.

"What's the point of owning the car unless you can race the car?" Tony asked the Canal-Plus trackside commentator. It was a rhetorical question, of course, since he was in the car and about to race it. "You only live once, right? Joie de vivre! Sacre bleu! Ménage a trois! All that stuff."

He flipped down the visor of the helmet. Race time.

It was a beautiful car, built in the 70s and state-of-the-art then. Tony had made sure himself that this car stayed true to its original form. He'd fought an epic ethical struggle with himself over whether he should use improvements in materials science to his advantage . . . but no. In the end, he'd wanted the car to be the kind of car it had always been. He wanted the best 1970s open-wheel racer that could have existed in the 1970s. Specifically he had wanted this one because his father had owned one. Somehow it had been auctioned off after Howard Stark's death, but Tony had replaced it.

The old man would have loved the Monaco Historic Grand Prix. But because he'd died twenty-some years before the Monaco Historic Grand Prix had started, it was up to Tony to race in it for him.

Here's to you, Dad, he thought, and started the car.

"Did you know about this?" Pepper demanded as she shot up and away from the table, rattling the untouched drinks.

"I had no idea," Natalie said.

"This cannot happen," Pepper said. "You have to know where he is at all times. Where's Happy?"

Natalie looked relieved to be able to answer that question. "He's waiting outside in the car."

"Get Happy," Pepper ordered. "I need Happy."

"Right away." Natalie headed for the door. Pepper resolved to kill her star employee at the earliest opportunity.

CHAPTER 12

A long the track, Ivan had rubbed shoulders with the mighty, the plutocrats whose favorite toys were the sports cars of their fathers. None of them had cared to find out who he was. He had even brushed past Tony Stark as Stark had prepared to start his own car. That might have been a time to do something, but it would have been too private, lacking the necessary spectacle and drama. Ivan had a plan. He would stick to it.

How he loved the machines. All machines. In Ivan's veins ran the blood of a born engineer. His father, too, had been destined for engineering greatness. A Stark had derailed that plan. Ivan would get it back on track.

Engines roared to life around him. He faded into the crowds of technicians and journalists who stood back, their jobs done for the moment, and watched the drivers run last-minute checks. One after another, the cars headed to the starting line.

Ivan had his own preparations to make. He melted away into the crowd, aiming for a spot he had scouted out under the grandstand near a turn from which almost any spectator would be able to see the great moment that was about to occur. He would make his entrance from there. What sort of exit he might make, Ivan did not know. To plan for an exit in this case was to plan for defeat. Ivan did not plan to lose.

"I didn't know," Natalie said into the phone. "He told no one."

She looked up at the televisions, like everyone else in the Bar Américain was looking up at the televisions. The race had begun, and there was Tony Stark driving, in the Stark car. As both the English- and French-language commentators gave the play-by-play, in which Tony featured prominently, people in the bar were having their own conversations about Tony joining the race. They were about evenly split. Half of them believed it was a travesty, that Tony was a dilettante who would ruin the race, and by extension the sport, by turning into his personal playground instead of a celebration of the history of motorsport—which was what the Monaco Historic Grand Prix was all about. The other half thought that a star like Tony Stark was exactly the kind of star power the Monaco Historic Grand Prix needed. All of them, Natalie got the feeling, were hoping he would crash, just for the spectacle of the thing. This was a sentiment more common to NASCAR and funny-car fans than partisans of open-wheel racing, but anyone who spent a lot of time watching cars go really fast also spent at least part of that time entertaining fantasies about what it would look like if some or all of them stopped very suddenly.

More specifically, Natalie reflected as she hung up the phone, a whole lot of people were hoping Tony would crash. Not all of them for the same reason.

Natalie looked around the Bar Américain. There was Justin Hammer, his expression equal parts fury and admiration as he watched Tony gain on the Hammer car as they came around a hairpin turn. There were two more turns until the tunnel. If Tony was going to make a move, right after those turns was where he would likely make it.

She caught herself thinking like a race fan at the exact moment when the first car exploded and the race became something else entirely.

Ivan's left-hand whip slashed through the chain-link fence under the grandstand like it wasn't there. This was an overused expression but in this case exactly correct; he felt no resistance whatsoever as he swung. The whip vaporized the chain link and skipped off the sidewalk the grandstand was built over, leaving a gouge like someone had dragged a stick through the concrete when it was wet. Two more flicks of the whip, right and left, opened a section of it that Ivan could walk through. He came to the safety barrier bordering the track, a three-tiered metal railing that offered little more resistance than the chain link had. He slashed a V-shaped opening through it as one of the cars thundered by, the wind of its passage rocking Ivan and blowing his hair across his face.

He shook it back over his shoulders and glanced back up at the grandstand behind him. A security guard, de-

tailed to keep people from leaning over the front railing
of the grandstand, was shouting at him and reaching for a
walkie-talkie. Too late, Ivan thought. There's nothing you
can do to stop me now, is there?

Most of his practice with the whips had involved slash-
ing them across things, getting a sense of how they reacted
to contact with various thicknesses of various substances.
While doing that, however, Ivan had also managed to get
a fair sense of how far the whips extended if he snapped
them like you would snap a towel. If he was right . . .

And he was. The tip of his right-hand whip cracked
exactly at the point of contact with the security guard's
forehead. The results were spectacular. Ivan raised both
arms, letting the whips trail and crackle like snakes made
of light; he drank in the shock from the grandstand, then
stepped out onto the track.

Since Tony's car had qualified behind the Hammer car,
he was still racing behind the Hammer car three laps in.
That was all right. He had the better car—he knew that
because he had refurbished it himself. And he had the
better driver—he knew that because he was Tony Stark
and by definition better than anyone else at anything he
chose to care about. So he bided his time through three
laps, getting to know the way the car responded to each
feature of the track, and then as the race hit the tunnel that
led into the course's only long straightway, he made his
move. Tony lived for the pass, the inside move on a tight
curve, the clever draft and slingshot around a wide turn.
If he was in front, he didn't want to win by an inch. He
wanted to lap everyone, to see the checkered flag rippling

in front of him before any of the other cars had gotten
their last-lap messages from their crews. He wanted to destroy his competitors, then shake their hands with a grin
after the race and make them wait at the podium while the
assembled media asked him all the questions.

All of that ambition and know-how and desire came
together as Tony ripped past Hammer's car at the mid-
point of the tunnel, engines screaming and Tony screaming right along with them. He couldn't help himself. This
was high-adrenaline stuff. "Yeeeaaahhh!" he screamed,
really screamed, like a caveman exulting over the corpse
of a sabertooth tiger. These historic cars were something
else. How come he'd never taken this one out of the
garage before?

In the Bar Américain, cameras were starting to focus on
the on-course disruption. Someone had invaded the track
and was using some kind of electrified rope to hack away
at the passing cars. The teams were going crazy trying
to get in touch with their drivers and tell them to avoid
the guy, and a yellow flag was coming out that all of the
drivers ignored in their haste to get around the invader
and escape to the pit. He was big, the track invader, and
shirtless, with long, lank hair and a kind of metallic exo-
skeletal frame that linked his two—what, ropes? Cables?
Whips?—to a power source that glowed from the center
of his torso.

"Jesus, it's like a lightsaber," one of the bar patrons said.

The French announcers were nearly hysterical, and
even the more laconic commentators on the English-
language feed were getting worked up. "I've never seen

anything like this," the color guy was saying. "You've got to have quite a pair of attachments to do this."

"The Monaco Historic Grand Prix is making another kind of history," said the lead announcer. "Track invasions have happened before, but never has an interloper destroyed a car. This is a terrible day. Where are the police? Who is supposed to be protecting the drivers and crews against an attack?"

"Shocking," agreed the color man.

A car exploded as it passed the invader. Pieces of it sailed down the track and crashed into the barriers and the chain-link fence that separated the grandstand from the course. "That can't be good," Pepper said. She was trying to figure out how he was doing whatever he was doing. She was also trying to pick up where Tony was on the course and simultaneously she was choosing among several different potential ways of killing him for entering the race and thus causing the whole situation to begin with.

Someone was on the track of the Monaco Historic Grand Prix with what looked suspiciously like a miniaturized arc reactor. This meant that one of three things: Obadiah Stane had leaked the design to someone while he was plotting against Tony's life; there was a spy inside Stark Industries who had sold or leaked the design after cracking Tony's private servers; or someone with a serious hate for Tony Stark had independently arrived at either an arc reactor or a technology that looked and acted very much like it.

None of those were desirable scenarios.

Happy came in. "Where's the football?" she asked. He held it up—an aluminum briefcase lacquered in the deep red that had become one of Tony's favorite colors since he built the Mark IV suit. It was shackled to his arm. Pepper stood. Time to make sure Tony wasn't in over his head, for the millionth time. "Let's go."

They passed Natalie in the lobby on the way to the car. She was talking on the phone, and Happy wasn't sure, but he thought she was saying something about the race. "Natalie! You on this?" Happy said.

She hung up. "Yes."

"Good," Pepper said on the way out the door. "As soon as he finishes up, you should be thinking about how we're getting him home."

"The plane is fueled and on the runway," Natalie was saying as the door closed behind them.

Hurrying to the car, Pepper said, "Give it to me." Happy handed her the key and held out his arm so she could reach the lock on the football. She worked at it as they ran together out of the hotel toward the VIP lot.

They'd never done a field test of it, but Pepper thought this might be the time. After all, shouldn't a field test be done under conditions that simulated as closely as possible actual combat? Presto! An armed maniac destroying the Monaco Historic Grand Prix! Perfect.

Now if only they could get to Tony before said armed maniac did.

And if only she could get the key to work. "Hold still, Happy," she said.

"What, and run at the same time? You try it," Happy said, but he tried to hold his arm steadier as they ran. When they got to the car, she still hadn't gotten the lock open. Happy had to hold his arm out to her and drive one-handed while she jerked the football around this way and that trying to work the lock while he drove maniacally in the direction of the track gate. These were not optimal conditions for working on a small and temperamental lock. Pepper grabbed Happy's wrist to hold it still. She looked out at the streets of Monaco. Word of events on the racetrack had apparently not spread. Happy violated every traffic law in France during the first ninety seconds of the trip. Perhaps the police, Pepper thought, had heard about the track invasion and were already on it.

She called Tony but he didn't answer. This was surprising because he usually patched his phone through to wherever he was, even the Iron Man suit. Why wouldn't he have done it in the car?

"Let's go, let's go, let's go," she said.

Happy shot her a look. "You want to drive?"

"No, I want you to drive faster," she said. "And I want you to hold still so I can get this goddamn key to work."

Tony came out of the tunnel and accelerated down the longest straightaway on the Monaco course, the harbor on his left and a sharp turn coming up real soon. Hammer's car was tight on Tony's and he could only imagine what Hammer was thinking right at this moment. Oh, the joy of making your competitors suffer. They stayed that way through the hard decel into the turn and then the acceleration out of it. "Suck it, Hammer," Tony said. Monaco was so tight, Hammer's driver would never be able to pass him. He was going to have to look at Tony's rear end for the whole rest of the race. Beautiful.

That was the thought in Tony's head when he saw the

cars in front of him veer crazily away from something in the center of the track. One of the cars disappeared in a fireball that swallowed up his view of the middle distance—but just before that, Tony could have sworn he saw a man on the track, and something sparking like live wires . . .

The initial fireball cleared and Tony saw that there was in fact a man on the track, walking against the direction of the race. He was big and slabbed with muscle, looked kind of like a wrestler, and had some kind of metal framework around his arms and torso. From his hands dangled a pair of whips that glowed and sparked as he flicked them against the concrete.

The car in front of Tony braked and swerved. Tony went with it, using it as a screen; his rear-view mirror told him that Hammer's driver had the same idea. A flickering line of energy shot out and destroyed the car, splitting it just behind the cockpit. The two parts of the car, spitting vapors and flame, tumbled into the crash barrier. Now Tony really stood on the brakes, but there was no way he was going to be able to avoid the guy. He hauled on the steering wheel, felt the car shudder into a skid, and watched in what felt like slow motion as the guy flicked one of the whips out toward Tony's car.

"What the f—?" Tony opened his mouth, but before much more could come out, the whip sheared through the chassis of Tony's irreplaceable one-of-a-kind historic car like a Weed Whacker through a dandelion stem.

CHAPTER 13

"You speak French?" Happy asked as they neared the gate. The gendarmerie looked as if they might have already gotten wind of what was happening out on the track. They were nervous and armed, and there were more of them than was typical.

Happy was just nervous. He still only had one arm to drive with, and his other arm was getting a little sore, what with being hauled around in the back seat while Pepper tried to figure out how to get the key into the cuff and release the football from Happy's arm, an outcome both of them were heartily rooting for.

"Yes?" Pepper said, meaning sort of, although after that tart Natalie's display today she was a bit ashamed to say so.

Happy heard the uncertainty in her voice. He weighed the possibility that they could talk their way past the guards given the emerging chaos, the language barrier, and the briefcase handcuffed to his right arm. Then he considered the likelihood of successfully driving the limo through the gate without damaging either members of the gendarmerie or limousine passengers.

"Me neither," Happy said, and gunned it.

The gendarmes scattered. One of them fired a couple of shots at the limo just for appearance's sake, but the limo was built to handle much heavier ordnance than the standard five-five-six fired by your AR-15-type assault rifle. By the time Happy had registered the pings of the ricochets, they were through the gate, across the margin, and out onto the track. Two cars went screaming by, their engines loud even through the limo's sealed windows. Ten thousand rpm meant a lot of noise. Now to find Tony before the nutcase with the laser whips or whatever they were chopped him up like he'd chopped up half of the other cars in the race.

"I'm a big believer in ten-and-two for safety," Happy was saying, "and right now I'm rocking just the ten, which is cool, but two would be nice . . . "

"Are you sure you brought the right key?" Pepper snapped.

It was going to be a hell of a thing if they got there and then couldn't use the football.

In the bar, Natalie tried to track what was happening on the racecourse, what Hammer was doing, and what was happening on her phone all at once. "He is extremely vulnerable at the moment," she said, looking around to make sure that Colonel Rhodes and Happy Hogan weren't around. Several times they had nearly buttonholed her in what would have been an extremely uncomfortable way.

She was extremely vulnerable at the moment, too. Her support network was a long way off, and it would be very easy for a misunderstanding of her operational role to escalate fatally. That could not be allowed to happen. What she had done with Hogan had been stupid, almost unforgivably so. If something like that happened again, the consequences might be much worse than a frosty relationship with Pepper Potts.

Natalie listened into the phone for another moment, then said, "Understood," and hung up. She looked around. Neither Rhodes nor Hogan was anywhere in sight. Allowing herself to relax a little, she started dialing her phone again. The one thing she could do at the moment was make sure that—as she had told Rhodes—the Stark Industries plane was ready to go when Tony was.

Tony came to a full and complete stop upside down in the truncated remains of his car. He popped the steering wheel loose and flipped it out onto the track so he could wriggle out of the driver's seat, which—counterintuitively— was much harder to do upside down. His helmet had cracked in the crash and he stripped it off. Blood stung in his left eye. The remains of his car were between him and the marauding guy with the whips and the metal exoskeleton, which was a good thing. An even better thing would be if he could get to the football, or if someone could get the football to him, or if maybe some kind of airstrike could incinerate the guy with the whips.

Who at that very moment reached the wreckage of Tony's

car and slashed it methodically into small pieces, shouting in what sounded like Russian the whole time. Well, Tony thought. I can go out one way or another. He bided his time, grabbed hold of the nearest bit of wreckage that could readily be weaponized, and when the whip guy looked up from his work having not found Tony in the wreck, what he found instead was Tony cracking him across the face with the rear wing from the disintegrated car.

Tony put everything he had into the swing. It was a good one. It landed solidly, square on the side of the whip guy's head . . . and it had no visible effect whatsoever.

He paused, switching tactics to psychological diversion. "Are we beyond talking this through? Finding some common ground?"

"Stark destroyed my family!" the whip guy growled. The accent was definitely Russian, or something from that part of the world. Tony hit him again. Still no visible effect.

"I'm sorry," he said. "That was rude. I cut you off."

The whip guy roared like an animal and slashed at the space recently occupied by Tony Stark. But Tony was off and running, looking for any cover at all. What he saw were pieces of race cars, beautiful machines turned into fabulously expensive junk.

Aha. They said necessity was the mother of invention, and Tony had just invented a plan.

There was a big piece of chassis, the better part of a race car upside down at an angle that would provide brief and incomplete cover. With a plan in mind, Tony shifted into Br'er Rabbit mode, running from the whip guy fast enough to stay alive but slow enough to lure him along. He accelerated and dove under the car. Timing was going to be key here, he thought as he yanked the gas cap off and scrambled forward past the stream and splash of high-test fuel. If this didn't work, he was going to have bigger problems than plasma whips or laser cables or whatever it was this guy was using.

And how in the hell was he powering it all with an RT? There was no time to think about it at the moment, but that was a question Tony intended to have answered.

Right now it was Br'er Rabbit time. There was gas everywhere and a sociopath approaching with whips that apparently made fire. So. Tony ran as the whip guy got close enough to strike.

The whip slashed down through the race car's engine and into the track surface, coming into contact with the spreading pool of fuel along the way. The explosion that followed blew the car to unrecognizable pieces and sent Tony pinwheeling into a wall of hay bales at the edge of the track. He started to right himself and looked back toward the dissipating fireball.

There was the whip guy, walking through the flames like they weren't there and coming toward Tony like he was the only thing in the world that mattered.

"I see him!" Happy cried out. They were moving against traffic, but there wasn't any traffic anymore. There were hulks of destroyed cars, pit crews running out to save drivers, spectators rushing up and down the stands in waves . . . there was fire on the track, everywhere. As soon as he'd said it, he lost track of Tony again. Another fireball on the track hid everything down around Tabac, which was where the action appeared to be. Happy floored it and headed that way.

"Where is the key?" Pepper yelled.

"Check my front pocket." Happy careened around a wrecked car as Pepper leaned forward and dug into his pants. He glanced over at her and saw her face in profile, turned slightly away from him. Her hair spilled onto his shoulder. The feel of it and the smell of her and the general sense that both of them could be dead at any second loosened Happy's tongue. "I've always loved you!" he cried out.

She froze. Happy swerved around a volunteer crew digging a driver out of the ruins of his car. "I should have said that before you had your hand in my pocket," he said.

Pepper didn't answer. She dropped into the back seat and started working on the briefcase again. Happy had the limo floored and his mouth clamped shut. Of all the stupid times to let her know about his stupid feelings . . .

There was Tony again.

Happy took in the situation all at once. Tony was down, half-buried in a collapsed pile of hay bales or whatever it was they set up on the inside of the crash barriers. He was moving, though. A big part of the track near Tony was on fire. Through the fire, strolling as if he was made of asbestos, came the big nutcase with the laser whips, cracking them on the pavement and grinning as if the sound was his favorite thing in the world.

There was one thing to do and Happy did it. He cut the wheel hard and hammered down on the brake, sending the limo into an old-fashioned bootlegger's turn and burying the whip-wielding freak at a speed that should have been sufficient to punch his ticket once and for all. The limo slammed hard into the crash barrier, crumpling the railings, setting off every airbag and spiderwebbing even the bulletproof glass. It came to a rocking halt, still running.

Happy noticed just then that the limo's hazard lights were still blinking. He felt a bit stupid, like he'd been driving for miles down the freeway with his turn signal on.

What to do next, Happy wondered. Talk to Pepper? No possible way. Death by embarrassment. Get out of the car and peer at the mess that was surely stuck to its undercarriage? Much preferable to the idea of talking to Pepper right then.

He was about to open the door when he noticed the boss approaching the limo.

"You got the football?" Tony asked before Happy had a chance to lower the window all the way down—but it didn't really matter since the spiderwebbed glass disintegrated as soon as he hit the button. Pepper raised the briefcase to show him. Happy was acutely conscious of the bruising on his wrist from the cuff, and of the bruising on his ego.

"Thanks?" Tony said. "Is that what I'm supposed to say?"

"You're welcome," Pepper managed. She spat airbag powder.

As Tony reached for the case, the car jumped and the maniac reared up from underneath it, whistling one of his whips past Tony's head with a barbaric yell. The whip tore through the armored hood of the car like it was aluminum foil. Tony spun back and away.

Happy was in combat time, seeing and reacting all at once. He slammed the damaged limo into reverse, got some clearance, and rammed it forward again, pinning the lunatic against the track wall. Jesus, he thought. This guy must be made of something more than flesh and bone.

The whip guy heaved against the car, but Happy held down the brake pedal. He wished he had a gun. Then he wished he'd never gotten out of bed that morning, because the whip guy started in on the front end of the car. Crack! Crack! Crack! He slashed off pieces of the hood, the front fender, and the left front tire. Crack! He slashed off the front roof strut and the corner of the roof itself. Crack! That time Happy had to dodge out of the way as the whip seared through the dashboard and straight down into the transmission housing.

From the back seat, Pepper called out to the boss while the whip guy went to town on the limo's front end. "Tony!" She opened the door and spun the football across the slick pavement in his direction.

Incredibly, the lunatic whip guy—who was wearing, could it be, an RT on his chest?—had hacked enough of the car into pieces that he was almost loose. He kept at it until with a final heave, he shoved free of the limo's bumper and stalked through the wreckage after Tony.

But by the time he got there, the situation had changed dramatically. Tony caught the football and entered a code into a pad next to its handle. It chirped its acceptance. He opened it and placed one foot in either open half. Then the football proceeded to build a light, portable prototype suit Tony was calling the Mark V from the bootsoles up around Tony's body. It wasn't the same as the full Mark IV, that was for sure. But it was still a formidable piece of smart, weaponized body armor. This whip-cracking gulag refugee had ruined—absolutely ruined—Tony's Monaco Historic Grand Prix driving debut. There would be hell to pay for that.

The first crack from an energized whip left deep scoring in the suit. Troublesome. Tony dodged the next several swings, getting a sense of how this guy wanted to use them.

Also he was incredulous at the RT on the whip guy's chest. How was that possible? The RT, and arc reactor technology, were so Stark-proprietary that even the Department of Defense had never touched the tech. Who was this guy who had just showed up in Monaco and started wrecking the place with his RT-powered buggy whips?

A whip sparked across Tony's torso, coming dangerously close to his own RT. Tony grabbed the arm holding it and flung Whip Guy into the smoking wreckage of two cars. He bounced up like a boxer who takes a shot and comes right back, like he needed the first one to really get his head into the fight. The next time he and Tony came together, the dance was a little different. Whip Guy came in high and low, vertical and horizontal, like he was only just discovering the possibilities of his toys and couldn't wait to try them all out. Tony got in a shot when he could and ducked away from as many as he could, but he was starting to have some trouble. If he'd been in the Mark IV, everything would have been fine. But in the Mark V, he had a fight on his hands. The football suit didn't have the same kind of weapons; its repulsors were pretty rudimentary and there were not internal missile or projectile systems. It was like instant coffee if the Mark IV was Jamaica Blue Mountain; all it did was make you wish for the real thing.

What it did have was pure physical strength, so that's what Tony put to use. He pounded Whip Guy every time an opening arose. He barraged him with pieces of cars, pieces of track, anything that came to hand. He got in close and delivered punches until he could feel the heat from the whips. Then he danced away and started the whole thing over again.

His heart was pounding. He was tired. It didn't seem possible, but he was wearing down without the Mark IV's energy boost. If he'd been linked in, Jarvis would no doubt have been telling him that his palladium levels were problematic.

Time to end this, Tony thought as the two of them crashed back into the wreckage of the limo, which they'd batted around until it was barely recognizable. He swatted the limo aside and dove into a clinch with Whip Guy, pinning him down and just plain pounding him until he quit.

Breathing heavily, Tony tore the RT from Whip Guy's chest and looked at it. He couldn't quite believe what he was seeing. Sirens and chaos, and he felt like he was the only one in Monaco who had anything like a clear idea of what had just happened. Problem was, he had no idea how what had happened could have been possible.

Gendarmes swarmed around the lunatic destroyer of the Monaco Historic Grand Prix, who smiled with blood on his metal teeth as they dragged him away. "I win," he said.

Well, not exactly, Tony thought, seeing as I'm still standing here and you're being dragged away by the local gendarmerie, who were apparently trying to make up for the lateness and incompetence of their response by flooding the track now that everything was over and they could get in front of the TV cameras without endangering the creases on their uniforms. He walked away, looking at the RT, fascinated by it. It shouldn't have been possible, but there it was.

"Pepper," he said. "We need to get to the plane and test this."

"Test it? This is the most important thing we can do right now?"

"As a matter of fact it is," Tony said. "See, that's because this thing cannot exist. Because if it exists that means that there is someone out there who has access to either my servers or my brain. Neither one of those things should be possible. Perhaps we can find out what has really happened, once our whip-happy Russian pal there gets interrogated. But if he doesn't tell them anything," Tony finished, holding up the RT, "this will. So. Yes. We need to test it. Okay?"

"Okay," Pepper said.

"And by the way," Tony added, "this Mark V thing worked okay. Not great, but okay. Needs some tinkering."

CHAPTER 14

By the time Tony walked into the police station, he'd had enough time to calm down. Some. He'd run some preliminary tests on the RT recovered from Whip Guy, and the results were provocative. It was almost like the Ten Rings guy from Afghanistan had read his mind and recreated the RT exactly based on what Tony had done in the cave with Yinsen, only with better results because he hadn't been freezing his ass off in a cave the whole time he worked. The world, in Tony's opinion, was not big enough for two separate organizations to have a viable arc-reactor technology, any more than it was big enough for two organizations (or states) to have an Iron Man suit. The existence of this RT was deeply problematic and had to be dealt with pronto, with extreme prejudice, readyfireaim. In this frame of mind, Tony was ready to press Whip Guy hard to see where the RT had come from. Muscle like him didn't usually know much, but they often knew more than they thought they did, and if you had a little patience it wasn't difficult for a professional interrogator to get that information—in some cases without the subject of the interrogation ever knowing exactly what he had divulged or why the interrogator had wanted to know it.

The French cops in charge were reluctant to let him talk to the guy, who apparently was named Ivan Vanko. But Tony, his head full of large ideals and spine stiffened by heartfelt determination, was under no circumstances going to leave before he got a chance to ask this Vanko a couple of sharp questions. Eventually the cops gave in and walked him back to the holding cells. They even found him an escorting officer who spoke English.

"So where did he come from?" Tony asked along the way.

"Not sure yet. He's covered in gulag tattoos, so we're assuming he's Russian."

He'd sounded Russian out on the track. Tony tried to think of Russians who might want to put together energized metal-filament whips to dismember him. And who might be able to build an RT.

None came to mind. Maybe Jarvis would know . . . but here they were. No time for research.

The French officer glanced at his watch. "Go now. He's about to be taken to an Interpol way station outside Nice."

A second French cop—this one silent and glowering—let Tony into the holding cell where a manacled Ivan Vanko sat facing the other way. Ivan was a big man even without the RT apparatus and the whips, and the officer had been right about the ink. Somewhere Tony had read that Russian prison ink had its own language, that inmates used it to tell their stories. He'd have to put someone to work deciphering Ivan's tattoos. Natalie Rushman spoke Russian. Maybe it was a job for her.

This was not one of those guys you saw who had one huge tattoo of a multi-towered Orthodox church covering most of his back and/or chest. Ivan's tattoos were many and uniformly bad, in Tony's opinion. He'd never gotten a tattoo, but he thought he knew good work when he saw it in any field of endeavor, and the ink adorning Ivan's body looked like it had been applied by a seven-year-old. There were a few exceptions, but overall Ivan was a walking advertisement for the principle that any tattoo should be considered carefully and its irreversibility fully understood.

Apart from the ink, Ivan was head to toe the walking stereotype of villainous muscle. Long hair, radiating attitude, comfortable in his confinement because he'd been there before. Tony debated how to approach him.

"Is that you, my friend?" Ivan said softly. Tony didn't answer. Ivan shifted his weight a little but didn't turn his head. "Tony Stark?"

Tony walked around to where Ivan could see him. He held up the RT where Ivan could see it. "It's pretty good," he said, and meant it. "Cycles per second are perfect. Elemental composition is pretty decent." This initial compliment out of the way, Tony got to the point. "Way too good for a dirtbag like you to make. Where did you get it?"

As Tony spoke, Ivan's eyes drifted shut and he tipped his head back. A dream smile spread across his face. "You like it?" he said. There was no mistaking the pride in his voice. "I'll make you one."

"You didn't make this."

Ivan's smile got a little wider. "It wasn't so hard."

Come on, Tony thought. He can't seriously think I'm going to believe this. He took a step toward Ivan. "Who made this?"

Opening his eyes, Ivan looked Tony in the eye and mocked him. " ' . . . every country in the world is twenty years awwaaayyy!' " He laughed. "Your technology is built from stolen goods. You come from a family of thieves. Today Tony Stark became a beggar."

A family of thieves. Tony stored that away. What did this Ivan know about his family, or think he knew? A question for another time, when he had some uninterrupted hours to spend with Jarvis. "Where did you get it?" he asked again.

"It came from the past."

"What?" Please don't be crazy, Tony thought. Because if you're crazy then I'll never be able to trust anything you say and that will mean that I'll never know where this RT came from and that will mean that I will grow old and die under the weight of an intolerable uncertainty.

"Anton Vanko," Ivan said reverently.

A name. At least he had a name. "Who's that?"

Suddenly enraged, Ivan surged against his manacles. "It is a name you should know!" he shouted. Veins throbbed from the base of his neck right up to his forehead.

"Why?"

Ivan cooled off. His expression changed, became at first cagey, then knowing. The ethereal smile returned, now with a bit of a predatory edge. "It's killing you, isn't it?"

He knows, Tony thought. How could he know?

It was true, though. He could tell that Ivan knew something about the effect the RT was having on Tony's body. And how could he know that if he hadn't done some serious work on RTs himself?

That wasn't possible, though. Nobody else was working seriously on arc reactor technology. He hadn't even been able to get Obadiah Stane to take it seriously until Obie had seen the first suit, the Mark I. And then Obie had gone . . . well, no. Who was Tony kidding? Obie had been plotting against him before that.

Which had nothing to do with arc reactors. Or with people appearing out of nowhere having built RTs that they used to crash the Monaco Historic Grand Prix and put half of the drivers in the hospital. This was a problem Tony had never thought he would encounter: someone else independently arriving at tech he'd thought was his own. Well, his father's; the initial designs for the arc reactor came from old blueprints Tony had found in his father's lab after the old man died. He'd taken it from there to the giant reactor that had run at the office until Pepper blew it up to kill Obadiah, and from that giant reactor to the miniaturized version that had saved his life after the unfortunate events in Afghanistan.

He looked back at Ivan and saw that Ivan was studying him.

"It's. Killing. You." Ivan touched his forehead, right by the temple. "I know these things."

For one of the few times in his life, Tony Stark was speechless. An hour ago he would have killed Ivan without a second thought. Now he wanted to know what Ivan knew.

The English-speaking officer entered and held the door. "Time's up," he said.

Ivan leaned his head back and closed his eyes again. He seemed happy. "If you can make God bleed, people stop believing in Him," Ivan said. His long, slow chuckle followed Tony back out into the hall and all the way to the security door.

After Stark left, Vanko went through a familiar routine. He had been in prisons before. He knew how they operated. He knew how to be patient. He could grow old and die in this French prison, or back in a Russian one, and it wouldn't matter . . . because he had looked Tony Stark in the eye and told him the truth. Now Stark would have no choice but to follow the story to the conclusion that would destroy him.

The CRS processed him out of the French system and put him in the back of a van that smelled like a jockstrap. The trip lasted about an hour; Ivan had heard them mention Nice and figured that they were going to warehouse him somewhere near there until Russian authorities came to pick him up or the French decided to keep him and prosecute him there. There were plenty of angles for both countries to play. None of it mattered to Ivan Vanko. "It's done, Papa," he said in the rank darkness as the van came to a jouncing halt and booted footsteps approached the rear door. "I did not kill Stark, but we won anyway."

An hour later, he was sharing a cell with a terrified Frenchman. Vanko spoke no French. He relied on expressions to communicate what his cellmate needed to know, which was one thing: stay away and survive. Two hours after that, a guard arrived at the cell door and tapped on it to let Ivan and his cellmate know to stay back while he opened it. The cellmate was only too happy to stay as far as possible away from both the door and Ivan, who stayed sitting on his bunk while the guard came in. Ivan didn't move. He had learned that if you gave prison guards a little push right away, they either picked a fight or learned to leave you alone.

The guard looked Ivan in the eye. For a moment Ivan thought it was going to be fight, and that was fine with him. Then the guard set a tray down next to Ivan, caught Ivan's eye, and scratched at the side of his neck. Ivan noticed what he was supposed to notice: the Ten Rings tattoo on the side of the guard's neck. Ah, he thought. An unexpected twist to events.

"Drink up," the guard said. In Russian.

CHAPTER 15

Things happened quickly after that. Ivan took a look at the food. Mashed potatoes—but it didn't smell like mashed potatoes. It did not in fact smell like any food substance Ivan had ever smelled, and in his tour of the Russian penal system he had learned to detect the slightest food value. He picked up the cup of juice and noticed a note underneath it. Ivan read the note, then looked over at the number on his cellmate's uniform. He looked from it to the number on his own uniform.

They were identical.

The next thing Ivan noticed was something he initially thought was a digital clock with a malfunctioning display. It said :30. Then it said :29, then :28, . . . and Ivan put it all together. He knew what the mashed potatoes were, and he knew what this small LCD device was, and he understood why the guard had left it all here, and he knew that if he didn't act now he was going to die.

He acted. His cellmate, who did not know that the mashed potatoes were not real, was staring at them with undisguised desire. Ivan crossed the cell in two steps and had his cellmate's head in the crook of his arm by the time his cellmate's eyes refocused from the potatoes to Ivan. A twist and pull of the jaw snapped the cellmate's neck. Ivan let the body fall.

The detonator read :24.

Ivan slapped the mashed potatoes up against the wall and stuck the detonator into the center of the gooey mass. It said :17. Ivan turned back to the door just as the guard opened it again and led him down the hall. Prisoners shouted in French. Ivan wished that he could speak French so he could tell them what was about to happen. Then he reconsidered, and was glad he knew no French so he couldn't say anything and ruin what was clearly a daring and ruthless plan to break him out of jail before he vanished into the Interpol bureaucracy, probably forever.

Who was this benefactor? Ivan could not think of a single person on Earth who could reasonably be expected to take a risk on his behalf. Apparently, however, if he survived the next few minutes he would meet exactly such a person.

Just as the guard opened a door and got Ivan into a stairwell, the charge went off with a thunderous boom that echoed down the prison's halls and—for a moment— left the prison in perfect silence. Then noise crashed back in from every direction and source. Prisoners screamed, debris rumbled and clanged as part of the prison wing collapsed. Sprinklers kicked in, soaking Ivan to the skin as he headed down the stairs at the guard's direction. Three floors down he came to a fire door. As he walked through it, he was ambushed. He started to resist, but held back. He was in a foreign country, sprung from a jail by a mysterious organization that appeared to have taken an interest in him beyond their initial financial transactions. Perhaps what he needed to do was relax and see where it was all going to lead. Hooded, cuffed, and bundled into a van, Ivan felt himself bouncing along an access road.

He was being erased. Someone had enough of an interest in Ivan Vanko to remove him from the realm of the living. Clearly the duplication of inmate numbers and the instructions contained in the note revealed a plot to dupe the world at large into thinking that Ivan Vanko was dead. Questions would be asked about how he could have gotten hold of explosives during his first hours in prison, and how far the conspiracy to get him those weapons reached. Ivan had to assume, however, that the as-yet-unrevealed conspirator who had made all of this happen was not so stupid as to leave hard evidence behind. The Ten Rings, he thought. Perhaps this is how one is initiated into that organization. All that remained to be seen was whether Ivan had been removed from the roster of the living so that his kidnapper could demand the secrets of the arc reactor.

If this was the case, the kidnapper was in for some disappointment. Ivan had suffered deprivation. He had been tortured physically and mentally. He had endured solitary confinement and sensory deprivation and sleep manipulation. He was highly confident that if he did not want to share the secrets of the arc reactor, he would be able to withstand whatever lay in store for him. And he had destroyed the original blueprints back in Moscow, so there was no chance of the kidnapper finding anything useful there.

The other possibility, the one that shone like a beacon in his mind but was probably a mirage, was that Ivan had been plucked from the fire and chaos of the prison because someone had seen what he had done and wanted him to do more of it. There were forces in the world, Ivan knew, who operated in such rarefied strata of influence and power that they remained hidden from those people who thought they had influence and power. True power was as understated as true wealth. If one of these hidden forces—either the Ten Rings or someone so elite that he could order the Ten Rings to act as saboteur and courier— had broken Ivan out of the jail, then perhaps the mirage was not a mirage.

Perhaps Ivan Vanko had been killed in the eyes of the world so that, in the perfect privacy of death, he could do the work he was destined to do.

Far more likely, he knew, that what waited for him was a series of progressively more brutal interrogations and then an unmarked grave. But ah, it was fine to imagine working with no restrictions, no responsibilities beyond creating what he could create. Thinking of this, he lost track of time for a while, the way one did when one's mind struck out through the landscape of wish fulfillment. The hum of tires on pavement became a kind of white noise in his mind. Ivan Vanko sat, and daydreamed, and wondered whether Tony Stark was at that moment lying awake wondering how Ivan Vanko had known so much about him. The world was full of possibilities.

Some time later, the van stopped and Ivan was led out of it into a large, echoing space that he immediately knew to be an airplane hangar.

The hood was stripped away, and Ivan blinked until

his eyes adjusted to the stark fluorescent lighting. He had guessed correctly about his surroundings. Across an expanse of oil-stained concrete stood a Gulfstream G5 jet adorned with a corporate logo Ivan had seen but never before remarked upon: Hammer Industries. The G5 was a sixty-million-dollar plane even before all of the custom touches that a company like Hammer would insist upon. The man who traveled in such a plane might not have Tony Stark money, but he had money to spare.

This man was currently seated at a table between Ivan and the plane, eating a meal off fine china with a decanter of wine at hand. He watched Ivan and Ivan watched him.

Ivan started to put two and two together. He had been broken out of jail by an arms merchant. A highly illegal act had been performed to secure his services. This meant that whoever had performed this act considered Ivan's services highly valuable and worth significant risk—or that whoever had performed this act considered himself above the law. Either possibility was present. Just as Ivan had known that he was in a hangar, however, he knew that this man sitting before him had willingly taken a risk because he wanted Ivan to do something critically important.

It was good to know this. Someone was beginning to recognize Ivan's talents and was not immediately inclined just to squeeze him for knowledge and dispose of him. Ivan relaxed ever so slightly—not enough that anyone other than him would have known it had happened, but enough to let him look at the situation in a dawning new light. It might just be, he thought, that his mirage imagined in the back of the van was becoming real.

The man gestured at a chair opposite his own and said, "Please. Sit." Ivan did, noting the American accent.

"I'm Justin Hammer and I would like to do some business with you."

Ivan said nothing. He wasn't ready to say anything yet. Clearly this American wanted to call the shots, and for the moment that was fine.

"Dig in," the American said. Ivan did, scooping food with his manacled hands and stuffing it in as fast as he could get it from plate to palate.

"What I saw you do today," the American continued, "was deeply impressive. I just couldn't bear to see you shipped off to God knows where . . . it would have been such a waste of talent." He reached across the table to pour Ivan a glass of wine. Ivan took a moment to savor the smell. He did not know what good wine was supposed to smell like, but this man across the table did. This was a man who appreciated the good things Ivan had never had a chance to appreciate. So Ivan inhaled, and learned how good wine smelled.

"You have a real hard-on for Stark, don't you?" the American said.

This was a bit of a disappointment. Ivan knew this type. There were some Americans—and some Russians who had learned from American gangster movies—who thought that excusing themselves from all societal norms was a way to flaunt their power and strength. The easiest way to do this was to use inappropriate language. Ivan saw no reason for this, just as he saw no reason for casual brutality. He used violence as a tool. It was a tool he happened to enjoy using, but he never let himself get carried away with it. The man who did that was at the mercy of his own baser instincts. Ivan was motivated by duty and obligation to family, to his patrimony, to the legacy stolen from him in the cradle. What higher ideal could there be?

But if Ivan Vanko knew anything about a given situation, he knew what was expected of him, and those expectations in this situation did not include critique. So Ivan nodded.

Seeing Ivan's nod, the crass American also nodded. "Yeah. Me too. But you want to know how to get to that guy? Really get him? You don't just go and try to kill him. No. You go after his legacy. That's what you kill."

Ivan drank wine so his mouth would be full and he wouldn't tell the American that Stark's legacy—and his patrimony—were exactly the point, and that Ivan had already figured that out without the help of a self-absorbed and foul-mouthed American with a Gulfstream jet.

"See, you got 'it,' " the American said. "I don't know what 'it' is, but you got it. What you need is someone behind you. A benefactor. I'm building my own version of the suit, and truthfully? I'm hitting a few rough spots."

Imagine that, Ivan thought. You, a pompous blowhard with Hollywood mannerisms and showboat instincts, are having trouble duplicating the technological advances of Tony Stark and Anton Vanko. Of course he said nothing. This was going to be his way of dealing with the American. He would say nothing, and the American would take that silence to mean assent. To assist himself in saying nothing, Ivan began to eat. It wasn't easy with manacled hands, and Ivan resented the show of power on the American's part—he could easily have broken the manacles and sat down with Ivan to a civilized meal. These were the kinds of slights that Ivan Vanko remembered and paid off when the time came.

"If you're with me, I'll set you up," the American went on. "Now, I'm not going to lie to you. This isn't without its challenges. Let's face it, you're one of the most wanted men in the Western world. You can't exactly show your face. For the time being, I'll need to keep you in the shadows. You'll have to work within the parameters. But if you can . . . I think you will find it very rewarding."

The American wiped his mouth and stood, dropping the napkin on a meal that had cost as much as Ivan's groceries for the previous three months. "Any interest?" he asked.

Ivan finished chewing. "Yes."

"Good. Then we have a plane to catch." The American started walking toward the G5. He stopped halfway there and looked back at Ivan. "Coming?"

Ivan was. If nothing else, he wanted to see what that plane looked like on the inside.

CHAPTER 16

Sitting sideways in an antique sports car that had once belonged to his father, Tony Stark contemplated a picture he'd turned up with Jarvis' aid. In it, Howard Stark stood next to another man—about his age, of similar demeanor. You had to be careful about reading too much into old photos, but there was respect between the two. Also, if Tony wasn't mistaken, tension.

The problem was that he had a photograph of his father and the father of the RT-wearing, whip-wielding Ivan Vanko. But he had nothing else to connect the two men. The extensive records of Stark Industries, from its founding to the present, barely mentioned him. "Jarvis," he said, "open up projects Manhattan, Trinity, and Footprint. See if we get anything there."

"Nothing, sir," Jarvis said. "And I must inform you that the younger Vanko has died, apparently."

"What?" Tony said. "How?"

"Blew himself up trying to escape," said Jarvis.

Briefly, frustration threatened to overcome Tony's natural bulldog tendency to investigate, to learn, to master. He took a deep breath and sat very still. So. He wouldn't be getting any answers from Ivan Vanko. That made things harder, but it wasn't decisive. Not unless he let it be decisive.

Tony thought hard for a moment. "Okay, Jarvis," he said. "Search Vanko. Look into every Russian file, phone book . . . " Momentarily he lost his train of thought. What else? "Census report, hospital record, everything. Cross reference it with Howard Stark." Data exploded all over the desktop, all of it irrelevant. Tony's head dropped forward and he rubbed his eyes. "God, I'm tired."

There must be something else, he thought, looking back at the photo. All of it must lead *somewhere*. There must be *answers*. And he needed them fast, before palladium toxicity made everything moot . . . and how had Ivan Vanko known about *that*?

There, Tony thought, was a question that would never be answered.

Then he gave up and decided to let the problem stew for a bit, while he watched television accounts of the latest catastrophic collapse of the company his father had entrusted to his care.

Casa Stark, Pepper reflected, was very much an upstairs-downstairs kind of situation the day after the events at Monaco. Upstairs, she and Natalie were fielding calls from media and government. The media thought they were circling the dying corpse of Stark Industries. The government wanted to get its hands on the football, just like they wanted the Mark IV, just like they wanted everything else.

Downstairs, Tony was doing something. But he wouldn't say what, and he wouldn't let anyone else in. Pepper figured that he was sulking about something, but the way Tony had been lately, she wasn't sure whether he was worried about having such a hard time with a minor-league annoyance like the whip guy, Ivan Vanko, or just feeling pouty because he hadn't gotten to drive the rest of the race and show up Justin Hammer. With Tony these days, it was hard to tell where ego left off and id began.

She scanned the bank of TV screens on which various pundits and anchors were digging into the parts of the story they found most interesting and likely to seize viewers. A news anchor was talking about Ivan Vanko, although she didn't know his name. "Authorities are still baffled as to who exactly orchestrated the assassination of the man who tried to kill Tony Stark," she said. "Forensics teams have begun the painstaking process of recovering human remains . . . "

The next screen to the right displayed the bullet head of a conservative pundit. "Tony Stark says trust him," he was saying incredulously, "and then just yesterday gets his butt broken off and handed to him by some whackjob who decides he doesn't like the corn dogs in Monaco!"

Moving right along, Pepper thought . . .

On the screen below the pundit, a financial talking head offered advice about the average viewer's Stark portfolio. "Get out now," he said. "If you have money in Stark, and you might need it, take the hit and liquefy. STK down a whopping seventy percent on the day . . . "

This reminded Pepper of the days following Tony's return from Afghanistan, when he had announced that he would no longer be making weapons. The talking heads had killed him then, too. Stark Industries shares had taken a sixty-percent dive. But now, six months later, they were in better shape than they'd ever been.

Well, they had been in better shape until yesterday.

On a fourth screen Tony's old friend Senator Stern was taking his shots. "Until Mr. Stark realizes that it's a big world out there, a world that doesn't care whether he lives or dies . . ."

One of his senatorial colleagues, a sixtyish woman with a Beltway beehive, added, "And frankly, it's worth pointing out that a great many people would like to see the latter."

Very funny, Pepper thought. Once again a senator mistakes her own position for the general feeling of humanity. Although . . . how many people out there really might want Tony dead? The truth was, she didn't know. There were times when she felt like killing him herself, but she'd never wanted anyone else to do it.

All of this went through her head as she simultaneously kept up a stream of public-relations shucking and jiving. She'd been doing it all day and was doing it right now, saying, "Stark Industries itself is another matter," to someone on the other end of the line. Who, she didn't know and didn't much care. "Our growth remains strong despite the anomaly that surfaced yesterday."

If, she thought, by strong you meant a seventy-percent dip in shareholder value.

Natalie cupped her hand over the mic on another phone. "It's AP," she said to Pepper. "They're going to go with a no-comment if we don't give them a quote."

"So give them a quote," Pepper said.

"What do I say?"

What Pepper wanted to say was: Listen, you little chippy. Tony's got his eye on you and that means I have to deal with you until his famously roving eye roves elsewhere. But that doesn't mean I have to like it, and it sure as hell doesn't mean I have to pretend to like it or pretend to like you.

But that would have been unprofessional. So what Pepper said instead was, "You're in the big leagues now. Step up. Don't say anything Tony will regret."

"Okay, but are we saying that—"

"Just talk," Pepper said. "Be brief. Less is more."

The doorbell rang. Natalie looked from Pepper to her phone. "Should I get that?"

There were times when Pepper really could have sworn that Natalie's naive act was exactly that: an act. It felt like she was playing a role. Nobody with her combination of education, smarts, and travel could possibly be such an innocent.

But again, it would have been unprofessional to bring all of that up in the middle of a full-blown PR crisis with the boss hiding out in a snit in the basement. So Pepper allowed herself just a tiny bit of the sarcasm she felt entitled to. "That's usually the protocol for doorbells, yes," she said. "Start sweating the small stuff. Give me the phone."

Natalie went to the door as Pepper started handling both phones. When she opened it, Rhodey came right in and said, "Where is he?"

"Downstairs," Natalie said. "He won't come up."

"Why not?"

Muting both phones against her collarbones, Pepper said, "How should we know? He doesn't tell us anything."

Rhodey headed for the stairs. Time for a little tough love toward Tony Stark. "Good luck," Pepper said behind him. Then one of her phones rang again.

Rhodey got to the bottom of the stairs and did a bit of reconnaissance through the glass walls that divided the landing from the main part of Tony's basement lab. There was Tony, watching the same TV faces that Pepper and Natalie were watching upstairs.

Rhodey knocked. Tony glanced up and let him in. Rhodey looked around, alert for any clues to Tony's mental state that might be lying out in the open on a workbench somewhere. He didn't see any, so he opted for the direct approach. "You okay?"

"Yeah," Tony said.

"You look like crap," Rhodey said, partially to provoke Tony and partially because it was true.

"Why do people keep telling me that?" Tony complained.

"We need to talk," Rhodey said. "Dead or alive, that guy has changed the game."

"There's no problem!" Tony said, too loudly. "The guy was a one-off."

"Twenty years, Tony! Remember you said that? Well, you were wrong! Somebody had your tech yesterday!"

"Nothing has changed!" Tony argued. "I'm alive!"

"Listen, it's like I said on the plane. The decision about the tech is out of your hands. The government is going to roll tanks down the Pacific Coast Highway and take your suits. You said 20 years away, but someone had your tech yesterday," Rhodey said, and would have said more, but just then Tony grimaced and slumped as if his legs were going out from under him. He braced himself against the edge of the desk. "Whoa," Rhodey said. "You okay?"

"No," Tony said. "Did you see Natalie up there?"

"Natalie isn't part of this conversation, Tony." Rhodey leaned up against the side of the car. "You need to make a statement. Soon."

"Hm," Tony said. "You're right."

Nearly leaving a startled Rhodey behind, Tony charged up the stairs and into the kitchen, where they could hear the ongoing media disaster from the living room. With the efficiency of a heat-seeking missile he located the liquor cabinet and a bottle of tequila within it. He poured and knocked back a shot under Rhodey's disapproving eye before striding through the living room and out onto the balcony.

Over the sound of the surf and the sea wind along the bluffs came the chop of helicopter blades. Tony looked up. One of the cable networks, it looked like, although the logo was hard to distinguish against the flash of the sun on the copter's fuselage.

He took out his phone and invoked Jarvis. "Jarvis," he said. "Put me in touch with that helicopter."

"Done, sir."

"Hello? Who is this?" came a shout through Tony's phone. He could hear the copter's rotors twice.

"Is this the helicopter that's hovering over my balcony and blowing all the leaves off my plants?" Tony yelled. There was a silence. "Good," Tony said. "Okay, here's my statement in the aftermath of the events at the Monaco Historic Grand Prix. Iron Man won! That other guy? He's toast. The world is as safe as it was the day before yesterday. Iron Man is on the job!"

"Mr. Stark?"

"I said everything I'm going to say."

"Mind looking up at the copter so we can get a good shot? Real quick."

"Sure, you bet," Tony said. He squinted up at the copter, shot the cameraman leaning out the door a tycoon smile, then waved as he went back into the house.

Back downstairs, Tony fiddled around with random bits of electronic flotsam on his workbench. "There," he said. "I made a statement. Happy?"

"Well, it was sure in keeping with what they might have expected," Rhodey allowed. "Listen. You okay?"

"Am I okay? How do you mean okay? I'm handsome, rich, surrounded by competent people, some of whom are gorgeous women. What could be more okay than that?"

Rhodey said, "What would Jarvis say if I asked him?"

"Jarvis would say whatever I wanted him to say," Tony said. "That's why I made him."

"Do tell," Jarvis said.

"Shut up, Jarvis," Tony said. "Don't talk to Rhodey."

Rhodey looked at him. All insouciance and denial, no sense of responsibility for what he had or what it meant to the people he professed to care about. I need to get out of here, Rhodey thought, or I'm going to say or do some things I'll regret.

"I think I better go," he said. "What's that rash on your neck?"

"It's just a rash," Tony said. "It's under control. Stress or something. It'll go away."

He waited for Rhodey to say something. When Rhodey didn't, Tony added, "We good?"

"Yeah," Rhodey said, and mostly meant it. "I think I just needed to hear you say that."

"Cool. I'll see you at my birthday party," Tony said. "And remember: casual." He made disparaging gestures at Rhodey's uniform. "This starchy getup makes girls think you're a psychopath."

CHAPTER 17

What a world this was, Ivan thought as he sat in the back of Hammer's limousine headed for Hammer's research facility. Ivan had never been to the United States, and now his first time came as an international fugitive presumed dead. He was in the United States illegally, having never come anywhere near a customs official during the refueling stop in New York. Then Hammer's plane had landed on Hammer property. Ivan felt like contraband. He was dead but alive, in a foreign country where only one person knew both his location and identity.

And that one person, Justin Hammer, was proving to be a very useful idiot.

"You'll be able to work in absolute peace," Hammer was saying as they walked down a long corridor with a steel security door at its end. "I think you're going to like what you find." He was a little ahead of Ivan, who was flanked by two enormous security guards. Ivan Vanko was not a small man, but he looked like one next to this pair. Steroid muscles, he thought disdainfully. Gym muscles. They contain no real strength except to intimidate people who already know they are weak.

The two gorillas set their palms against a touch sensor next to the door. After a brief pause, it opened. All four of them entered. "Well," Hammer said. "Here we are."

Ivan took it all in. One week before, he had been working in two rooms in Novogireevo, with illegally tapped power and pirated computing access. Now he was looking at perhaps one thousand square meters of gleaming white space. There were more computers than he could imagine needing to use. At a glance he saw tools for smelting, machining, welding, wiring, plating, microwave circuit manufacture . . . all building processes, large and small. If my father had been given the use of a lab like this, Ivan thought, he would have changed the world.

But Stark had taken that away. It was now up to Ivan Vanko to reclaim it.

Apparently Hammer had some ideas about how to challenge Stark as well. Much of the lab's floor space was taken up with long rows of gleaming metal drones, humanoid in shape and visibly armed.

"They're combat-ready," Hammer said. All they need is an engine to make them run. Have a look."

Ivan held up his manacled hands.

"Oh! Of course . . . guys?" Hammer waved the guards over. They unlocked the manacles. Ivan feinted at one of them, who jumped backwards like he'd been bitten by a snake. Looking at Hammer, Ivan cracked the barest of smiles. All in good fun, yes? Then he went to the bank of computers that lined one wall of the lab. Before he could make any decisions about the drone, he needed to know how they were put together.

"You'll be able to access them as soon as we generate you some encrypted passcodes," Hammer said. By the time he was finished speaking, Ivan had already cracked through the security shell and opened codes and schematics that were proliferating across the monitors.

"No need," he said without looking at Hammer. "Your software is shit."

While the data compiled, he went over to one of the drones and began to examine it. They were humanoid exoskeletons, with a large empty space inside the torso. "That's where the operator goes," Hammer explained unnecessarily. "I'm starting to have a tough time getting volunteers."

No wonder, Ivan thought. These are death traps for a human operator. And you, Justin Hammer, are a technologically retarded fool.

"What you want them to do?" he said, in a rare effort at diplomacy.

Hammer considered this. "I was hoping to demo them at the Stark Expo. Take a dump in Tony's front yard, if you know what I mean . . . you'd like that, right?" He grinned encouragingly, as if they were jointly planning a great practical joke.

Ivan ignored the transparent attempt to draw him out.

"Long term?" Hammer said. "I want them to put me firmly in bed with the Pentagon for the next twenty-five years. Short term? I need them to look like they can take two steps without falling over."

The venality of Hammer's ambition disappointed Ivan.

This was a man with practically unlimited resources and enough technological know-how at his disposal to command an army—but what he wanted was the crown jewel of crony capitalism, long-term defense contracts. Were it not for the fact that Ivan needed to keep the power running in this facility for the next couple of weeks while he worked, he might have killed Justin Hammer right there.

Instead Ivan took a step back and looked at the rows of drones. His soldiers. They needed some work, but they would do nicely. Trying to make them work with a human operator was transparently stupid. It added one hundred kilograms and an extra stage in the command-and-control process. Without a human operator, the drones would be lighter, faster, and less prone to error. They would be superior to human beings in every way relevant to the battlefield.

That superiority, Ivan was confident, would extend over armored human beings as well.

He thought about Hammer's near-term goal: two steps without falling over. Already a much more ambitious path was clear to Ivan. "I will make them kill things," he said.

Hammer looked nervous. Ivan liked it when the people around him were nervous. "That'd be a nice bonus," Hammer said. Then Ivan forgot he was there and started working.

CHAPTER 18

I love it when a plan comes together, Tony thought. Especially a plan for a kick-ass monster party that's all about me. I got DJs, I got custom ice sculptures, I got a sound system that will reach right across the Pacific and get the whales bumping and grinding while they migrate up to Alaska. It's my birthday. On my birthday I get to forget all of my cares and just let it all hang out.

There were people under the impression that he did that all the time, that for Tony Stark life was one long, ongoing act of wish-fulfillment. One person who often thought this had the initials PP and thought she knew Tony better than Tony knew himself. The truth was that Tony could have taken all of his money and his Iron Man suit and a couple of his favorite cars and disappeared into the desert. He could have bought a five-hundred-foot yacht and spent the second half of his life floating around the Mediterranean with a crew consisting entirely of twenty-three-year-old ex-models with self-esteem issues. He could have built a house on the Moon, was the truth. He could have dropped out.

Instead there he was last fall dropping fire retardant over the Los Angeles foothills, and taking clandestine phone calls from the CIA about certain mistakes that were now having unforeseen consequences and needed to be rectified without anybody knowing about it, and heading off into the wild blue yonder to confront this or that menace every time someone asked him to. So where did anyone get off telling him that he was self-involved or that he owed them anything? He was there when they needed him.

And tonight, because it was his birthday, he was demanding that they be there when he needed them. Even though he was never going to admit that he needed them. Except maybe to Pepper, and then only in circumstances in which situational irony would make his sincerity uncertain. Because that's how he and Pepper did things.

There was one last thing to do—other than wait all day for Natalie to find the tie he'd sent her for—and that was get a little check on the progress the palladium leaking from the RT fuel cell had made toward killing him dead while it powered the device that kept him alive. Speaking of things Pepper didn't know. I am Irony Man, Tony thought. He pricked his finger and waited for Jarvis to process the result while he looked at himself in the mirror. The image looking back at him was a little frightening, he had to admit. He kept putting on a show when people were looking, but it was getting harder and harder to fool himself with the same song and dance.

"How we doing, Jarvis?" Tony asked. "Am I really healthy, or just really really healthy?"

Jarvis gave it to him straight, no chaser. "Bio-toxicity is at its apex. Further strains placed on your body will result in almost certain d—"

Tony cut him off and stood there absorbing the news. Welcome, everyone, to my birthday party, he thought. My last birthday party. Morituri te salutant. He gazed at himself, partly out of narcissism and partly out of despair, until he heard Natalie calling from one of the walk-in closets.

"I can't find it," she said.

Tony rallied. "No problem," he called back, coming out into the main bedroom. "Bring in whatever."

"There are sooo many," she said, bringing in a tie that Tony thought Pepper might have gotten him as a joke on Bosses' Day a year ago. She looped it around his neck and started tying it. "This is going to look very snazzy," she said. Snazzy, Tony thought. He liked this girl. A lot. He liked the touch of her fingers on his neck and the look on her face while she did it—and Natalie, he was pretty sure, liked putting on that look because she knew he was watching.

Maybe he could be just a little bit late for his own party . . .

"Voila," Natalie said, buttoning his collar up and tightening the tie perfectly. "I'll go downstairs and make sure everything is perfect," she said, flipping her phone open as she left.

"Thanks," Tony said. "You're a gem."

And she was. In addition to being all kinds of hot, as well as smart, she was sweet. She wanted to take care of him. In a world where it sometimes seemed that everyone wanted something Tony had, it felt nice to know that someone just wanted to take care of him.

*   *   *

Natalie saw the discoloration spreading across the upper part of his chest and the base of his neck and put two and two together. Was the RT doing something to him? If so, he was going to need some serious technical assistance, and there weren't too many people who were going to be able to provide it. She made a phone call and started talking. There were people who needed to know about this, and needed to be ready to take action.

First, though, she needed to finish getting him ready for the party. And the next stage in that preparation was the martini she was currently carrying from the upstairs minibar back into the bedroom. He was looking in the mirror when she returned and handed it to him, then watched as he took the first sip.

"Is it dirty enough for you?" she asked, feeling a little brazen.

Tony regarded her for a moment, then asked, "If you were about to go to your last birthday party ever, what would you do?"

"I would do whatever I wanted to do with whomever I wanted to do it with," Natalie said. She meant it.

Her boss looked her up and down, taking his time about it. "That's a classy getup," he said when he was done with his appraisal. "I'm going to need you to change."

Keeping her eyes locked on his, Natalie said, "Certainly, Mr. Stark."

In three days, Ivan had transformed the Hammer research lab into a more comfortable setting. Many of the wide-open wasted spaces were now covered in nests of cable and small machines of Ivan's design. The lights were lower and the overall space carved into smaller units, each of which was dedicated to a particular purpose. In short, Ivan was making the Hammer Industries lab more like his despised flat back in Novogireevo. He had even constructed a small replica of his Tony Stark gallery. The only thing missing was Irina, really. The superintendent was checking on her. Before going to Monaco, Ivan had left instructions that if he did not return to Moscow in a month the superintendent was to adopt Irina as his own. He had suggested to the superintendent that friends of his might stop by to see how Irina was doing, and that their displeasure should she be unhealthy or poorly cared for would be intense. Ivan believed that Irina would be well taken care of. Even so, he missed her. She would have been good company here in this America he was not seeing except on a monitor screen. He watched cartoons here too, keeping two and three and four screens going while he worked. He had yet to find Nu Pogodi anywhere but the Internet, but the presence of Bugs Bunny and Johnny Test slaked his cartoon thirst for now.

One of the monitors lit up with an incoming call and the face of Justin Hammer replaced a schematic Ivan had just tuned up that morning. "You don't answer my calls these days," Hammer said.

Ivan had no answer for that, either, so he didn't answer.

"How's it coming?" Hammer asked.

"Good."

"Little harder than you thought, right?"

Ivan looked to the side, where rows of miniaturized arc reactors covered a worktable. "Not really," he said.

"Okay," Hammer said. When he finally got the message that Ivan wasn't going to talk to him, he said, "Well, let me know if you run into any prob—"

Ivan ended the call. He had better things to do.

At some point, Hammer would turn on him. Ivan knew this, and understood it. In Hammer's position, he would do the same. But he was not in Hammer's position. All of the elements of their interaction that Hammer considered advantages were in fact weaknesses. When Hammer chose to act on his perceived advantages, Ivan would be ready. He hoped the timing would be correct. It would have something to do with the Stark Expo, which Hammer was planning to exhibit in the next several days. Ivan cracked his neck and looked around; for a moment he had expected to see Irina there waiting for a seed. But no. His father was dead and Irina was gone. All that was left for Ivan Vanko was the task at hand, which was revenge. He bent to it.

Pepper hunched forward to get the right angle between the dome light and her compact mirror. In the front of the limo, Happy sat fidgeting. She was hoping he wouldn't say what she knew he was sooner or later going to say, but then he went ahead and said it.

He was anguished over what he'd said at Monaco, she could see that. And the truth was, things had been damned awkward for a little while. "You should come in," she said, knowing he wouldn't but wanting to give him something.

"No, thanks," Happy said, shaking his head.

He got out and came around to open her door. Thunderous bass from Tony's house reached across the lawn. "I don't know if this is a good idea," Pepper said.

"He'll be really disappointed if you don't go."

"Really?" She glanced up at the house. "You think so?"

"You're the boss now. Go in there and have fun," Happy said, leaning on the door. "You're networking."

He handed her the gift she'd brought. She regarded the house with dread. "Stay close. Just in case," she said.

Poor Happy, Pepper thought. He's loyal to a fault, honest . . . and completely in over his head. With Tony and with me.

CHAPTER 19

The scene inside Tony's house was about what Pepper might have expected. If it was a style, she would have called it Arrested Frat, subcategory More Money Than Was Healthy. The DJ spun behind an assembly of sound equipment that would just about have sufficed for a show at the Staples Center. There were other famous faces at the party, too—Hollywood types who got a kick out of being close to someone with a real alter ego instead of a bunch of pretend ones, mostly, but the occasional athlete as well. Mostly what jumped out at her as she walked in with her present clutched in two hands was that she felt like she had on those few occasions in college when she'd walked into a frat house party. Everyone appeared to be convinced that there was a certain way they had to act, and they were acting that way. Young women pretended to be ditzy and a little vulnerable; slightly older men competed to see who could most wittily insult their friends' favorite things while also competing to see who could drink the hardest and fastest.

At this last game, few people could beat Tony Stark. When Pepper found him in the kitchen, he'd clearly gotten a head start. He was cradling Natalie Rushman, one of whose arms was encased in a gauntlet from the Mark IV Iron Man suit. A power cable ran from it straight to Tony's RT, creating the unsettling impression that Natalie and Tony were wired together as one person. The impression was reinforced by the fact that Tony was wearing the other gauntlet.

He and Natalie were currently involved in some kind of game that involved Natalie pointing the gauntlet's repulsor in the general direction of an ostentatious drinks table crowned by an ice sculpture of Iron Man that was the Taj Mahal of machined water, only without any of the grandeur or artistic value. Pepper's initial response to this was to note the proximity of partygoers and calculate the likelihood that one or more of them would be hospitalized when the repulsor went off. Lawsuits were sure to follow.

To Tony, however, the situation apparently appeared much different. "Hostage crisis," Tony said ominously. "You gotta find the bad guy." Guiding Natalie's gauntlet, he went on. "There's the bad guy. Three . . . two . . . one . . . go!"

Natalie closed her eyes and the repulsor went off, disintegrating the ice sculpture and a pyramid of glassware next to it, along with a magnum of champagne that sprayed its foam far and wide.

"Direct hit!" Tony crowed.

"Wow!" Natalie said as she opened her eyes and looked

at the gauntlet. "It's powerful. It packs a big punch. It's got a lot of kick." Then she burst out laughing. They leaned into each other, laughing harder . . . and then they saw Pepper. Natalie sprang away from Tony as far as the gauntlet's power conduit would let her.

"I'm styked to see you," Tony said.

Hm, Pepper thought. "Stoked or psyched?"

He pointed at the gift. "What is that?" She handed it to him and Tony considered it. "See, that's my peeve," he said. "I don't like having things handed to me." He shook it and reached no conclusions. Then he started to hand it to Natalie.

Natalie held up her gauntleted hand. "We're attached."

"Let's do shots," Tony proposed. "Oh." He looked back at Pepper. "She likes martinis with three olives."

Pepper took her gift back from his ungauntleted hand. She spun on her heel.

"Give me back my hand," Tony said, aghast, as she walked away. "You have no idea where it's been."

She ran into Rhodey in the front hall and had practically never been happier to see anyone in her entire life. "Hey, Pepper," he said.

"I need some air," she said.

He looked past her to the unfolding bacchanalia inside. "Is it Tony?"

"It's a disaster," she said, flipping her present onto the pile that had drifted up against the wall inside the front door. "I shouldn't have come."

A squeal from down the hall just about pierced their eardrums. They turned to look and Pepper saw a mini-skirted blond wearing not one but both Mark IV gauntlets, hovering in midair while Tony cheered her on. Pepper saw Rhodey's face turn to stone. "This is a new move, apparently," she said.

"Wait here while I go talk to him," Rhodey said. He stalked down the hall to the edge of the living room, where the blond was saying, "Don't look up my skirt," in a way that made Rhodey think she wanted everyone at the party to look up her skirt.

"I'm not," Tony said. "I won't."

The girl pivoted accidentally in midair, noticing Rhodey as she steadied herself. "Rhodey!" she exclaimed. "Hi!"

He had no idea who she was. Ignoring her, he went straight to Tony and said, "Really. Are you going to make me say it?"

"What, you want to go next?" Tony joked.

"That's not what I was going to say."

"Best party you've ever been to?" Tony waited for a response. When he saw that Rhodey wasn't going to play along, he dialed it down a notch. "What are you drinking?"

"Not the Kool-Aid," Rhodey said. "Now let me get this straight. The military can't have access to this technology, but you can use it as a party favor with . . . "

"Rebeca!" the levitating girl said. "That's with one C."

"Yeah. That's really important for me to know right now, Rebeca," Rhodey said. He leaned in close to Tony, who didn't back down. "Put it away, Tony."

For a minute Rhodey thought Tony might take a swing at him. Instead, he backed up a fraction and said, "Point taken." To Rebeca he said, "Hey girl, you're grounded."

She lowered herself slowly and carefully onto Tony's shoulders. Looking up brightly at Rhodey, she asked, "How was my landing?"

"As an Air Force man, Colonel," Tony added, "would you call it a three-point landing?"

"Tony . . . " Rhodey was almost at his limit.

Tony seemed to notice. He held up both hands. "I get it. I got a better idea. Let me put this to bed." He slapped the girl on one perfectly tanned and gym-toned thigh.

"Thank you," Rhodey said. As he started to walk away, Tony—incredibly—called out, "Won't you come?"

And then Rebeca said, "Why are you so angry? It's a *party*."

About forty-five minutes later, from the balcony that looked out over Tony's living room, Rhodey and Pepper looked down and observed the results of his recent intervention. Tony, fully armored in the Mark IV, with the face shield up, called out, "Pull!"

A champagne bottle flew up into the air, arcing across the living room until Tony vaporized it with a repulsor blast. Over the cheers that ensued, he called out, "Here comes the Annie Oakley! Are you ready for the Annie Oakley? One . . . two . . . pull!"

Another bottle sailed up to be blasted into bubbles and sand. Pepper and Rhodey exchanged a look.

"Our little talk did a lot of good," Rhodey said.

Pepper nodded. "I think he's going to calm down now."

Back downstairs, Tony gave up skeet shooting and ascended the DJ platform, a bottle of champagne in one hand and a microphone in the other. "Rhodey, DJ, ladies and gentlemen. Ms. Potts. I've had too many secrets and it's time to reval the most intimate details about myself. You know, the question I get the most from people about this suit is, 'Tony, how the hell do you go to the bathroom in that suit?' "

There was a long pause. Tony let the suspense build. All over the living room, partygoers leaned forward to get the secret.

Then Tony said, "Just like that."

The crowd went wild. Over the wave of sound from below, Pepper said to Rhodey, "He's going to blow some-one's head off."

"Probably," Rhodey said. He was an inch away from not caring anymore.

Down in the living room, another one of the seemingly endless supply of gorgeous women in the house stood up and held a watermelon over her head. "Tony! Tony!" she called out. "Do it. Do me! Let's get this party dirty!"

It turned into a chorus: "Do it!" "Yeah!" Someone started belting out the opening notes of the William Tell Overture.

Tony turned toward the girl and grinned, swaying a little on his feet. "Tony!" Rhodey called out. "Come on, Tony! Stop that!"

He and Pepper got downstairs as fast as they could. Pepper headed for the DJ platform. Tony raised his arms. "Really?" he said. "You want the Gallagher? Put on your raincoats, people." He stood up and drew a careful bead on the watermelon. "I'm about to explore my inner Gallagher."

The girl threw the watermelon up in the air and Tony blew a storm of pulp, rind, and seeds all over the ecstatic partygoers. The noise was deafening. The DJ put on something fast with lots of squealing.

"We have to stop this," Rhodey said.

"Okay," Pepper said. "You do what you have to do. What should I do?"

"Start clearing people out," Rhodey said.

That was it. Decision time. Rhodey turned and left the room. He was about to do something that Tony might never forgive, but for the life of him, Rhodey couldn't figure out what else to do. He remembered Tony saying that what people needed was not more suits like his, but more guys like him. Right now, Rhodey was of the opposite opinion. One Tony Stark was plenty. More than enough, in fact.

But one Iron Man suit was not enough at all. Not nearly.

CHAPTER 20

Pepper took the microphone from Tony's hand before Tony—who was too busy accepting the adulation of his fans and ogling the more forward of the young women present—noticed she was there. Pivoting to face out into the room, she put on a big fake smile and called out, "Does this man know how to throw a party or what?"

A huge cheer answered her.

"Thank you so much for coming," Pepper said. "This has been a wonderful birthday."

"What are you doing?" Tony interrupted.

Pepper covered the mike and turned to him. "Listen to me. You're done. That's enough. You just peed in your pants and it's not sexy."

"You could drink that water," Tony protested. "It's recirculated."

Pepper was in no mood to hear it. She offered him the

microphone. "You want to say goodbye to your guests or should I do it?"

Tony took the microphone. He turned to the crowd, which had fallen mostly silent as he and Pepper had their tete-a-tete. "Pepper Potts, everybody," he said, and everyone dutifully clapped even though it was obvious they had no interest in leaving. "The party is over," Tony said, affecting a crestfallen demeanor. He paused to let everyone present moan and boo. Then he brightened up and said, "But there's going to be a raging afterparty!"

Thunderous cheers. Pepper turned and glared daggers at Tony. She would have incinerated him where he stood if only she'd had the power. "And anybody who doesn't like it," Tony went on, "there's the door!"

As he pointed at the door, the repulsor in the hand he used to point went off. The beam nearly decapitated any one of a dozen partyers standing in front of the glass waterfall over the basement stairwell, shattering it into thousands of glittering pieces that rained down the stairs. Water pattered on the floor in the silence that followed.

And revealed by the accidental destruction of the wall was Air Force Lieutenant Colonel James Rhodes, wearing the Mark II Iron Man armor.

"Everybody out," Rhodey said.

There was a flat-out stampede for the door. Watching Tony get wasted and play with his expensive and dangerous toys was one thing. Even watching him screw up and nearly kill somebody was kind of fun, in its way. But when a second guy shows up in armor? A second, real pissed, humorless guy who looks like he's spoiling for a fight?

That's when everybody in Malibu knew it was time to go home.

As they passed Tony, he rescued a bottle of booze from someone and took a look at it. Remy Martin. Rhodey walked up to him and Tony held out the bottle. "Nightcap?" he asked, his voice brittle and face tight with anger and embarrassment.

Rhodey swatted the bottle out of Tony's hand, shattering it. "No thanks," he said.

"Suit yourself."

"Tony," Rhodey said. "You brought this on yourself. Don't do anything stupid."

The Mark IV face shield snapped shut and Tony headbutted Rhodey straight across the room into the opposite wall. Plaster dust settled in a cloud around Rhodey as he got up. "Don't do anything stupid?" Tony echoed. "You already have."

He flipped the face shield open again and looked to the DJ, who was edging toward the door, not wanting to lose his gear—or miss the show—but also not wanting to end the night in the emergency room. "You. DJ," Tony said.

"Yes, Mr. Stark?"

"Still on the clock?"

"Whatever you want, sir," the DJ said. "Just don't headbutt me."

Tony nodded. "Give me something fat to beat your friend by."

The DJ nodded and spun up something wall-shaking as Rhodey caught Tony in a bear hug from behind. "You're not leaving me any options," Rhodey said, dragging Tony backward. Both of their face shields closed in the split second before they crashed into the wall together. Their combined weight and momentum was far too much for one ordinary wall to withstand, and they crashed through it like it wasn't there, grappling together into the gym.

For a few seconds Tony couldn't see through all the dust, and that was all Rhodey needed. A volley of fifty-pound free weights hammered into Tony, knocking him off balance.

"Time for bed," Rhodey said. He looked serious.

He batted a second group of them out of the air and came after Rhodey with an entire barbell—his favorite military-press bar, which he would now use to press that military bastard until his brains ran out his ears. Swinging it like a baseball bat, he rattled a couple of blows off Rhodey's arms and shoulders before knocking him down with a shot to the knees and then belting him straight into the boxing ring with an uppercut to the helmet. Tony flung the bar away; it punched through the gym's windows and spun away over the bluffs and out across the Pacific surf.

What happened in the ring was more MMA than boxing. They grappled and pounded the hell out of each other with fists, feet, elbows, and whatever heavy objects came at hand. Tony uprooted a corner post and nearly took Rhodey's head off with it; Rhodey got one of his own and the two of them went at it like broadsword-wielding medieval knights until the posts were too bent and broken to be useful anymore. Then Rhodey blew Tony through the wall with a repulsor, and the fight moved on to wreck the bedroom. A girl Rhodey had never seen before—or, wait, was she the one who had been wearing the Mark IV gauntlets and a bikini earlier?—leaped screaming out of Tony's bed and barely made it to the door before Rhodey went flying backward through the space she'd just been occupying.

"You know that's mine, right?" Tony said, pointing at the suit.

Rhodey nodded. "I do."

"Just checking," Tony said.

"Come and get it if you can," Rhodey said. Tony did, with a thrust-assisted lunge that crushed Rhodey through the bathroom doorway and broke the granite sink top into handy missile-sized pieces. Rhodey put them to good use, zipping them discus-style at Tony hard enough that the impact on Tony's shoulder spun the Mark IV around into Tony's bed, smashing it. Rhodey was no puritan, but he took a special pleasure from this moment.

"Sleeping on the floor tonight, looks like," he said.

"Can't believe I invited you up before," Tony said, and came after him again.

They went through a walk-in closet and the wall behind it, coming out into the kitchen in a flurry of punches, plaster fragments, and flying ties. "You steal my suit," Tony said between throwing punches and debris, "and now you steal my clothes? What's next, you want my company too?"

"I'd put it to better use than your drunk ass is," Rhodey shot back as he smashed a convection oven against the side of Tony's helmet. "But hell no, I don't want it."

He looked around at the wreckage of the house as the living room balcony, undermined by their rampage, settled to a dangerous angle. Part of it broke off and fell.

"Used to be I wanted this house, though," Rhodey said. "Shame how you've let it fall apart."

And that, both of them reflected later, might have been the last straw.

Happy had come back in when he saw Pepper come out in her state of baffled and wounded fury. The boss was the boss, but there were some things you didn't do. One of them was make Pepper Potts cry. And boss or no boss, Tony Stark needed someone to set him straight.

As he walked into the house, he felt the entire structure shiver and heard an immense crash from somewhere inside. Picking up the pace, he cut into the kitchen and ran into Natalie, who was talking on the phone. Happy caught part of what she was saying: " . . . should move in now! He is vulnerable."

"Who the hell are you talking to?" Happy demanded. Then both Iron Man suits blasted through the wall separating the bedroom and the kitchen. Happy figured the boss—well, the former boss—was in the Mark IV, but he had no idea who might be in the old suit. In fact Happy was only then starting to figure out exactly how much he didn't know.

The wall kept collapsing. Happy started moving people toward the exits. He was going to have that conversation with Natalie real soon, though. That was three times recently he'd seen her on the phone at odd times, usually times of some kind of crisis. It didn't take a genius to sniff out that something might be going on there.

The two suits squared off. Happy saw the glow of repulsors, just beginning to build. He looked around at the number of people still in the house, and the crowd that had gathered outside on the patio to see what they could of the battle royale through the rapidly disintegrating walls and windows. Oh, man, he thought. No way this has a happy ending.

"Everybody out!" Happy shouted. Tony's house was

pretty well put together, but no way was it going to stand up to a couple of full-on repulsor blasts, especially after what had already happened to it. Those things could knock a tank over. God only knew what they would do to Casa Stark or the inebriated guests therein.

Happy ran. Seeing him, everyone else still in the house ran. Seeing them, everyone on the patio started to run. Just as they got to the door or an already-broken window or a brand-new hole in the wall, or the patio steps that led out to the lawn, every remaining window on the ground floor blew out in a blinding flash.

For a while there was silence, or so Happy thought. Then, when his ears started ringing, he figured out that he'd just been temporarily deafened. He rolled over on the lawn. The house was in ruins and dazed partygoers were patting themselves down to see if they still had all their arms and legs.

Inside the house, he saw another flash. Then he saw the Mark II suit, rising on twin spikes of light into the sky over the Pacific. It gained altitude and then arced around and accelerated away to the northeast.

Uh oh, Happy thought. Now he had a real bad feeling.

When it came time to act, Rhodey thought, a man had to have the courage of his convictions. He was committed. He had done what he had done for the right reasons—reasons anyone would understand.

But that didn't mean he liked it.

After the buzz of the fight, the adrenaline, the plain old joy of bringing the house down around you while you fought to a standstill with your bullheaded and self-centered and infuriatingly witty best friend . . . after all of that, the hangover. Not in an alcoholic sense, but in the sense of feeling wrung out, paying for the exhilaration with gloom and bodily distress.

Rhodey's head ached from the impacts on the suit's helmet and his body felt like one big bruise. The after-image of that final repulsor blast felt like it would never leave his retinas. Also, he knew that when he put on the suit—no. That was one thing. Tony would have under-stood that. When he flew away from the ruins of Tony's house in the suit, he had changed the nature of their rela-tionship. Forever. Maybe he had ended it.

He had wanted to believe Tony's spiel about being committed to using the suit for the right reasons, and pro-tecting it from those who shouldn't have access to that kind of technology. The world would have been a better place if it was true, or if Tony was the kind of man who could be trusted with a trump-card superweapon. But the world wasn't like that, and Tony Stark was not that kind of man. Rhodey could be sad and disappointed about it, but that wasn't going to change his duty. He had given Tony all the rope you could give someone, and all Tony kept doing was tying new nooses on the end of it. Well, if he was going to hang himself, at least he wasn't taking the Iron Man tech with him.

There was one other factor in Rhodey's stew of feel-ings. He remembered the first time he'd ever seen Tony use the suit. Right then and there he'd sworn that he would get a crack at it himself one of these days. Too bad events had unfolded the way they had, but Rhodey wasn't going to lie to himself. This was fun. No wonder Tony liked it so much. And no wonder he didn't want to share it. Hell, now that Rhodey was up in the air in the Mark II, he didn't want to share it, either.

Right there, though, was where he and Tony parted ways. Because Rhodey knew where his duty lay, and he intended to fulfill it.

Edwards Air Force Base was ninety miles away. Rhodey called ahead, using a direct line to Major Julius Allen, who would be the duty officer. Their conversation was brief. When he landed in a hangar at Edwards fifteen minutes later, the major was still yelling at everyone in sight. "I want this entire area on lockdown!" he shouted at a beleaguered lieutenant. "Get those guys out of here! I want only necessary personnel!"

Rhodey flipped up the suit's face shield and walked over toward the major, who saluted him. "Colonel," he said. He looked at the Mark II like Orville Wright seeing an F-16, equal parts lust and amazement. It was Julius Allen who had first clocked Iron Man's actions in the Caucasus, as Tony Stark had gone rogue destroying all of the weapons his company had sold—or allowed to be sold through intermediaries—to insurgent and outright terrorist groups. He was a career advanced-weaponry specialist and research coordinator, so it had about killed him not to know what was going on, and it had also about killed him to know that Rhodey knew more about the situation than Allen did.

Now, with Rhodey standing before him in the Mark II, Major Julius Allen was about to have a whole bunch of his fondest wishes come true.

"Major," Rhodey answered with a nod. "Let's talk inside."

CHAPTER 21

It was morning. Tony didn't like mornings as a general rule and he liked this one less. The only things making it bearable in the midst of a shattering hangover, veiled threats from Jarvis about the dangers posed by palladium poisoning, and the certain knowledge that Rhodey had betrayed him to the generals who would turn the Iron Man suit into . . . whatever they were going to turn it into . . . the only things making this morning bearable were the sunglasses on Tony's face, the box of jelly doughnuts in his lap, and the view from the roof of the doughnut shop, which was ornamented with a giant plastic doughnut seven or eight feet in diameter. Tony sat inside the hole of this doughnut and regarded the San Diego Freeway's finest stretches, plus a couple of planes taking off from LAX.

Tony asked himself how he'd gotten there, and had no good answer. It must have had something to do with doughnuts, and some lingering childhood memory of having come to this same doughnut shop with his father, although that might never have happened. Beyond that, his own motives were inscrutable to him, beyond the clear impulse to squeeze the jelly from each of the doughnuts in his possession into his mouth.

"Mr. Stark," someone called from down on the ground. "I'm going to have to ask you to please exit the doughnut."

"I got five more," Tony said around a mouthful of jelly.

"Don't make me come up there," the man said, which was a sufficiently ridiculous threat to make Tony look down and see who was making it. This party turned out to be a stern-looking black guy in an eyepatch and leather jacket.

"Oh, brother," Tony said. "Aren't you the nut I kicked out of my house a while back?"

"We were going to have this conversation sometime," said the bald-headed pirate wannabe. "Now seems like a good time."

Tony shook his head. "Not interested. I got a lot on my mind." He turned his attention back to his doughnuts.

After a brief silence, Eyepatch tried again. "How about I buy you a cup of coffee?" he said pleasantly.

Well now, Tony thought. A civilized approach. Coffee with doughnuts. That could work.

Ten minutes later, there they were inside waiting for coffee. It was taking a while because Eyepatch—whose name, Tony seemed to remember, was Fury—had with him a cadre of menacing and probably armed people in black outfits who had cleared employees and customers alike out of the shop. One of those highly skilled operatives was now getting coffee, which Tony was realizing he needed badly.

"Look," he said. "I told you I have no interest in joining your super-secret whatever it is."

"Oh, yeah, yeah," Fury said. "That's right. You're doing it all yourself now. How's that working out for you?"

"I don't want to be rude, but can you just tell me which eye I should be looking at?" Tony asked. "I'm not sure if you're real or if I'm having delirium tremens."

Fury reached across the table and slapped Tony hard enough to make his eyes water. "Oh, I'm real, all right. You don't get realer than me."

It took Tony a minute to work out how he felt about being bitch-slapped by a stranger in an eyepatch. "Wow," he said, putting his hand to his face. "That stings."

"You're not looking so well," Fury said. Tony saw him looking at the side of Tony's neck, where the marks of the skin rash were spreading. For all Tony knew, it might have crept right across his face.

"I've been worse," he said.

"That's not the word I'm getting," Fury said, to which Tony might have said something acerbic, but at that moment he heard Natalie's voice.

"We have the perimeter secured. I don't think we should hold it for too long," she said, as Tony turned and saw that instead of her drop-dead stunning business suit, or drop-dead stunning evening gown, she was wearing a drop-dead stunning navy blue combat uniform, made of something form-fitting and accented by dominatrix boots and a belt from which dangled a gun and a number of other tools.

"You are so fired," he said, momentarily forgetting in his daze that he had signed away most of his power to fire anybody.

"Tony, I'd like you to meet Agent Natasha Romanoff," Fury said.

"I've been a S.H.I.E.L.D. shadow," she said, "embedded for over six months. I was tasked by Director Fury once we knew you were ill."

"That's very courteous of you," Tony said. Six months . . . so she had been on this case since before everything with Obie Stane had blown up? How had this S.H.I.E.L.D. outfit known that he was getting sick? "I'm just going to need a moment to process this," he said, marveling at the way Natalie—or Agent Romanoff—looked in her midnight-blue fighting catsuit. "Just let me take this visual in for a minute. It's too good. Give me a second to—"

She cut him off. "I suggest you sit back and listen to this man," she said, suddenly not Natalie anymore. She was mysterious and lethal and deadly serious. "Carefully," she finished.

"You've been pretty busy lately," Fury said, picking up the thread. "Naming your girl CEO, giving away your stuff. You even let your friend fly off with your suit. If I didn't know better I'd say that—"

"You don't know better," Tony cut in. "I didn't let him, he took it."

There was a silence during which Fury looked Tony dead in the eye, leaning forward slowly until his face was out over the table. "Don't. Talk," he said. "When I'm talking." He paused. Tony decided not to push anything. Fury went on. "You're blowing my mind. So he just took it from you? Oh, I'm sorry, I must be mistaken. See, I thought you were Iron Man. So he just took it?"

Fury reached across the table and deliberately

plucked Tony's last doughnut from the box. "Like I just took this cruller?" he said. "I can just take stuff? I want something, "I can just take it, and you can't take it back? I see."

"According to your own database security guidelines, there are redundancies," Natasha added. "To prevent un-authorized usage."

Tony took a breath to decide how to proceed. "We're out of doughnuts," he said. "What do you want from me?"

"What do I want from *you*?" Fury's one eye popped. "What do *you* want from *me*!?" He stabbed a finger at Tony. "You're becoming a real problem. A problem I now have to deal with. And believe it or not, you're not the center of my universe. In fact, you're not even my biggest issue I got in the Southwestern sector."

Fury cast his eyes to heaven, then down at the table. "What do I want from you," he muttered. "Hit him."

Hit me? Tony thought. Then he felt a sting in the side of his neck.

He jerked away from it and saw that Natalie—Natasha—had injected him with something. "Ow!" he said. "What, you're going to steal my liver and sell it? That's what you want? Can you people please not do any-thing weird for five seconds?" Looking up at Natalie and back to Fury as he rubbed the side of his neck, he said, "What did you do to me?"

"It's what we did for you," Fury said. "Lithium diox-ide. It'll take the edge off."

This was too good to be true, which meant that Tony couldn't believe it for a second. "Good," he said. "Get me two boxes of that. I'm cured."

Natasha shook her head. "It's not a cure," she said. "It just abates the symptoms."

She held up a small mirror from a pouch on her belt. In it Tony could see the rash recede down the side of his neck and disappear into his collar. How about that, he thought. It worked. Even if only for a little while, it worked. He wanted to ping Jarvis and get a sample to see what the palladium toxicity level was.

"There's not going to be an easy fix," Fury said.

"Trust me, I know," Tony said. "I've tried every combination of every permutation of every known element."

Fury was shaking his head. Very slightly—the S.H.I.E.L.D. honcho was not given to elevated displays of emotion—but he was shaking his head. Tony stopped. "I'm here to tell you," Fury said, "you haven't."

Tony opened his mouth, then shut it again. He looked outside, where a crowd had gathered. Some of them had phones out and were taking pictures. Tony tried to work out the consequences to Stark Industries' stock price if pictures of him sitting in an eight-foot plastic doughnut in the Mark IV with a guy in an eyepatch got out. He couldn't reach a firm conclusion. The S.H.I.E.L.D. guy who had been hanging around before everything went wrong with Obadiah, what was his name . . . Coulson. Coulson was outside with the crowd. He looked like he was saying something to them. Then he took out a smallish device of uncertain purpose and did something with it, whereupon its purpose became clear because everyone in the crowd started yelling and waving their phones at him.

Fury was looking at him, his expression part impatient irritation and part smug gotcha. "Have I got your attention?" he asked.

While Tony was figuring out how to get his mouth working again, Natalie reacted to something only she could hear. "Copy that," she said. "We might want to get those doughnuts to go, boss," she said to Fury.

For the first time, Fury appeared to notice the crowd. "Fine," he said. "What do you say we go get some fresh air?"

"The thing in your chest," Fury said later when they were sitting in Tony's kitchen under a beautiful afternoon sky striped with high cirrus clouds, "is based on an unfinished technology."

"No, it was finished all right. It powered my factory for a while," Tony said. "All it did was square my electric bill."

Looking up at the sky, Fury said, "Howard knew the arc reactor was just a stepping stone to something greater. He was kicking off an energy race that would dwarf the arms race. He was onto something big, something that would have made a nuclear reactor look like a triple-A battery." Fury paused to make sure Tony was paying attention. "He was about to change the balance of global power."

They took in the ambience of the destroyed kitchen for a while. Man, Tony thought. Rhodey and I sure did a number on the house. "What did Anton Vanko have to do with it?" he asked after a while.

"Anton Vanko," Fury repeated. "Yeah. The other side of the coin. Anton, now, he saw the arc reactor as a way of getting rich. When your dad found out, Vanko was deported. When the Russians found that he couldn't deliver, he was shipped off to Siberia where he spent the next twenty years in vodka-fueled rage." Here Fury paused to cast a significant glance in Tony's direction.

Yes, Tony thought. I get it. Drinking, rage . . . sure.

"Not an ideal environment to raise a son," Fury went on. "Who, by the way, you happened to cross paths with in Monaco. Sins of the father and all."

Something beeped deep in the house. A notification from Jarvis, perhaps, who had been instructed not to act like a full-on AI when Fury was around. Tony wasn't sure and at the moment he didn't care.

"Sometimes you're paranoid," Fury said. "Sometimes you have people coming after you. You just happen to be both."

"My dad was exacting. If there was something there he would have left bread crumbs," Tony said, thinking out loud. Could Fury be right that Tony had missed something? Had he missed it because he hadn't seen a clue his father had left? "What did you mean when you said I haven't tried everything?" he asked. "Is there something you're not telling me?"

"Your father knew that you are the only one with the means and knowledge to finish what he started," Fury said.

"Hey, Obi One-eye," Tony said. This got a ghost of a smile from Fury. "I don't know where you're getting your information, but my father didn't even want his own son around the house. The best day of both our lives was when I was shipped away to boarding school."

"That's not true," Fury said.

Tony was struck by his tone of voice. Not argumentative, not defensive. Fury was simply stating a fact. "Well, then," Tony said, "you must have known him better than I did."

"In some ways I probably did," Fury said. "He was a founding member of S.H.I.E.L.D."

Tony wasn't sure how to handle this. How was it possible? He distracted himself by putting something else in front of this new information in his mind. The kitchen. He kind of liked it that way; in the back of his mind he was already sketching out blueprints for a new kitchen with a glass roof. It didn't work. One of the founding members of S.H.I.E.L.D.? Tony was a bit stunned by this. How had he never heard of any of this?

"Well, I got a two o'clock," Fury said, standing up. "You got this? We're good, right?"

"Got what?" Tony stood too. "I still don't know what I'm supposed to get."

"Natasha will remain a floater at Stark with her cover intact," Fury said. "And you remember Agent Coulson."

"Roughly. But I don't get it and we're not good," Tony said.

Ignoring this, Fury started to walk away. "And Tony, remember," he said as he headed for the S.H.I.E.L.D. car waiting in Tony's driveway, "I got my eye on you."

Good one, Tony thought.

He was ready for a good solo think, perhaps aided by Jarvis, but Natasha appeared with a brisk status report. "We've shut off all communications. No contact with the outside world. I'll be administering your medication. Tacos and sodas at six."

Then she too left and Tony was sitting at the kitchen table with Agent Coulson, who had been there the whole time without anyone noticing him. Coulson was that kind of guy, Tony thought. The perfect operative because he was practically invisible.

"If it's going to go down like this," Tony said to him, "I mean, if I get to do this celebrity rehab thing, I'm going to need a shiatsu massage and whatever is next on my Netflix."

"I'm not here for that," Coulson said. He smirked a little. It was the kind of expression you saw on a man who nobody ever thinks is in charge, and everyone is always a little surprised to see running things.

Tony waited for him to get it out of his system.

"I've been authorized by Director Fury to use any means necessary to keep you on premises. If you attempt to leave or play any games, I will taze you, give you knockout drops, and watch TV while you drool into the rug." When he was done, Coulson looked pretty satisfied with himself.

"I'll just chill," Tony said. "Okay. I get it."

"Now give me the thing," Coulson said.

"What thing?"

Coulson mimed tapping the keys on a cell phone. "The thing."

"I have no idea," Tony began. He stopped when Coulson reached behind himself for something in his belt. "Here," he said, producing the glass Jarvis chip. "Here."

Coulson took it and slipped it into his coat pocket. "And there's your evening's entertainment," he said.

Tony looked down at a box sitting on the floor next to the kitchen table. When he looked up, Coulson had walked out of the kitchen, maybe to find a comfortable seat somewhere else in the ruin.

CHAPTER 22

Finally Hammer seemed to have gotten the message. Ivan hadn't heard from him in more than twenty-four hours. This was good. Optimal, in fact. It meant that Ivan could work, and that Hammer was a little frightened of him. Ivan wanted this, because he knew how men like Justin Hammer reacted when they were afraid. Sooner or later, when he had gotten everything from Ivan that he thought he needed, Justin Hammer would make his move to get rid of Ivan. One complication for Hammer would be that Ivan knew this move was coming. A second complication for Hammer was that Ivan was smarter than he was, as well as more ruthless and infinitely more driven. Hammer wanted to get rich? Ivan had no desire for money except for its function in providing him with things to build and deploy to destroy Tony Stark. Hammer could have his pretense of Pentagon contracts extending until long past his retirement age; while he was indulging this fantasy, Ivan was working.

There were thirty-two drones in what Ivan called final preparations. He was styling them according to Hammer's wishes even though there was much about each drone that Hammer did not know. They stood in four groups of eight.

The first thing Ivan had done was redesign each drone so it did not need a human operator. This necessitated rebuilding much of each drone's torso to eliminate wasted space—and, in the case of those drones designed to fly, reconfigure the aerodynamic surfaces to account for the new distribution of mass. The cranial armor, originally designed to protect a human head, now protected an array of sensors and navigational equipment, all of which could be controlled from right here in this laboratory or from anywhere in the Hammer Industries complex. If the user had the correct authority. The thoracic space, originally configured to contain and protect a human torso, now contained the complex of exchangers, circuitry, and energy-management systems necessary to get power from each unit's RT to where it was needed.

And in the center of each unit's torso, deliberately placed to echo the Iron Man Mark IV armor, glowed a mini arc reactor. One of these, Ivan thought, would be the last thing Tony Stark saw in this mortal life.

Unless—and this was the only more desirable possibility—the last thing Stark saw was the apparatus Ivan Vanko was building for himself.

The drones were not the only denizens of this laboratory whose combat capability was being refined. Right now Ivan was holding back on the number of hours he put into a refinement of the Whiplash system because he was intrigued by the problems the drones presented and because he felt some glimmer of obligation toward Justin Hammer. After all, if Hammer had not broken him out of jail, he would be in no position to be installing RTs in an army of drones destined to destroy Tony Stark. So Ivan owed Hammer a certain debt of gratitude.

Soon that debt would be discharged. When it was, Ivan would feel free to embark on his own lines of research. Until then, he would take what Whiplash time he could, and he would work knowing that whether he constructed drones for Hammer or improved arc reactor-driven systems for himself, he was working toward the goal of Tony Stark's humiliation and demise. This could keep him going.

Now that he had committed, Rhodey felt good about the decision. This was going to be a transformative moment in the history of the security of the United States. For the first time, infantry was about to become armor, and armor was about to become air power. This was a newborn revolution in strategy and geopolitics. If it pissed Tony off, well, that was Tony's fault for being such a self-centered arrogant prick.

And Tony was guaranteed to be pissed off, especially once he found out who was going to be doing the prototype of the fully weaponized version.

Screw him, Rhodey thought. He can spend the rest of his life getting girls in bikinis to shoot the windows of his house out with repulsors when they aren't getting him drinks. If that's what he wants, that's what he can have. But that doesn't have to mean that the United States throws away the advantage it might have gained by Tony's innovation . . . back when Tony was still innovative instead of just drunk.

All of this went through his head in the few seconds it took for a staff sergeant to gather a select group of Air Force engineers who had been waiting in the machine shop attached to the hangar where the Mark II lay on a table more or less exactly in the spot Rhodey had landed it. Rhodey, with Major Allen just to his left, stood next to it and nodded at the engineers as they came in. These were the Air Force's best and brightest combat engineers, together with a few lab guys who were there to glean what technological goodies they could while they were putting the new version of the suit together.

"What you will be weaponizing," Rhodey told the assembled team, "is a flying prototype of the Iron Man Mark II, for the purposes of an offensive footing."

"Yes, sir," the engineers said, more or less in unison. Everyone waited around for a minute. Rhodey realized they were waiting for more from him, but he didn't have any more. They'd been briefed that they were supposed to be disassembling and retrofitting an advanced mechanical system. Now they knew what that system was. What he wanted was for them to get to work. He took a step back and made an after-you gesture in the direction of the Mark II. The engineers approached it, wrenches and screwdrivers in hand. One of them picked up the helmet.

"Don't forget," Rhodey said. "This thing was made by Tony Stark, so chances are—"

He was cut off by an actinic flare that knocked one of the engineers flat on his back. *He was prepared for this*, Rhodey had been about to say. But now they already knew.

"There's a lot we could learn here," Major Allen said, eyeing the semiconscious engineer.

"You're not going to learn everything," Rhodey cautioned. He unscrewed the suit's RT and held onto it just in case. "We're just arming it."

But just arming it meant gauging its aerodynamics all over again given new distributions of weight and differing shapes of external armature. So Rhodey was deliberately oversimplifying, and they knew he was doing it, but they also knew that the task at hand had to be kept very simple or it was never going to get done in time for the impending visit of General Newcomb in forty-eight hours. The general, it was understood, expected a fully functional prototype and would be deeply displeased with anything less.

"Just arming it" also meant figuring out how to touch it without being shocked into a stupor. Rhodey had glossed over that, too, figuring that they were the engineers and it should be them who figured it out.

For a moment the assembled crew stood in a rough ellipse, of which the Mark II and the KOed engineer would have been the two foci. The engineers didn't appear certain about what they were supposed to do next. Their comrade who had gotten the initial shock stirred and sat up. "Whoa," he said.

The energy in the room—primarily dread, if Rhodey was any judge, but tinctured with anticipation and boyish excitement at the sheer excellence of the gadget in question—changed with the bulldozing entry of Justin Hammer, who slammed in through the machine shop door and walked straight up to the Mark II. He stood almost reverently before it, but when he started talking, he reminded everyone present that if there was one word that could rarely be used to describe Justin Hammer, that word was reverent.

"You have got to be kidding me!" Hammer exclaimed, all visible evidence to the contrary. "I got here as quick as I could."

Rhodey shook hands and said, "You think you could hook it up?"

While they were greeting each other, Hammer's flunkies were bringing in an array of crates and setting them near the Mark II.

Hammer winked and popped the lid off the closest crate, bringing out a blocky matte-black submachine gun. "Heckler PDW," he said by way of introduction. "Fires a nine-millimeter round, deadly at close range. Deadlier with hollow-points. Not a bullet you want to reach out and touch you."

Rhodey shrugged. He'd seen the PDW before and could recite its specs from memory: muzzle velocity 2379fps, et cetera and so on. It was a fine infantry weapon for close work, but Hammer's choice betrayed a lack of imagination. This was an Iron Man suit they were talking about.

Tossing the PDW to an aide, Hammer said, "Really? Looking for something more?" From the same crate he lifted a full-length assault rifle and slapped a banana clip into it. "Barret M468 assault," he said. "Collapsible stock. Five-point-five-six-millimeter round. Lots of punch. Fast movers. AKA, the Skin Ripper."

The Skin Ripper? Rhodey was wondering if Hammer's usual clients went for that kind of video-game blahblahblah. The Barret was a typical M-16 clone, nothing more and nothing less. Didn't jam like the M-16 used to have a tendency to, but it was nothing special. Skin Ripper, my ass, Rhodey thought. Any gun in the world will rip your skin. And who the hell cared about a collapsible stock when the weapon was going to be built onto the Mark II? It wasn't going to need a stock at all.

"Be more imaginative," he said. He was starting to enjoy having Hammer work for him instead of feeling like it was the other way around. "Go large."

"Silly me. Of course." Hammer handed off the M468 and waved to someone just outside the hangar door. "Please . . . "

One of his aides borrowed a pallet jack stored against the hangar wall and used it to bring in a man-sized crate covered in Hammer's corporate logo. After a bit of a struggle, he came up with a heavy machine gun, multibarreled and slick with oil. "Outfitted to our Apache Longbows," he said. "Fires AK's seven-point-six-two suppressor rounds. The torso taker, leg breaker, the powder maker. Our boys in uniform call it Uncle Gazpacho. If guns were porn stars? Meet John Holmes."

This got a chuckle from a couple of the engineers. Rhodey was no prude, but he didn't go for porn humor when the national defense was under discussion. And the gun was fine, but if he'd been Hammer, he'd have gone with Uncle Gazpacho first and brought out heavier stuff from there. So, fine. The weaponized Mark II would have a Gatling gun as its go-to small-arms default.

"What else?" Rhodey said.

Taken aback, Hammer said, "Anything bigger would need to be fitted to an aircraft."

What the hell did he think they were doing here? Rhodey wondered. This was a new paradigm. Hammer was disappointing him. For a moment Rhodey had a daydream of how this same presentation would be going if it was Tony Stark doing the pitch. By now the Mark II would have been bristling with armaments the world had never seen, or thought of. That was the difference between men like Tony and men like Justin Hammer. Because Hammer wanted to get rich, he spoke the language of the pitch and the deal. Because Tony was an engineer at heart rather than a businessman, he spoke the language of the barely possible, the thing that could maybe be done if the brain could be stretched enough to see the way to do it.

He wished he was having this conversation with Tony, but it was a wish like wishing you could have dinner with an ex-girlfriend one more time, just because of the way she'd made you laugh and gotten you thinking about things you'd never thought about before.

But the reason you were broken up was that she was a drunk with a wandering eye, and you couldn't trust her, so here you were with the next best thing.

"Dream a little," Rhodey said to Hammer.

From yet another crate Hammer extracted a red missile, approximately a meter long and about as thick as Rhodey's flexed bicep. It was almost entirely featureless except for small fins near the exhaust. Looked like a miniature cruise missile with on-board continuous command-and-control systems. Rhodey liked it.

"If I can find a way to mount them, this is your lady," Hammer said, caressing the missile like a man in love. An unintentionally revealing moment, Rhodey thought. He was glad when it passed and Hammer got down to his standard ridiculous pitch shtick. "A kinetic-kill sidewinder vehicle with a secondary cyclotrimethylene trinitramine-PDX burst. It can intercept incoming ballistics but it's better at just vaporizing whatever's downrange. Capable of busting the bunker under the bunker you just busted. If it were any smarter it'd write a book. A book better than *Ulysses*. It's my *Pieta*. My Rachmaninoff's Third. My Eiffel Tower. Completely elegant, bafflingly beautiful, and capable of reducing the population of any standing structure to zero."

Rhodey looked it all over. "Done deal," he said after a brief—and calculated—pause. "Get busy."

"Which ones do you want?"

"All of 'em," Rhodey said on his way out of the hangar. All of a sudden, he had a hell of a lot to do.

CHAPTER 23

In addition to his many other salutary characteristics, Tony Stark was a collector of outdated technologies. One item in this collection, luckily, was an old Kodak Ektagraphic CT1000 sixteen-millimeter film projector. This was lucky because the box Coulson had left on the kitchen floor had contained, among other interesting items, a reel of sixteen-millimeter film. As a result of Tony owning the CT1000, he was now sitting downstairs in his lab playing this film, which in turn meant that he was watching old footage of his father working on the footage he'd prepared for the first Expo, back in 1970.

"Everything is achievable through technology," Howard Stark said, just as he had on the archival Expo footage Tony had shown at the new Expo's opening ceremony a couple of weeks ago. "Better living, robust health, and for the flirst time . . . sorry . . . the flirst . . . " He burst out laughing. "Damn, I gotta untie my tongue." Getting himself back to his mark, he waited while the film crew got ready to do the shot again. "You think Steve McQueen has this problem?"

Tony couldn't help but smile himself. Whatever else came of his meeting with Nick Fury, he had to admit that it was nice to see this footage of his father in unguarded moments. Hey, Dad, he thought. So this is what you were like when you weren't being Howard Stark.

Off-camera, someone said, "Okay, and action, Howard!"

"Everything is achievable through technology," Tony's father began again. He trailed off. After about five seconds, the crew started to chuckle. "Except remembering my dang lines!" Howard said. "What is it again?"

"Better living . . . " the same off-camera voice reminded him.

"Of course," Howard said. "Better living. I'm sorry, Ron. Let's finish this tomorrow."

"Cut," said the off-camera voice. The screen went blank . . .

. . . and then came to life again, with a pajama-clad Howard Stark, in his laboratory with an Expo model behind him and a baby cradled against his shoulder. It was dark, and much of the lab was in shadow. Jesus, Tony thought. That's . . .

"This is the third night you've kept me up crying," said Howard Stark to his son across the years. "Thought I'd give your mother a rest."

My mother, Tony thought. When he said that, my mother was alive. It was a difficult idea for him to get a handle on. Sometimes it seemed to him like his parents had always been dead, like he'd only really begun to exist when he was at MIT and he'd gotten the phone call about the car crash . . . for a long time, he realized, he'd unconsciously dated the beginning of his life to the moment that he'd been orphaned.

"Right now you haven't mastered English yet so I thought I'd put this on film for you," Howard went on. "I want to show you something."

He stepped aside to let the Expo model fill the frame. "See that? I built that for you." Sometimes Tony's father was talking into the camera, and sometimes to the infant Tony whose older, wiser, more cynical self watched with a dazed smile on his face. "And someday you're going to realize that it represents a lot more than just people's inventions. It represents my life's work. Someday you'll figure it out. And when you do, you'll do even bigger things with your life. I just know it. You're the future."

Nick Fury had said the same thing. Only not in the same way. Tony started to shake off his sentimental response and engage his intellect. This footage was something more than a Hallmark card; his father was starting to get at something, and he expected Tony to figure out what it was.

"I've created so much in my life, but you know what is the thing I'm proudest of?" Howard was talking to the baby Tony, but now he looked right into the camera. "You. My son."

This hit Tony hard. He wasn't the kind of man who cried, but alone in his ruined house, abandoned by friends and staring death in the face, he felt a little prickle in the corners of his eyes. Yeah, Dad, he thought. I love you too. And I'm ready. What are you trying to get across? Is it a puzzle? Show me. Show me.

I can do it, Dad.

"You are and always will be my greatest creation. I love you. Now let's get you to bed." Howard paused before he'd walked out of the frame. "The secret to the future is here," he said over his shoulder, looking back and forth between son present and his imagined son of the future.

Fury had been right, Tony thought. I never knew how the old man felt. He welled up, there by himself with everyone he knew either angry or alienated.

And there, Tony thought. I was right too. He left me something . . . the lesson. Don't leave anything unsaid.

"Jarvis," he said. "I'll be right back."

Having broken some kind of land-speed record for an electric car on Los Angeles streets, Tony got to Stark Industries, walked in the front door, and only then realized he was still in his bathrobe and slippers. At least he'd remembered the strawberries from the fridge back home. There was something with Pepper and strawberries, he couldn't quite remember what, but he was pretty sure they'd break the ice. He brushed past everyone who said hello, ignored the ones who stared, and dove into an elevator. On the trip up to his office's floor he invented a hundred different ways to make elevators faster. When the doors opened at last he barged out into the executive reception area and came to a halt at the desk which had once hosted his secretary and now hosted Pepper's. Whose name, Tony realized with something akin to horror, he did not know.

He waved at her as he went by . . . and ran straight into

the door when it didn't open at his touch. Confused, he looked back at the secretary.

She let him hang for a long moment. More than long enough to let him know that while he might have gotten away with all kinds of outlandish behavior when he was CEO of the company his father had founded, things were going to be a little different now that Ms. Potts was in charge and he was just the wayward founder's son with no executive position requiring deference.

Then she went to the door, touched a code into a pad set into the jamb, and poked her head in. Through the opening, Tony saw Pepper on the phone. She glanced up and waved the secretary away.

Bambi, Tony remembered. That was the secretary's name.

Before he lost his chance, Tony slipped right by the secretary and into the office. Pepper was saying something about illegal seizure of Stark Industries property and associated trademarks. "I'm sorry, Miss Potts," Bambi said when Tony shoved past her. "Mr. Stark is here and he refuses—"

"Thank you, Bambi," Tony said.

Pepper glared at both of them and kept talking. Bambi left and Tony stood fidgeting while Pepper represented the interests of the company in a forceful manner. "It's our position that Stark has and continues to maintain proprietary ownership of the Mark II platform," she said. "No. Listen, Bert, don't tell me that we have the best patent lawyers in the country and then tell me not to pursue this." She paused while the overmatched Bert presented his case. "Well, then," Pepper said, "let the president sign an order. This isn't done. I want to force the issue here." Another pause.

"I will see you at the Expo," she said. "Will Mr. Stark be attending the Expo?" She looked over at him. "No, he will not."

Pepper hung up. Now that she only had Tony to glare at, she glared twice as intensely. "You got a minute?" Tony asked.

"No," she said. "I don't."

"How about thirty seconds? Come on."

"Twenty-nine," Pepper said. "Twenty-eight . . . "

"I want . . . wow . . . gee," Tony said. Suddenly on the hot seat, he was tongue-tied. "Oh, boy. I want to say . . . express . . . I never knew until just a minute ago . . . look. Listen. I. Okay. Umm. I need you to know . . . " He paused. "Life is short. And I . . . I . . . "

"Let me stop you," Pepper said, "because if I hear you say the word 'I' one more time I'm going to throw something at your head. I'm trying to run a business. I care about the future, which means I need to provide peace of mind to my shareholders, who at this moment are running for the hills because of your antics. I'm trying to do the job that you were meant to do."

She noticed the strawberries Tony was clutching like he didn't know whether to give them to her or throw them away. "Are those strawberries?"

Tony held them out to her. "Uh-huh."

Her eyes narrowed. "Do you know there's only one thing on earth that I'm allergic to?"

"Strawberries?" Tony said.

"Bingo," Pepper said.

"I knew there was something with you and strawberries." Tony looked around for somewhere to put them, but he couldn't find a trash can.

"I need you," Pepper said slowly.

"I need you too," Tony said. "I think I'm in—"

"To leave," Pepper finished.

Tony couldn't speak. For one of the few times in his life, he was utterly at a loss. He didn't have to say anything, however, because at that moment Natasha walked in, acting as Natalie Rushman again. "Ms. Potts," she said.

"Hi. Come in," Pepper said. Behind Natalie, Happy came in. He picked up three suitcases that Tony had just noticed on the other side of Pepper's desk.

"Wheels up in twenty-five minutes," Natalie said. She handed Pepper some papers.

"Thank you," Pepper said.

Happy had the luggage to the door. "Anything else, boss?" he called.

Reflexively Tony answered. "I'm good." At the same moment, Pepper said, "I'll be right down."

There followed a difficult silence. Neither of them knew exactly what to say. Tony stepped in when he couldn't stand the idea of silence anymore. "I guess you got both kids in the divorce," he said to Pepper. Then, nodding at Natalie, he said, "Blending in nicely."

"Natalie's been incredible, I have to say," Pepper enthused.

"Seamless transition?" Tony asked skeptically. "I thought you two had a problem with each other."

"It seems the only problem is you," Pepper said. She turned to Natalie. "Please speak to Mr. Stark about the matter of the . . . you know what. Now that he's here, maybe you can discuss what to do with his personal belongings."

"Absolutely," Natalie said. Turning to Tony, she said,

"Would you like to go through your things before I put them in storage?"

Strange echoes of the scene with me, Rhodey, and Pepper on the plane, Tony thought as Pepper followed Happy out the door. And he asked the question that he thought someone probably had wanted to ask him that day. "How do you sleep at night?" he asked her. "Could you possibly be more duplicitous? You're a triple impostor. You're a black widow. Do you actually speak Latin?"

"*Fallaces sunt rerum species*," Natalie said.

Amazing, Tony thought. "What did you just say?" he said. "Did you cast a spell on me?"

"It meant get your ass home before I have you collected," Natalie said quietly.

Then she walked out, leaving Tony alone—except for a carton of strawberries—in the office that once was his. How things do change, he thought. "You're welcome," he said softly to no one. He walked over to Pepper's desk, ate a single strawberry, and threw the rest in the trash can that he found at the far side of her desk.

Well, he thought. Personal belongings. He figured he'd grab what he could before that perfidious Natasha had him collected. There, leaning against the bookcase under a sheet, was a model of the original Expo that Howard Stark had constructed in his first pitch meeting with New York's movers and shakers. Would you look at that, he thought. He undraped it and set it level. Sins of the fathers, Fury had said. No joke.

Then something about it caught his eye.

Something in the shape of it . . . the organization of the buildings. There. Tony leaned forward, tracing his finger along the miniature skyline as if he needed his sense of touch to confirm what his sense of sight was telling him. It would have looked like an accidental angle highlighting the geometric arrangement of the whole . . . unless you had a certain line of research in your head because in that certain line of research were contained all of the possibilities of your life and your death . . .

Then the structures looked like they were arranged the way the atoms might be arranged in a certain molecule.

The horizons of Tony's life suddenly receded back into an indeterminate future, or at least the possibility of one. What an incredible feeling it was. "Bambi?" he called. "I need a dolly."

When Tony got home, he put the model in the lab, coming in through the garage because he didn't want to deal with getting it down the stairs. He set it up near the virtual desktop, shoving various other partially completed projects out of the way. On the virtual desktop he projected an image of the film frame at the end of his father's outtake—the one with the partial image that had begun to make the shape, and his father's plan, clear to him. Looking at it, Tony started to work out the implications of what he was considering. Even if he was right, the lab setup he had wasn't going to do the trick; the power draw was going to be immense, and he had a hunch he was going to need a lot more computing power than was available in the house network.

First things first. Tony went out into the garage and came back draped in cables and carrying a sledgehammer. He dropped the cables in a pile, closed his eyes for a minute to dredge up the memories of how he'd wired the house, and then looked at the wall in front of him.

"Jarvis," he asked, "is this a load-bearing wall?"

"No, sir," Jarvis said.

Man, was this going to feel good. Tony got a grip on the sledgehammer and started to swing.

CHAPTER 24

It had been a rough forty-eight hours, that was for sure. Rhodey thought he might have slept for as many as four of those hours, but it also might have been only two. He was barely keeping his head together, and was passionately looking forward to about sixteen hours of rack time whenever this little show was over.

He thought it was all worth it, though. The Mark II was transformed. It was an incredible piece, the cumulative expression of Tony Stark's intuitive genius and the United States Air Force's battlefield savvy. It was, as the politicians liked to say, a game-changer. General Newcomb, who Rhodey was currently escorting from a fancypants C37A transport to the hangar, was another one of those people who liked the expression game-changer. Like lots of top brass who did things like travel in the C37A—the military version of the Gulfstream V—he was making the transition from soldier to politician and had a tendency to confuse the dialects of the two tribes.

"I think you will be very impressed," Rhodey said as he walked with General Newcomb into the hangar. He was grateful to be out of the sun, which was savage at Edwards every single day, or at least every day Rhodey had ever been there. If he ever saw it rain there, he was going to start looking for four horsemen. "I selected many of the armaments myself." It occurred to him to wonder if he was ever going to get stars on his epaulets and start talking like a politician himself. He had a mild preference for developing a terminal disease.

His mind was jittery, so his train of thought was jumping the tracks. Rhodey breathed in the temperature- and humidity-controlled air inside the hangar. He caught the scents of fresh paint, machine oil, solvents . . . and a slight overtone of nervous sweat coming from the assembled crew of engineers, who were at least as fatigued as Rhodey was. Some of them hadn't even let themselves take a nap during the determined march toward this premiere. This was one fried group of geeks.

"Well," Rhodey said. "Major Allen, would you mind doing the honors?"

Allen saluted and walked to the tarp that hung from a frame of two-by-fours built to enclose the star of the show. After a glance back at Rhodey, he unveiled it with a flourish. Everyone present caught their breath—the engineering team because they were waiting to hear what the brass would say, Allen and Rhodey because they'd both worked so hard to make sure that the armed forces of the United States had a necessary edge over all enemies foreign and domestic . . . and General Newcomb because he was looking at the finest piece of military hardware that any general had ever laid eyes on.

It stood two meters tall, and still held the burnished silver hue of the original Mark II. Where the Mark II, and its successor Mark IV, had kept a design emphasis on a humanoid shape, the new suit was part human and part armored vehicle. From one shoulder sprouted the heavy multi-barrel machine gun Justin Hammer had called Uncle Gazpacho; from the other, a partially recessed magazine of missiles. The upper torso and extremities of the suit were bulked up to accommodate small arms in both five-five-six and nine-millimeter, engineered from the basic firearms provided by Justin Hammer. The lower torso and legs were less differentiated from the Mark II origin, their functionality oriented toward flight and ballistic-control systems. Rhodey ran through the specs: eight missiles, one thousand rounds of ammunition in each of the three sizes slotted into external and ejectable magazines; acceleration and maneuver capabilities improved from the Mark II; heads-up and communications capabilities derived from highest-grade military packages combined with the existing protocols Tony had built in during initial development. This was the next step in the development of warfare, and perhaps it was one more lever in the maintenance of a durable peace. At least that's what Rhodey tried to tell himself.

"Unbelievable," General Newcomb breathed. He looked it up and down, and Rhodey could see him envisioning superiority in theaters from Venezuela to the Swat Valley. "What do you even call something like that? It's like a . . ."

They had talked about various names while working on it over the past two days. The possibilities ranged from the bombastic to the whimsical: Terminator, Silver Surfer,

Squeaky, Overlord, Captain America, the Maitre D', the Murder D . . . it was something to see what a group of sleep-deprived engineers could come up with.

But in the end, there was really only one thing to call it.

"It's a war machine," Newcomb finished.

At first Newcomb couldn't take his eyes off it. After a while he managed to tear himself away from the War Machine and get down to the business of asking the kind of questions generals were supposed to ask. "It's functional?"

Nobody had yet flown it, but Rhodey had stood in it while they spun all the systems up and fired everything from the ground on a target range outside the hangar. Targeting and command-and-control systems were all green. The heads-up commlink was working exactly as it should. The only thing Rhodey hadn't tested were the flight systems, since he'd just wound the suit up to Mach 5 on his way out here. Unless the engineering crew had done something to the aeronautics, it would fly just fine. They had run exhaustive simulations on the new weight distribution and shape, and from those it looked like the team had done a superb job installing the retrofits so that the existing thrust and navigational systems would still operate.

Rhodey wasn't about to piss on the general's obvious good mood by telling him that last bit, though. "One hundred percent online," he said.

"Good." Newcomb faced Rhodey and Major Allen. As quickly as he had been swept away by his first sight of War Machine suit, he pulled himself back together. Now he was all business. "The Pentagon has asked that I issue your first orders."

"But sir," Rhodey said. The suit wasn't ready for actual operations. When he'd said it was online, he meant that it had tested out without killing anyone or falling on its face. "I've asked that . . . "

"Hammer is doing a weapons presentation," Newcomb said, cutting Rhodey off with a look. "We'd like this to introduce it."

Rhodey didn't have to hear the rest, but he knew what was behind this. The Pentagon wanted to put Hammer in the spotlight again after his embarrassment at the Senate hearing. They'd turned their backs on him for a while, and now, in true Beltway fashion, they were going to welcome him back as if all of it had never happened. And since billions of dollars and arms prestige were at stake, they were going to give him a little boost as they welcomed him back into the fold.

The problem, of course, was that when Rhodey had brought the Mark II out to Edwards, he had done it with the understanding that the weaponizing of the system would be conducted with an eye toward creating it as a shield—in terms both Tony and Justin Hammer had used—rather than a sword. General Newcomb, by making the War Machine a centerpiece of Hammer's presentation at the Expo, was redefining its function. He was turning the War Machine into an ostentatious threat instead of the behind-the-scenes trump card Rhodey had intended.

"With all due respect, General," Rhodey said, "I feel strongly that we only use the suit when absolutely necessary."

He said it knowing that he had to say it but also knowing that it wouldn't make any difference. Pentagon brass had never waited to show off a new toy, and they weren't going to wait to show this one off. Rhodey's feelings on the topic had no bearing on the decision. He'd been a fool even to phrase his objection that way. What he was really wanting to say was: General. I betrayed a friend to put this machine in your hands. If you use it in exactly the way he feared, that makes my betrayal that much worse. In fact it means that he was right all along, and that the whole time I was arguing for him to give the machine to you, I was misguided. Now I see this. Now it is too late. Now there's no way to explain to Tony Stark that I was trying to do the right thing.

Men like General Newcomb, however, were unlikely to be persuaded by their subordinates' sense of personal obligation. Particularly when shiny new pieces of dominant military technology were in question.

Newcomb respected Rhodey enough to finesse his response instead of airing him out in front of Major Allen and the engineering team, though. "Colonel, the world needs to see this," he said. "Fast. With Iron Man unable or unwilling to fulfill any of his tasks right now, I assure you it is absolutely necessary."

He waited for Rhodey to acknowledge what he'd said, or contest the point. Rhodey, conscious that he had already received quite a bit of indulgence from a man who was not in the habit of granting any, did neither.

"It's also an order," the general finished.

And that was the end of the conversation. "Yes, sir," Rhodey said.

"And very nice work, gentlemen!" General Newcomb beamed at the assembled team. "You've made your country proud."

CHAPTER 25

When he got to the point in a long experimental odyssey at which things were either going to happen the way he wanted them to or go spectacularly off the rails, Tony had two strategies. One was to be completely laconic and pretend to everyone within earshot that he didn't care one way or another what happened. The other was to acknowledge the importance of the occasion by way of over-the-top behavior like quoting Shakespeare or blasting "Night on Bald Mountain" over the lab stereo.

Today, although he kind of felt like some loud music or perhaps an impassioned performance of the bit about screwing courage from Henry V, Tony played it cool. He ran diagnostics. He made sure that he had his math right. He calculated possibilities and analyzed likely outcomes. He acted, in short, like a working scientist. And when he had done all that, he came to the conclusion that he might not be able to do exactly what he wanted to do with the resources available to him at the house. This was an annoying conclusion, but Tony couldn't make it go away. "We're going to draw down a lot of power, Jarvis," he said. "Let me know if you start to feel a little logey."

"I've calculated the necessary computing power and energy to effectuate your experiment," Jarvis informed him.

I have, too, Tony thought. Why are you just now telling me this, and why did you let me spend the time doing it if you were just going to do it too?

"And?" he prompted.

"It is not possible without drawing from an outside source," Jarvis said.

Tony was fairly certain that he detected a self-satisfied note in Jarvis' voice. He inferred, in his palladium-poisoned and sleep-deprived and Vanko-obsessed state, that Jarvis had been waiting for Tony to finish his power consumption calculations so he could watch Tony get them ever so slightly wrong and then inform him that he had, oh dear, gotten them ever so slightly wrong.

It was enough to make a guy wish that he'd never wondered if it was possible to create an artificial intelligence.

"Close and lock the system," Tony said. He considered the next step, wondering if it would cause more damage to the company than the possibility of saving his life was worth.

Ha ha, he told himself. Very funny. Even Pepper, in her newly tightassed role as CEO of the company Tony still considered his, wouldn't begrudge him this. Lost computing time meant lost productivity meant decreased shareholder value meant pressure from the board on the executive suite meant Pepper would come looking for him wanting to know why every Stark Industries computer in the world shut down at the same time because it had been commandeered for an off-the-books operation that nobody could characterize with any specificity.

That was okay. Or would be, if this little exercise worked. If not, when Pepper showed up to yell at him, she might find herself having to make funeral arrangements.

"Then tap into the Oracle grid," he told Jarvis. "Get every Stark computer from here to Hong Kong involved."

While Jarvis was arranging this extremely complicated network that was larger than any in the world and would only exist for a few minutes before splintering and having everyone involved pretend it had never existed, Tony focused on getting the material elements of the process exactly right.

He was working with four components. One, a set of mirrors designed to focus anything that hit any of them on a single specific point in space inside the set. Two, a cube of pure glass whose position in space included the specific focal point of the set of mirrors. Three, a high-energy laser array whose beams would be focused and intensified by those mirrors. Four, a non-ferrous centrifuge designed to spin up to ridiculous g-force values and initiate high-energy reactions that could only happen in the absence of highly magnetic metals such as iron.

The centrifuge was a special little item created in this very lab as a way to experiment with trans-uranium elements and other short-lived chemical anomalies. Tony had designed it along the same lines as a uranium-separating gas centrifuge, only with better abilities to handle solids and a built-in linkage to the laser system to create both high-acceleration and high-energy situations. He liked it as a toy, but he'd never really found a worthwhile use for it until seeing the answer to the puzzle posed by the Expo model in the old filmstrip.

The lasers were derived from the European HiPER project to develop laser-powered fusion. Like HiPER, Tony was using neodymium glass in his lasers, but he had made a few tweaks, including a much-improved chirped pulse amplification to get more focused delivery of energy from each laser, as well as the King Kong of optical frequency multipliers that took the frequency of each pulse way up into the ultraviolet. And like HiPER, Tony was after a kind of fusion, but this was a demonstration model. He didn't need industrial qualities of anything. He needed proof of concept, which would come in the form of a molecule that would or would not appear in the cube of glass under the right conditions.

Tony's understanding of those conditions derived from his interpretation of the pattern of buildings in his father's Expo model. If he was wrong about that, then everything else would be wrong as well and he was as likely to blow up the house and bring down the entire network of Stark Industries computers as he was to make any contribution to scientific progress, or extending his own life beyond the next few days.

But he didn't think he was wrong. Tony felt pretty strongly that he had this figured out, and that when he fired those lasers and spun up that centrifuge he would see something that no man had ever seen before.

Except Howard Stark, in his imagination of a future he would never live to inhabit.

Dad, Dad, Dad, Tony thought. Nick Fury was right about you. The world wasn't ready for you yet when you were here.

How might things have been different if the Starks hadn't died in that crash during Tony's freshman year? What might the three of them have accomplished together? How might they have brought together the drive for innovation and the drive for a better way of life?

Would they have found a way out of arms manufacture sooner, or was that always going to happen only if carefree ironmonger Tony Stark found himself watching his own weapons slaughter women and children in the remote passes of forgotten parts of the world?

Live and learn, Tony thought.

He ran checks on the mirror array. It was perfect. He spun the centrifuge up to test acceleration and let it run back down. Exactly according to specs. He fired off a test burst from the lasers, checking for spread of frequency and pulse duration. All well within the experimental tolerances he had estimated.

The only thing left to do, really, was run the experiment and see if it would work.

"Jarvis, spin up the non-ferrous centrifuge," he said, unnecessarily adding, "Be ready to capture whatever floats through it." Jarvis did not comment, an uncharacteristic bit of restraint for which Tony was deeply grateful. As Jarvis spun the centrifuge up, Tony ran his internal checklist again. He'd performed every step. If this was going to work, here was where he would find out.

"Let 'er rip," he said.

The laser array flared into life, first in a deep red and then modulating in frequency well up into the ultraviolet. Tony kept track in a simulation on the virtual desktop, run in real time from information delivered via Jarvis from the actual experiment. Everything looked perfect.

"Fingers crossed," Tony said. Jarvis didn't answer.

The centrifuge hit its target acceleration. Tony was about to tell Jarvis to spike the energy delivery of the lasers up, but Jarvis knew the experiment better than Tony did, and he'd already given the command before Tony could say anything.

He was holding his breath. The lasers had gone cold, the centrifuge had spun down to silence, and the glass cube at the center of it all—the center of the experiment, the center of Tony's understanding of his father's great unrealized ambition, the center of Tony's belief in his continued existence on this planet—that glass cube sat in a sterile enclosure with a tiny grain of imperfection at its center.

Tony exhaled, long and slow. "That's it, Jarvis," he said. "Read it."

"Dissecting now."

As Jarvis spoke, a holo spawned on the virtual desktop representing Jarvis' analysis of the molecule that would either save Tony's life or be the biggest single expenditure of wasted energy in the history of Stark Industries, and probably the history of human civilization. Time slowed to a stop. Tony lived and died a thousand potential lives beyond this exact moment when he was about to find out how much more living of this life he would get to do before dying out of it for good.

"As soon as you get its atomic structure," Tony said, "tell me what the name—"

"Unknown element," Jarvis said. "Contains similar transgenic properties to the chemical compound Vibernum. Also has characteristics known in uranium, or Ourains."

This was good. This was what he had hoped for even though he wasn't yet sure it was what would save him. "Name it," Tony commanded.

"I couldn't possibly," Jarvis said, with as much emotion as he ever displayed about anything. "I am hardly the International Union of Pure and Applied Chemistry."

Whatever, Tony thought. "Project it!" he said. A three-dimensional image appeared on the desktop, endless interlocking triangles joined into a perfect sphere. Tony enlarged it, focused on different parts of it, threw it into various refractory and hostile environments. No matter the degree of magnification or the deforming pressures he put on the molecule, it was triangles all the way down. It was like a buckyball only based on the triangle, and composed of an element with astronomically more ability to contain and deliver energy than carbon. Carbon was great for building things, but not so good for powering them. Vibranium, on the other hand, looked like it might be exactly the opposite.

"It's beautiful," Tony said. Let's run the play, Hail Mary. Gimme an RT."

An RT diagram appeared. Tony tinkered with it, creating interfaces with this new molecule and seeing how it all fit together. "Spin it," he said. It spun, and emitted light. Tony started to think that he might actually have done the impossible. "This might actually work," he said, and set about finding out.

Later that day, he was smelting, pouring, catalyzing . . . and remembering the last time he'd done this on the fly, in the cave with Yinsen knowing that he might be killing both of them by working on a mini–arc reactor instead of reverse-engineering the Jericho missiles the local warlord had wanted. That was real living, when you knew that any action you took might kill you and might save you. It was relying on your natural intellect and believing in your hunches. Yinsen, Tony thought. You got your wish. I'm trying like hell not to waste my life. If you're out there somewhere, I sure hope you've noticed.

The moment of truth was nearly at hand in the transition of the grand vibranium experiment from creation of a single molecule to production of usable quantities of said molecule. Tony stood with a pair of tongs, the pincer end of which extended into a mean high-energy electromagnetic blast furnace where, with any luck, a whole lot of vibranium was precipitating into a kettle that the pincer would shortly grasp and remove.

"Jarvis, ramp reverse currents," he said. "How much do we got?"

"Accumulating twelve billion angstroms per minute," Jarvis replied.

Tony thought about it. "Just a bit more," he said. He waited, hoping the alloy wouldn't cool too soon after precipitating. Even the small temperature differential between the interior of the kettle and the more open space inside the furnace might turn out to be a critical obstacle to getting the kind of purified vibranium he was going to need to make this all work. There hadn't been any time to test it, though. Everything had worked so far, and Tony was going on gut instinct—and, he wasn't too modest to admit, natural brilliance.

A chime sounded. "Transversal complete," Jarvis said. Tony extracted the kettle, pivoted to hold it over a waiting mold, and began to pour.

Ivan had completed all of the work that Hammer required from him. This meant not that he had stopped working, but that he had at last been able to undertake his real task. Deep inside the intricacies of a circuitry diagram, he did not look up as Hammer strode into the lab flanked by the two overinflated guards who never seemed to leave his side. Hammer looked ebullient. When he spoke, he would be too loud. He would be over-friendly. This would be a cover for the betrayal that he had been planning all along, and which Ivan had awaited since the moment he had first walked into this laboratory and seen the rows of drones waiting for their rebirth.

"Tonight's the night, my friend!" Hammer said. "The time we finally get to destroy the Stark legacy! Show the world what we've done!"

He approached Ivan's workbench and sat down on the only stool. "Which is also what makes this so hard," he added.

Ivan paused and waited for him to go on. All of it—the conversation and what would come after—all of it was predictable. Because it was predictable Ivan had already incorporated it into his own planning, which meant that for Ivan to oppose Hammer's betrayal now would be to interfere with his own larger goals. So he waited. It didn't take long before Hammer went on. He was a creature of measured pauses and calculated breaths; Ivan had long since measured and calculated them as well.

"I've been thinking," Hammer said.

Me too, Ivan thought.

"And you're going to think that this is really lame, but lately I've been getting kind of nervous." Hammer shifted on the stool and looked away out over the lab floor. Ivan wondered what he saw. When Ivan looked out over that floor, he saw the place where he had made another man's plan his own. "See, I need to make sure that you stay put for this," Hammer said. "I like you—hell, I've even grown kind of fond of having you around. But I don't necessarily . . . God, this sounds bad . . . I don't trust you. I need to make sure you stay put for a few hours while I do this." He gave Ivan a look that Ivan thought he must have learned from watching his father saying something along the lines of *This is going to hurt me more than it hurts you.* "You can understand that, right?"

Ivan waited just long enough to convey the impression that he had perhaps been expecting something else. "Of course," he said.

"Swell," Hammer said, and stood. "You're a pal." With that, he headed for the open door. "Be nice to the babysitters," he called, turning to walk backward for a moment as he approached the guards, who stood flanking the door. "I'll be back soon. And hey, you should watch me on TV!"

I just might, Ivan thought. *Except . . . no, sorry, I think I will have other plans.*

As Hammer passed the guards, he said, loud enough that Ivan knew he was intended to hear, "Make sure that our friend is taken care of."

The door locked behind him. Ivan returned to his work, making sure he had everything out of the way and set up the way he wanted it once he could return to it after the coming interruption. When he had it arranged, he looked over at the guards. They were halfway across the lab toward him, walking easily, idiotic and malevolent grins on their faces. They were larger than Ivan, and there were two of them . . . but technology, as the military scholars liked to say, was a force multiplier. Ivan was not fighting by himself.

He wasn't going to have time to use all of the new toys he had designed in parallel with his work on Hammer's drones. This was a pity, since if he didn't do a dry run now, the next opportunity that arose would be quite a high-stakes occasion. Ivan hated to go into a fight unsure of his weapons. However, this appeared to be the situation and he would adapt to it. Adaptability. This was a Russian virtue.

All this ran through his mind as he rose to meet Hammer's guards, rolling up his sleeves as they approached. When they saw the hardware on his forearms, they didn't stop coming; but by the time things had gotten to that point, it had long since ceased to matter what they did.

CHAPTER 26

There it was, Tony thought. Either it was going to save his life or he was going to leave it. The shape of the new RT reflected the fundamental structure of its power source; he had defaulted to a circle in previous designs, with theories of radiant energy stuck in his head, principles of equidistance . . . but this time, the triangle. He would need a new housing for it eventually, but for right now he was going to have to improvise. There was no time for finish work.

He had managed to cobble together a sleeve that went inside the existing RT socket, so at least the new one wouldn't be rattling around in there. He set the RT against the rim of the socket. It fit. It looked good.

It looked really good, as a matter of fact. He held it up and wished there was someone around who could admire it with him. "Jarvis, what do you think?" he said.

"Eminently triangular, sir," Jarvis said.

How was it, Tony wondered, that he could engineer a sense of humor into an artificial intelligence but not figure out how to make sure a human being maintained one? Wasn't he funny? Wasn't he charming? And didn't he know when to quit being funny and charming because it was time for directness and honesty?

He thought he did, but his recent interactions with Rhodey and Pepper seemed to indicate otherwise.

Humor. Programming it was easy . . . well, easy if you were as smart as Tony Stark. But figuring out how it actually worked in real life? Nobody could do that.

At least, Tony thought, I have this fine-looking RT. It gleamed in the carefully designed light of his lab, with the vibranium power source generating roughly twice the power as the previous palladium compound—and with less than five percent of palladium's troublesome leaching property. Although to be fair, Tony probably couldn't blame the leaching on the palladium; it was a combination of the design of the RT and the amount of energy he was focusing through the palladium. There were very few compounds known to man that would not shed some of their mass when used as a medium for the circulation of such intense energies.

This is the greatest thing I have ever invented, Tony thought. And it is entirely possible that nobody will ever know about it. Because it is entirely possible that this is a great and ambitious failure, and I will keel over dead the minute I put it in, and this tremendous advance in elemental chemistry and metallurgical engineering will look like the last-ditch, desperate ploy of a dying alcoholic.

What the hell, Tony thought. Either way, there's a good story.

"Teleconference incoming," Jarvis said.

"Who is it?"

"Hammer Industries."

"With pleasure," Tony said. "Put him up." He glanced aside to set the new RT out of the field of Hammer's teleconference view and saw the screen open out of the corner of his eye. "What do you want?" he said with the jovial scorn he reserved for business competitors—or people who thought they could compete with Tony Stark.

Then he saw the face of Ivan Vanko.

"Tony," Ivan said. He was in some kind of lab, a cross between a rat's nest and a mad scientist's sanctum. Tony could only imagine what it smelled like. There were cables and conduits knotted and tangled everywhere, instruments and components stuck together with electrical tape . . . and in the background, a pair of legs dangled into the top of the frame.

"Today is the day the true history of the Stark name will be written," Ivan said. "As thieves. As murderers. At your own Expo, the world will learn what kind of criminals you really are."

"Let me tell you, Ivan—as one guy with daddy issues to another," Tony said. "I don't think this day is going to turn out the way you want it to. At the end of it, I'm still going to have the Expo, and Stark Industries, and you're still going to be a homicidal freak working with stolen tech in Justin Hammer's garage. Unless you're dead. How's that sound?"

Ivan blew him a kiss. "Today, Stark," he said, and cut the connection.

*   *   *

Natasha was sick of playing Natalie, but Fury had said in no uncertain terms that Pepper Potts was not to know of her undercover infiltration. So here she was, with a headset and clipboard, waiting around the entrance to the Tent of Tomorrow for Pepper to show up and sit down. Hammer's demonstration was due to start in fifteen minutes. Shows like this always started late, but part of the reason for that was people showing up late because they assumed the show was going to start late. Natasha considered punctuality a cardinal virtue and was deeply annoyed when people didn't take time—especially other peoples' time—seriously.

The Tent of Tomorrow was a tent in name only. In reality, it was an open auditorium space under a soaring glass roof, with a high-tech stage and an even higher-tech backstage setup. The distance from roof to stage was maybe seventy feet and at a glance Natasha thought the place might seat two thousand people. Soon the lights would be dimmed, but at the moment the spectators were amusing themselves looking at the diorama of progress painted on the walls, valorizing every invention from fire straight up through the cell phone. The backstage area, part of which Natasha could see from her angle at the top of the concourse, was swarming with Hammer Industries tech personnel making last-minute adjustments to their imminent demonstration. The front rows of seating were packed except a few way down low reserved for VIPs. Like Pepper Potts, if she ever showed up.

Natasha scanned the crowd, glanced at her phone, scanned the crowd again. Ah. There she was, with Happy Hogan coming from the Expo personnel parking lot behind the Tent of Tomorrow.

"Ms. Potts!" she called out. Pepper and Happy saw her and started in her direction, moving with the crowd and making no effort to hurry. "How was your flight?" Natalie asked when they were close enough to not have to shout.

"Fine, thank you," Pepper said with her usual—at least where "Natalie" was concerned—excess of chilly politeness.

Happy didn't even greet her, or look her in the eye. Nothing like wounded male pride to screw up a social interaction, Natasha thought. Maybe she should have taken it a little easier on him. On the other hand, he was a liability if he thought that his old-fashioned boxing skills were going to be any protection at all for Tony Stark. Or anyone else.

"I'll wait for you right here, Ms. Potts," Happy said. "Call if you need anything."

"I'll show you to your seats," Natasha said. Her phone rang and she answered it without looking at the number. "Natalie Rushman."

Tony wasn't teleconferencing with Natalie because he had his shirt off in preparation for transferring the new RT in and he didn't want her to see the state of his skin. Purple and black streaks radiated outward from the old RT, covering Tony's torso and crawling up his neck like bad tattoos. Sometimes when he looked at them he thought they might be moving. This was obviously a delusion, or hallucination on his part, but it was interesting, so he indulged it. The idea that there were palladium-powered worms under his skin eating him little by little was pulpy and outrageous enough that he wished he could share it with someone. Like Pepper. Or even Natalie, who was now answering her phone and pretending again to be the young legal assistant instead of the lethal S.H.I.E.L.D. operative.

But it was the S.H.I.E.L.D. operative Tony needed.

"Ivan's alive," Tony said before she'd even gotten her name out. "And at Hammer Industries."

There was the barest of pauses. "Yes, Ms. Potts has just arrived," Natalie—Natasha—Natashalie said briskly. "Okay. I'll be right there."

She must have already been at the Expo, Tony thought as Natalie—he couldn't stop thinking of her as Natalie—hung up. Good. Maybe she could get the S.H.I.E.L.D. personnel who were undoubtedly creeping around the place to slow Ivan down. Or at least be on the lookout for whatever Hammer was planning. That part Tony couldn't figure out; Justin Hammer was greedy, that was for sure, but he'd never struck Tony as power-mad or really evil. He was no Obadiah Stane, that was for sure. What the hell was he doing working with Ivan?

And not just working with him. Breaking him out of a French jail and killing more than a dozen inmates in an explosion meant to cover up the jailbreak, not to mention jump-starting a riot in which who knew how many more people had been killed . . . Tony thought he might have to revise his opinion about Hammer. Clearly Hammer was a bad guy, plain and simple.

Which would make it easier and more fun when Tony showed up to crash whatever party Hammer had planned.

First, though, he had to do a couple of things. He needed to suit up and fly off to the Expo for sure, and quick. But before he could do that, he had to take this new RT out for its shake-down cruise. Because if that didn't work, there wouldn't be any flying off anywhere, except maybe to the hereafter. The palladium toxicity in Tony's body had reached a point of no return. If the new RT didn't stabilize everything and give him enough baseline strength to let his immune system start to purge the palladium, then Tony Stark was not going to be part of events at his very own Expo.

And that idea was intolerable. "Jarvis," Tony said. "Let's get ready to swap in this new toy. How does that sound?"

"Marvelous, sir," Jarvis said.

Hanging up, she handed Pepper both of their tickets. "Press out front is getting grumpy that you blew right past them. I'll handle it," she said. "Section A, seats one and two. I'll be right back." She left Pepper there and headed for the exit, a plan already forming in her mind. On the way she made another call. Nick Fury answered on the first ring.

"Fury," she said. "Tell Coulson to lock down the Expo."

Happy saw her coming and she hung up again before Fury could ask any questions or Happy could say something both of them might regret. Seemed like every time she was making a phone call she couldn't explain, there was Happy to get suspicious about it.

Only right now he looked about the farthest thing from suspicious. He looked, in fact, like he was working himself up to an apology. "Hey," he said.

"I need a ride," she said. He caught the urgency in her voice and fell into step with her.

CHAPTER 27

This is going to be a big day, Jarvis," Tony said as he ran through the last checks on the new RT. Pretty soon he was going to run out of ways to put off actually installing it.

And why would he want to do that?

Because if it didn't work he would die. Better to prolong the uncertainty a little, maybe, except while he was prolonging the uncertainty the palladium was slowly—well, not so slowly anymore—killing him.

The problem with being a cyborg was that the -org part was never nearly strong enough to really compete with and survive alongside the cyb- part. If he lived through the transfer, Tony thought he might try to do something about that. It would be an interesting project to occupy the rest of his life or so.

"Apart from the obvious, sir," Jarvis said, "in what way will the size of this day exceed the size of an average day in your life? Or should I understand you to be speaking solely of the new RT?"

"And here I was thinking you had a sense of humor," Tony said. "Those two," he added, pointing at You and Dummy, "are more keenly attuned to my humorous stylings than you are, and they're not even sentient."

"There may be a connection there," Jarvis observed.

Tony paused in the act of unscrewing his RT from its housing. "Droll," he said.

As soon as he removed the RT, his heart would begin to go into cardiac arrest. That would leave him perhaps thirty seconds of more-or-less full function to get the new RT in. If it took longer than that, the odds of him surviving the transfer got longer, and fast. He rehearsed the motions for the hundredth time:

Unseat old RT.

Loosen magnetized disk attached to heart muscle and clean away foreign matter that might have stuck to and around it.

Remove old RT from wiring assembly.

Attach new RT to wiring assembly.

Seat new RT inside housing.

Go on with life, first priority delivering sharp and possibly fatal rebukes to Justin Hammer and Ivan Vanko.

As he went though each step, Tony mimed the motions. Except for the last, which was too complicated to mime.

"Wish me luck, Jarvis," he said.

Symptoms preceding cardiac arrest often included fatigue, fainting, blackouts, dizziness, chest pain, shortness of breath, palpitations, or vomiting. Tony felt approximately half of these as soon as he detached the old RT from the wiring assembly. His heart began to slow and immediately he felt like his blood was thicker, pressing hard against the walls of the veins. Through a sudden roaring in his ears he thought he was talking, but either Jarvis wasn't answering or Tony's mouth wasn't actually making any sounds. Attach new RT, he thought. Have rehearsed this many times. Attach new RT.

His hands were very slow. And weak. He held the new RT in those hands and looked at it, forgetting for a moment what it was for. Ah. Yes. Now he remembered. It was for attaching. Attaching equaled saving his life. And for it to save that very valuable life, it had to be plugged in.

He plugged it in.

The first thing that happened was Tony felt like someone had sent a mild electric shock through his entire body as his heart thumped back into action and blood started moving through his veins again. The second thing that happened was he felt strong. Not leap-tall-buildings-in-a-single-bound strong, but healthy. Like he wasn't in danger of keeling over dead at any moment.

God, what a feeling. It had been a while. Tony wiggled his fingers and wasn't sure why; it just seemed like the kind of thing you should do when you've just brought yourself back from the brink of death into an entirely new physical state. You wiggled your fingers on the off chance that they seemed different.

Tony's didn't. He took a deep breath and loved the way the air filled his lungs. He loved the way he could feel his heart beating, strong and steady.

He turned to look at himself in the mirror. The transfer hadn't sent him into irreversible cardiac arrest, which was good. Excellent, in fact. But if he died from some kind of palladium-related toxicity, his ingenuity would turn out to have been fruitless. Nothing I hate like fruitless ingenuity, Tony thought. His heart felt strong. He felt like he could put on the Mark IV Iron Man suit and race off to deal with whatever might need dealing with. Terrorists, criminal masterminds, Ivan Vanko . . . Tony was ready.

In the mirror, something extraordinary happened.

The purplish streaks darkened to a pure black. Tony's eyes popped. He reached reflexively for the new RT, thinking he'd go back to the old one if it meant dying slowly instead of all at once . . . for a long, breathless moment he goggled at himself and the intensifying symptoms of acute palladium toxicity.

Then the black streaks started to get fainter. Tony reached out to his reflection in the mirror, so amazed at what he was seeing that he momentarily forgot which side of the mirror was real. His fingertips rested on the mirror's surface over a branching black pattern that spread across his right pectoral muscle. At nearly the same moment that Tony touched the mirror, the streaks began to turn silver. Startled, he drew his hand back. What the hell was going on in there? It looked almost like the silvery color of the RT was spreading along the pathways where the infection had gone. Was that possible?

By the time he had the question articulated, the streaks were gone. Now Tony looked down and touched the real him, his real torso. The skin felt like his skin, the hairs like his hairs. There was no trace of the streaks. He took a deep breath and felt his heart beating strong and steady.

"I did it, Dad," he whispered. There was a silence in the lab for a while after that, until Jarvis broke it.

"How do you feel, sir?" the AI asked. It was an empty

question, really. Tony was sure Jarvis had already run a dozen screens on Tony's metabolism and overall health without Tony even knowing it. He'd want to look at them all over the next few days to see what, if anything they had learned from the new RT's actions in the initial moments after its installation.

Even if the question was motivated by simple politeness, Tony appreciated it. After all, Jarvis had been there when none of the humans of Tony's acquaintance were. Which was, of course, his fault . . . but now was not the time to dwell on that.

"Alive," he said, and did want to dwell on that. He took a deep breath and another sensation occurred to him. "But weirdly a little horny."

Now that business was taken care of with Hammer's guards, and now that he had spoken to Stark to do the gentlemanly thing and let him know of the coming reckoning, Ivan got to work finalizing the grand finale he had engineered for Tony Stark's Expo. The confrontation with the guards had damaged some of the equipment Ivan would need; in a moment of lost temper he had caused a problem that he would now have to rectify. There were network junctions to bypass, workstations to commandeer and repurpose, servers to hide and others to put into service pretending they were the servers he was going to hide. Some of this Ivan would have had to do anyway, but he had made his task more complicated by succumbing to the exuberance of battle. Now he would do the penance of working to repair his mistakes.

First he reconstructed the parts of the network he had

ruined. This was the work of a few minutes. Then he located a bit of code he had put together not long after arriving at Hammer's laboratory, when he had first envisioned this ending to the second act of his pursuit of Stark. Because of some other things Ivan had done to the Hammer system in the meantime, this bit of code was no longer exactly suited for its task, so he spent another few minutes revising it.

Then he compiled it and just like that he was in complete command of any computer that worked through a server at Hammer Industries.

"You made yourself a metal man, Stark," Ivan said in the stillness. "Now you will find that you don't need the man at all. All you need is the metal."

And if that failed—if the metal in question did not finish what Howard Stark had started so long ago—Ivan Vanko stood ready to administer the coup de grâce.

He had watched the suit of armor grow from the suitcase and build itself around Tony Stark's body on the track at Monaco, and in that moment Ivan Vanko had seen that armor did not have to be clumsy. It did not have to slow its wearer down. It could make up for many of the human body's weaknesses, and amplify many of the body's strengths. Chastened by his defeat and by the cavalier way he had previously dismissed the idea of armor, Ivan had himself gone to work designing a suit of armor that would serve his purposes. It would magnify the power of the whips, and be designed so that he could move quickly enough and gracefully enough to use the whips the way they ought to be used. In addition, it would be an ironic tip of the cap—or in this case the helmet and mask—to Stark for his unintentional guidance. Without Stark, Vanko would never have built this armor. With this armor, Vanko would destroy Stark.

He put it on himself, without the aid of a gantry like the one Tony Stark had put on display at the opening of his Expo. Ivan did for himself what Tony Stark needed an army of machines and men to accomplish; so much for the myth of the doughty American, improvising and creating on his own what the lazy European or the drunken Russian could never do. Ivan Vanko had designed and built this armor with the use of the Hammer facilities, yes; but Hammer's facilities might as well have been a medieval smithy compared to what Tony Stark had to work with.

Even so, the suit was a thing of beauty. Ivan thought his father might have appreciated it. He was inclined to call it РЕМЕНЬ КНУТА, because in English that translated best as Whiplash.

"Crack," Ivan whispered. He gave the dangling guard's legs a push, and went to work putting his armor on as the body swayed back and forth, a metronome to keep him in rhythm and on task.

The Whiplash armor was designed to prevent its wearer from being damaged by his own whips first and foremost, and also to repel projectile and energy attacks of the sort one might see deployed by Tony Stark in the Mark IV Iron Man suit. Flexibility and speed were paramount, so the joints were broad and covered only by a carbon-fiber mesh. The parts of the body most likely to come into accidental contact with the whips, Ivan judged, were the feet and lower legs. These were heavily armored. So were the shoulders and torso, to protect vital functions as well as the arc reactor, which Ivan had again situated directly over the heart. He hoped Stark would appreciate the gesture. The helmet was functional and minimalist, its eye slits modeled consciously on the Mark IV but the rest of it designed to look angular and predatory, an unapologetic aesthetic imperative that Ivan thought brought a deadly flourish to the overall impression.

And the pièce de résistance, of course, were the gloves and the armoring of the lower arms. The whips could be stored in a spool that wrapped around the forearms. They deployed from a slot at the inside of the wrist, and could be controlled without the user holding them. This was a game-changer, as an American might have said. By removing concerns about dropping the whips, Ivan had enormously increased the number of things he could do with them, individually and in conjunction. It was as if they grew from him, and he used them not as a tool but as an extension of his arm. Already he felt incomplete without them. To preserve all possible uses of the whips, Ivan had designed gloves that could hold them. The palms and fingers were reinforced with high-tech ceramics derived from spacecraft re-entry shields.

When he had dressed, Ivan set out. He could not fly, but he would have no trouble getting to the Stark Expo. He might even arrive before Tony could. Then perhaps he could get the show started early, while they all waited for the doomed star to make his final appearance.

CHAPTER 28

For all the well-known tension between Stark and Hammer, both personally and professionally, Justin Hammer sure did look to have borrowed a page from Tony Stark's Manual for the Presentation of New Gadgets at a Big Show. He was ever so slightly overdressed, the way Tony tended to be, with the tie not tightened all the way and the hair allowed to look a little unkempt. He strode the slick surface of a polished stage, with curvy women doing things all along the edges of the stage that had nothing to do with technological progress. If an observer did not know better, he or she might have taken Justin Hammer for a man supremely gifted with an ability to be at ease in front of large crowds in pressure situations. The same kind of man, perhaps, who might make a great quarterback or a great president.

But Pepper Potts did know better, and what she was seeing from her front-row seat was someone who could in all probability be sued for appropriating Tony's tech-show shtick from first gesture to last.

The irony, of course, was that Hammer was doing his best to present himself as the Next Best Thing, the thing that came after Stark Industries had proved itself to be a dinosaur, unfit for the new realities of commerce and global technological exchange. Give Hammer credit, he confronted this straight on a few moments into his remarks.

"Iron Man," Hammer said. "An invention that grabbed press headlines the world over. Today, though, the press has a problem on their hands. They're about to run out of ink." He arrived at center stage. "Today I give the world Colonel James T. Rhodes and the War Machine!"

From the ceiling, on a platform that nobody had known was a platform until it started moving, descended War Machine. Pepper caught her breath.

It was like an Iron Man suit completely given over to steroidal fantasies of battlefield glory. She could see the Mark II in there somewhere, the way you could still see Australopithecus there behind the countenance of every human you met on the street. But the War Machine had discarded all of Tony's design sense, his restless desire for the next better thing that he not only hadn't thought of but maybe couldn't think of, which infuriated him and made him think harder, look harder, until he found what he was looking for. The War Machine was brute strength, shining silver in the spotlights and the million flashbulbs and the shocked-and-awed collective WWWHHHHOOOOAAA that went up from the crowd. Where the Mark II had been sleek and humanoid, the War Machine reminded Pepper of the suit Obadiah had built. She was going to have nightmares. It was bulky, bristling with gun barrels and missile tubes, things that spun and rattled and obviously were designed not just to kill but to let everyone know that they were designed to kill.

It was a power fantasy come to life, a general's dream of theater dominance walking onstage. It was the expression "force multiplier" redefined forever.

Inside the suit, Rhodey looked like he would rather have been onstage at a Miss America pageant. As a contestant. Pepper felt terrible for him. She knew, maybe better than anyone in the world except for Rhodey himself, how hard it had been for him to take matters into his own hands and decide that Tony could no longer be trusted to have this technology to himself. And Pepper would have bet every last dime she had that he had fought the decision to exhibit the War Machine here. He was a soldier but he did not love war. He loved his country. Like Tony, she believed, Rhodey believed that the Iron Man armor was in fact best used as a weapon of last resort. Now it appeared that the Joint Chiefs of Staff had decided that its most effective role would be that of propaganda tool. See the new American soldier, invulnerable encased in armor and bearing enough weaponry to sink a battleship.

She could feel the adulation wafting from the crowd and she could see Hammer eating it up. "Nifty stuff, right?" he said. Then, in a more sober tone, he added, "But in a truly perfect world, men and women of the United States military would never have to set foot on the battlefield again." Music built and Hammer stepped around Rhodey to the lip of the stage. "Ladies and gentlemen, today we cross the threshold into . . . a perfect world."

Red, white, and blue smoke erupted around the stage as four lines of armored soldiers marched in perfect rhythm into the Tent of Tomorrow and stopped in formation along the sides of the stage. A deep voice boomed out each of their branches of service as they appeared in turn: "AAR-RRMMYYY! NNAAAAAVVVYYY! AAAAIIRRR FOORRRCE! MMMAARRRRIIIIIIIIINESS!"

The militaristic theater of the moment was perfect . . . or so Pepper thought, because right away Hammer topped it. When they met in their formation, slowly and in unison, the thirty-two soldiers pivoted and raised their right arms in a salute to War Machine.

And that was when Pepper—along with everyone else there and the who-knew-how-many watching on the various broadcasts and streams and live blogs of the event—realized that they weren't looking at armored soldiers.

They were looking at walking, synchronized, remote-controlled drones.

The new age of robot warfare had arrived. A perfect world.

Pepper had never heard a noise as loud as what came from the crowd and rebounded from the acoustically enhancing roof of the Tent of Tomorrow. Each group of drones was colored like the dress uniform of the service it represented, and each had particular design tweaks. The Air Force drones were obviously equipped to fly, with winglike additions to every limb and active control surfaces along their backs. The Army drones were squat and loaded with heavy weaponry, as if each one was capable of mounting an artillery barrage. For all she knew, they were. The Marine contingent was a bit leaner than their Army counterparts, looking like they were ready to storm a beach right then and there if only an enemy could be located. And the Navy stood streamlined and potent, midnight blue, racked and bristling with missiles that looked like they could turn any fleet in the world to scrap metal in seconds flat. Pepper experienced a moment of being simultaneously so proud to be an American that she wanted to tattoo a flag on her ass, and so disgusted with the American love of war machines that she wanted to run away to a commune in the Yukon and live off pemmican for the rest of her life.

Then, with timing so precise that later Pepper would wonder whether he had planned the whole thing exactly this way, Iron Man appeared.

Tony loved nothing better than crashing a party. It was hard to do when you were Tony Stark, because you got invited to anything that you might ever want to crash, but the Hammer presentation at Tony's very own Expo was the rare exception to this general rule. He took advantage of it with unseemly relish, rocketing down through the hole in the roof and landing to form a perfect equilateral triangle with Hammer and the traitorous Rhodey in that abomination they were calling War Machine. He would have winked at both of them, but he had the face shield down and wanted to keep it that way . . . because as much as he loved the entrance, he had a feeling that things were going to get real serious real fast. Ivan Vanko was around somewhere, and if he'd been in the Hammer lab, then Tony figured everyone ought to be real suspicious of what these ranked drones might get up to.

Whatever Hammer was feeling at seeing Tony crash his big party, he was a showman—you didn't get to be a dominant arms dealer if you didn't know how to pitch—and he rolled with this new circumstance. "And that's not all!" he said. "Here, ladies and gentlemen, is our very special surprise guest: Iron Man!"

Tony waved to the crowd while he popped a communications channel from his heads-up to Rhodey's. "Really?" he said. "A big gun on the shoulder? What ever happened to aesthetics?"

HUD-to-HUD, Rhodey said, "Tony . . . "

"That's mine," Tony said.

"It still is."

Which was the kind of lie you could forgive because you knew the person telling it meant well. Rhodey, Tony thought. You're too good to be involved with something as sleazy as the United States government.

"I knew that boyfriend of yours would get us into trouble," Tony said. "Next time do your homework."

"What are you talking about?" Rhodey asked.

Tony piped him a little something he had started on the flight over and finished up just now, with a quick scan of the drones flanking him on all sides. They were pretty well put together, and without a doubt would be a tough fight for anyone who wasn't in an Iron Man suit, but whoever had done their primary design phase work hadn't cared too much about hiding the specifics of their power systems and their command and control.

While Tony waited for Rhodey to assess what Tony had sent him, Hammer made it clear that his enthusiasm for his special guest was flagging. "Now, if Mr. Stark would step aside . . . "

"Oh, my God," Rhodey said.

That's right, Tony thought. That RT we took off Ivan Vanko and all these RTs in all these drones?

The same.

"Go home," he told Rhodey. "It's about to get ugly."

Then he commandeered the Tent of Tomorrow's loudspeaker and said, "Ladies and gentlemen, this pavilion is currently closed to the public. In an organized fashion, please find the nearest—"

He paused as he heard a ratcheting click and turned to find War Machine's heavy machine gun aimed right between his eyes. "Don't point that thing at me," he said.

"Tony," Rhodey said HUD-to-HUD. "Go."

"What?" In unison, all thirty-two drones on the stage pivoted away from War Machine, dropped their salutes, and focused their array of weaponry on Iron Man. "Oh God."

Hammer, edging toward the wings, called over to one of his technical support staff. "What the hell is going on?"

"We're not doing it!" the tech said. At that moment Iron Man shot upward and the eight Air Force drones followed him, shattering the glass dome of the Tent of Tomorrow into a blizzard of slivers that rained down into the crowd.

Pepper dove under her seat when she saw what was about to happen to the roof. Glass rained down everywhere, and the cheering of the crowd turned into screams. Odd, Pepper thought, how if you didn't know that there was glass falling out of the sky, you might not be able to tell that the crowd was panicking instead of being ecstatic over lethal gadgetry. She could hear people stampeding for the exits, and the occasional shouts of security guards trying to channel them into an orderly evacuation. Not much chance of that, she thought. Not with glass falling out of the sky and robots apparently taking off on their own.

Part of her thought: Already? We build robots and the minute they walk out into public they take off on their own?

It couldn't be that simple. Someone had to be pulling the strings. Hammer might even have been doing it, staging the whole thing so he could later blame it on someone else and present a prefabricated solution that he'd had ready since before the Expo. That wouldn't be beneath him.

Very little, in fact, was beneath Justin Hammer. Seeing Rhodey in the War Machine armor, embarrassed and ashamed, had convinced Pepper of that. Probably the order had come from a general, but you didn't have to be a genius to figure out that Justin Hammer had decided that a public demonstration of his War Machine armor would have him gobbling up defense contracts for the rest of his and his childrens' lives.

God, she was glad Tony was out of the arms business. But where had he gone?

CHAPTER 29

"Y ou want to do this?" Tony yelled as he did a series of barrel rolls and zigzags through the Expo. War Machine stayed hot on his tail. "Let's do this! I will smoke your ass!"

He was ready to do it, too. What with Rhodey taking his Mark II suit and handing it over to the military against Tony's express wishes, and then showing up at Tony's own Expo to model the misbegotten product of Hammer's greed and the United States military's Strangelovian mania for all that was new and glitzy on the tech front . . . if Rhodey was now going to take things to the point where the two of them were shooting it out in the sky over the Expo, Tony was ready to go there.

Of course, then Rhodey had to go and reassert his common decency, thereby reminding Tony that whatever faults Colonel James T. Rhodes might have had, a tendency to betray his friends was not one of them. "I'm not doing this!" Rhodey yelled back. "You need to get out of here."

I need to get out of here, Tony thought. Out of my Expo, that I put together, bringing all of these people together and—as things turned out—putting them in harm's way?

Not likely. "Jarvis, drone him," Tony said.

"Unable to penetrate firmware firewall," Jarvis said, almost apologetically.

Tony couldn't believe it. That was his firewall, in a version of his suit. "Unzip the codec," he snapped.

"Do something, man!" Rhodey said.

Tony gritted his teeth. Rhodey wasn't a tech guy, really; Tony couldn't explain the code stuff to him. "I'm trying," he said.

The Air Force drones, meanwhile, had spread out into a kind of double-wing formation, staying tight on Tony while fanning out far enough to either flank that any lateral move he made would be cutting right into ready fields of fire. The drones were smart, well programmed, and smoothly designed to function as a team. Tony had to tip his cap to whoever had done it.

Which meant, he assumed, tipping his cap to Ivan Vanko. That was fine. Vanko had proved to be more than a dirtbag, because no ordinary dirtbag could build an RT, find a way to mass-produce it, and retrofit a bunch of worthless Hammer Industries exoskeletons that no sane human would use until they turned into a fearsome airborne robot fighting force. That was pretty good, Tony had to admit.

On the other hand, none of those accomplishments meant Vanko was less of a dirtbag. You could be very intelligent, ambitious, and skilled human being and still be a dirtbag. This was not necessarily a position Tony would have taken a month ago, but he found himself drawn to it now. The facts of the situation were clear. Vanko was smart and determined. Vanko was also a dirtbag. Ergo those two states of being were not mutually exclusive.

QED, Tony thought. Light air-to-air missiles, suit-borne and not really up to the task of taking down the Mark IV, lit up the sky around him.

"So," he said to Rhodey. "Still happy you ran off with my suit?"

"You want to talk about this now?" Rhodey said.

"No. As a matter of fact, I don't. But we do need to get it settled, and since this army of drones might actually succeed in shooting my suit down and killing me in the process, it struck me that maybe you and I should clear the air." Tony dodged a fusillade of missiles and bullets—some of which, he couldn't help but resentfully note, were fired from the War Machine's rotating-barrel cannon. "See what I mean?"

"I'm not doing that," Rhodey said.

"You're riding around in the suit that's doing it," Tony said. "Jarvis, how's the whole thing with the decompiling of that suit's code so we can get control of it coming?"

"The situation is less than ideal, sir," Jarvis said. "But you may rest assured that I'm making the very best of it."

"Hey, Rhodey," Tony said. "Did I ever tell you that I was having trouble with the RT and that I was about to die because I couldn't figure out how to power it without using a substance that was slowly poisoning me?"

"As a matter of fact, you did not," Rhodey said.

"Huh," Tony said. "How about that. Well, it's true. I just thought I would let you know that I got it all figured out, and it's all good now. I'm not going to die."

"Terrific," Rhodey said. At that moment the War Machine suit fired off a missile, and for a while Tony was too busy to talk.

One of the problems with dodging missiles in a heavily populated area such as that surrounding the Expo was that if you dodged a missile properly in such an area, it tended to explode either on the ground or when it came into contact with a large standing structure. Neither of those outcomes was desirable at this point because either had a high probability of resulting in a large number of civilian casualties. So what Tony had to do was dodge the missile and get it to go off without hurting anybody. This was exactly the opposite of what the missile was designed to do, so Tony found himself in a struggle against the missile's designers as much as the missile itself. What had they focused on, and what had they ignored? The design of missiles was pretty standard, yet every model had its variations. Some of them were susceptible to flares or chaff despite being designed to fight through flares or chaff. Design was like that; the machines never did quite what you thought they were going to.

So what Tony had to do here was try to scrape this missile off against something substantial that contained no people and would not collapse on people. That narrowed down his options considerably, and meant that the best option might be just to let the missile hit him. He was ninety-nine percent sure the Mark IV could absorb the impact of any non-nuclear missile yet designed by human minds.

What to do, what to do . . . take a potentially fatal punch or try to evade it, possibly at the expense of numerous lives?

Tony sighed. He was developing a conscience. Much

too slowly for some people, but it was developing, and at times like this—when he was about to eat a missile explosion on purpose just because it was less likely to kill him than other people if they had to do it—man, at times like this he hated his conscience worse than the worst of his enemies.

The impact of the missile was like a combination of a moderately bad car accident and being inside a gong when it was struck by one of the enormous eunuchs gongs were always struck by in movies like the Elizabeth Taylor *Cleopatra*. Tony's eyes watered, his ears rang, he got a headache, and his entire body started sending out signals that it would be bruised and uncooperative tomorrow.

Following up on the impact, the Air Force drones strafed Tony with everything they had. Eight streams of machine-gun bullets pinged and ricocheted off the Mark IV, most harmlessly; occasionally one nicked an instrument or control surface and the HUD registered a corresponding loss in maneuverability or environmental awareness. "Jarvis," Tony said. "What do you think about the idea of fighting back?"

"That is certainly an option, sir," Jarvis said. "You are considerably outgunned, however, and it is uncertain whether your suit would survive combat with the eight drones and the suit occupied by Colonel Rhodes."

"Uncertain, huh?" Tony said. "When are you going to get Rhodey's suit back online for Rhodey so he can stop shooting missiles at me?"

"Oh, tout suite, sir," Jarvis said. "Tout suite."

*   *   *

For the attendees of the Stark Expo, the show at the Tent of Tomorrow was like going to the neighborhood bar on open-mic night and unexpectedly seeing Bob Dylan walk up on the stage to try out some new stuff he was working on. Tony Stark at Justin Hammer's show? Robot drones with missiles? A new armed forces version of the Iron Man suit!?

And then they took off through the roof—no, I'm not kidding—and they were shooting at each other!

A thousand phone conversations more or less like that cluttered up the local cell towers' bandwidth as the ion wakes of the Iron Man and War Machine suits twisted and curved across the sky, with the tight formation of drones close behind. A couple of people complained about being hit by falling glass, but the people who hadn't been hit were half-convinced that nobody had been hit, that it was all a show, that the whole point of the thing was some signal about Stark and Hammer working together. Before the first shot had been fired, rumors were already flying about joint Hammer-Stark projects, or even a possible merger of the two companies into a giant super-contractor that would dominate Pentagon procurements for decades.

The shooting was dismissed as a demo of new weapons systems. It was a fireworks show, put on to ooh them and ahh them. And it was working. The Stark Expo became the number one trending topic on Twitter thirty seconds after the collapse of the Tent of Tomorrow's glass roof.

A large crowd gathered on a pavilion outside the Tent of Tomorrow and another on a balcony across the Expo's main thoroughfare. The flickering of flashbulbs was enough to make anyone epileptic. All attendees agreed; it was one of the best shows Tony Stark had ever put on, and they'd seen (not to mention *heard about*) some killer shows.

All of that excitement lasted exactly until the moment when the eight Army drones marched in formation out the Tent of Tomorrow's front entrance. They extruded stabilizers from their legs, like the legs that come out from the side of a crane to keep it steady. Then they deployed heavy guns from racks on their shoulders and aimed them skyward. They waited like that, making minuscule movements that tracked the progress across the sky of Tony Stark and the War Machine.

Then, as the aerial show wound back over the main Expo grounds, the Army drones fired simultaneously into the air.

At nearly the same moment, the first stray bullets from the Air Force drones' pursuit of Tony began to ricochet off the pavement at the feet of the Expo attendees. For some of them, it was still a show; for others, it was the last best thing they ever saw in their lives.

Around the Expo's entrances and exits, S.H.I.E.L.D. personnel appeared and deployed from unknown sources. Their orders were to acquire and intercept Ivan Vanko, lethal force not only authorized but encouraged, and to apprehend Justin Hammer. Other mission parameters included minimizing civilian casualties and recovering the War Machine suit to delay—or, if possible, prevent—its final deployment as an asset of the United States military.

Ivan Vanko had done them a favor there. Already blog posts were appearing, with photos of War Machine's armaments aimed at Iron Man, to ask questions about whether the military was really in control of whoever occupied the suit. Could such a suit turn into more of a liability than an asset, given the grave consequences that would follow upon losing one to an enemy? What if an operator went rogue? What safeguards were in place to prevent something much worse than, say, the events at Stark Industries' Los Angeles complex two years before? Nobody believed the official story.

S.H.I.E.L.D. had another official story half-written already. But for their story to work, they needed Tony and Rhodey to survive the next thirty minutes. Right then nobody was sure how likely that was to happen.

CHAPTER 30

Here I am, bossed around by a messenger, Happy thought. "Why is your mom at Hammer Industries?" he asked, glancing in the rear-view mirror to make eye contact—and was rewarded by the sight of Natalie stripping out of her business casual. He cut his eyes away, then couldn't help it. He peeked again. Man.

She saw him doing it. "Keep a secret? She's not. Drive." She stared at him, half-dressed, until he looked back at the road. Then she said, "I'll explain later."

Ah, the life of a secret agent, Natasha thought. Changing in the back seat of a speeding car while a chauffeur ogles me and all of the real action is probably happening back at the site I just left.

She was hoping there would be something to find out at Hammer's research facility. Mostly she was hoping Ivan would be there. She wanted to see him. She wanted to fight him. Natasha Romanoff wanted accolades and glory and promotions. She wanted to be the best and the baddest. She wanted to kick ass.

Also she wanted Happy to stop looking at her in her underwear and keep his eyes on the road before he killed both of them. If there was one thing Natasha knew, however, it was that men rarely looked at something else for long when she was in the room. This was a mixed blessing. Right now it wasn't a blessing at all.

"So," Happy said. He was making an effort not to look at her too often. Natasha appreciated it. "I've seen you having these mysterious phone conversations for the past few weeks, you know, and it seems like you're always having one right when the shit is hitting the fan, like at Tony's party and at Monaco . . . so why don't you level with me?"

All of a sudden Happy's gaze, reflected in the rearview mirror, wasn't focused on any part of Natasha but her eyes. "Who are you calling? And why?"

"You want the truth, Happy? I'm a secret agent working for a mysterious organization called S.H.I.E.L.D." Natasha kept talking as she finished getting into her uniform. "I was deployed to Stark Industries because S.H.I.E.L.D. has been and continues to be worried that your boss's behavior is endangering the Iron Man suit and the American people. They sent me to L.A. to keep an eye on him and make sure that someone was there to call in the cavalry if things got out of hand." She zipped up her S.H.I.E.L.D.-regulation coverall and slipped a nearly invisible wireless receiver into her ear. Her phone and a speaker went into a sheath on the uniform's hip. It had a miniature wireless microphone speaker built into its collar.

Many S.H.I.E.L.D. operatives carried a gun. Natasha

preferred not to. She had nothing against guns in certain situations, but she had found that in close quarters, reliance on firearms could become a fatal liability. When they got to Hammer Industries, they wouldn't be looking at a pitched battle. They were infiltrating, with a single objective in mind. Firepower would be no asset there.

Happy, she thought, wouldn't be much of an asset either. Natasha hoped that his humiliation at her hands back in Tony's gym would keep him from wanting to do something macho and stupid like come in with her and fight. His loyalty spoke well of him, but Happy Hogan was a dinosaur. If she had to fight with him, he would only increase the odds of both of them not completing the mission.

What she could do about this, Natasha did not know. She had no authority over him. He wouldn't believe her if she invoked some arcane national-security statute that gave her any kind of authority. She was just going to have to make the best of the situation. If Ivan Vanko was still at Hammer Industries, Natalie thought, I'm going to be fighting as much to keep Happy alive as to remove Vanko as a threat.

Divided objectives were the perfect recipe for a failed mission. She didn't like it. Not one bit.

"Step on it, Happy," she said. "Come on."

"I think maybe I'm going to stop driving people around," Happy said, as he floored the limo's accelerator. "It turns them into jerks."

Natalie called Pepper. No answer. She called Coulson.

"Not much time to talk here, Natasha," he answered.

"I'm on my way," she said. "Almost there. Anything I need to know from the Expo?"

"Well," Coulson said, "people are stampeding out.

Other people are staying to watch what they apparently think is some kind of aerial show. There are a bunch of automated drones shooting at your employer. There is also a human-operated mobile armor apparatus shooting at your employer despite the fact that its operator protests that he is not making the suit do this." Gunfire and the roaring whine of flying armor in the background punctuated Coulson's summary. "One suspects that Ivan Vanko is behind some or all of these events. We're looking for him and for Hammer. No visual on either of them yet, although Hammer can't be far and we don't think it'll be long before Ivan shows up either. That enough for you to go on?"

"For now," Natasha said.

"Great," Coulson said. "Now maybe you can complete your mission and let me continue with mine."

"Maybe I can," Natasha said. She hung up and said to Happy, "Apparently Colonel Rhodes is shooting at your boss."

"Everybody wants to take a shot at the boss once in a while," Happy said. "Most of the time I don't think they really mean it. Most of the rest of the time, he brings it on himself and everything gets sorted out pretty quick. That's how guys fight. We throw the punches, we get it off our chests, then everything is okay again."

His eyes met hers in the rear-view mirror again. "Unlike certain women of my acquaintance, who sandbag me and then use nefarious methods to embarrass me in front of my boss and people who are important to me."

Ouch, Natasha thought. But he was right. She had done exactly that.

"Would it help if I told you that was part of the mission?" she said.

"It was part of your mission to put yourself between me and Mr. Stark?" Happy said. "Would it help to know that? No. I don't think that would help at all."

There wasn't much to say after that. Happy drove. Natasha rode. She hoped that—as he had just said—he had gotten it off his chest and everything would be fine again. Somehow, though, she didn't think that was as universally true as Happy had professed it to be.

Part of her was also rehearsing her mission objectives and trying to relate them to the question of Tony Stark's health. Should she have called in backup when she first noticed the discoloration on his skin, the night of the party? If she had, would things have unfolded differently that night? Possibly a different course of action on her part might have meant that Colonel Rhodes would never have given the Mark II suit to the military, and the current situation at the Expo would be quite different. Also, if Tony's health was compromised, that lessened his chances of surviving the current crisis—again, a situation that might have been averted.

Natasha had a feeling that Director Fury was going to have some choice words on her next set of mission evaluations. She was a good operative—she had no doubt of that—but as the director would no doubt point out, she had much to learn and she was not in a business that permitted mistakes.

So part of what she was hoping to do out at Hammer Industries was clean up after some of those mistakes by preventing Ivan Vanko from getting to the Stark Expo.

Failing that, she hoped to discover something that would hinder and compromise Vanko's plans for the Expo.

And failing that, the truth was that Natasha Romanoff was frustrated. What she really wanted was just to break some heads.

That, she thought, might just be something that she and Happy Hogan had in common.

CHAPTER 31

I'll tell you what," Rhodey said while his suit tried to kill Tony, "either Jarvis isn't all he's cracked up to be or whoever did this code on this item did a hell of a job."

"Congratulating your contractors, Colonel?" Tony said.

"Hell no," Rhodey said. "They're not running this thing." Rhodey got serious. "Do something, Tony. I haven't fired the big stuff yet."

"Here's hoping you won't get the chance to," Tony said. "Jarvis?"

"Some progress to report, sir," Jarvis said. "Unfortunately, that progress is solely in the area of determining that none of my existing methods are going to suffice to re-establish control over the War Machine apparatus. Its code has been completely rewritten and its security protocols now resemble neither yours nor Hammer's."

"Well, whose do they resemble, Jarvis?" Tony had, at

great pains, compiled an exhaustive sampling of security protocols used by his competitors in the arms and technological research fields. He avoided espionage, but he didn't want it happening to him, either—so he looked at what everyone else was doing, borrowed the good stuff, and put together a hybrid system that worked better. That's what hybrids did.

"I haven't seen anything like them before, sir," Jarvis said.

"Tony," Rhodey said. "What's going on?"

"Working, old pal," Tony said. "Working."

Pepper spotted Hammer heading for a backstage exit. She jumped onto the stage and made a beeline for him. Grabbing his arm, she said, "You're coming with me."

"No, I don't think so." He broke Pepper's grip and headed for the exit.

She followed him, getting her phone out to call Agent Coulson and let him know that if any S.H.I.E.L.D. people were around, one of them should probably be right here arresting—or detaining, or whatever it was they did—a certain Justin Hammer. "People are dead, Justin. Tony might be dead soon," she said.

"It's the arms business, Pepper. People die. That's what weapons are for. And if one of those people is Tony . . . " Justin trailed off and shrugged. "You know what? I like Tony. I wanted to embarrass him today. But I don't want to kill him. You know who wants to kill him? That crazy Vanko guy. I'm guessing he's behind this. He showed up at my lab wanting to work for me. I thought he was dead, but there he was. I turned him around and called the cops the minute he was gone. Where he's been since then, I don't know. But you want a villain in this whole thing? It's him. Not me. I'm a businessman."

Hammer's expression suddenly changed as something occurred to him. "Want to come work for me?" he asked. "Whatever you're making with Tony, I'll double it. Better hours, too. I won't make you get his laundry."

"I'm CEO now, Justin," Pepper said with a sweetly poisonous smile. "And you're a criminal. You should be thinking about plea bargains, not job offers."

"No," Justin said, shaking his head. "I'm not a criminal. I was in this to get rich. Just like Tony. You can't blame me for the rest of it."

Something exploded not very far away. Pepper flinched as the Tent of Tomorrow shook and things fell from the catwalks in the backstage darkness. When she looked up again, Hammer was gone.

She tried to call Agent Coulson. On the second try, he answered. "You've seen Hammer?" he said. "We are absolutely interested. I'm just inside the delivery gate. I'll head in your direction, you head in mine. We'll probably intersect near the front gate. Most people are being directed to evacuate that way."

Pepper came back out onto the stage picking her way through the broken glass. The Tent of Tomorrow was nearly deserted. "You've got to get out, miss!" a security guard called.

Miss, she thought. That was nice.

Where had all the drones gone? There had been twenty-four of them when she went looking for Hammer. Now there were zero. Pepper got part of her answer when, as she headed for the Tent of Tomorrow's main entrance, the guard directed her away. "Some of those robots are out front there, ma'am," he said, pointing with his flashlight toward a hallway that curved around the outside of the auditorium. "You should use the side door, over that way."

That figures, Pepper thought. From onstage, I'm a miss. Up close, I'm a ma'am. And he never even batted an eye.

She came out of the tent into chaos. Fires were burning in some of the Expo's buildings. There were bullet holes everywhere, like she'd stepped out of a science expo and into a war zone. Which she had. Overhead, the Air Force drones thundered after Tony. Rhodey, in the War Machine suit, was in there somewhere too. Pepper had an awful feeling that something was going to happen to Rhodey. If she turned out to be right, then Justin Hammer was going to have a lot to answer for. Pepper would see to it.

Heading toward her projected rendezvous with Coulson, Pepper rounded the front of the Tent of Tomorrow and stopped dead as she came nearly face-to-face with one of the Army drones. It was a foot taller than she was, at least. Maybe two feet. She wasn't a good judge of distances when she was in mortal fear of her life. Deep green in color and built lower to the ground and a bit bulkier than the drones designed for the other services, the Army drone looked made for close combat. She saw its targeting mechanisms acquire her, analyze her, and dismiss her in precisely the length of time it took for her life to flash before her eyes. Then the drone walked past without another glance in Pepper's direction. Seven more followed it. When they had reached an apparently predetermined point on the Ten of Tomorrow's raised external pavilion, they retrenched, set their stabilizers, and retargeted their heavy weapons in the general direction of the heart of the

Expo. Where they were going, or on what mission, Pepper did not know.

Tony thundered overhead, low enough that she felt the bruising wake of his passage. Firing wildly, the Air Force drones came close behind, with Rhodey an unwilling passenger in their midst. Around Pepper the world dissolved into explosions. She dropped to her knees. When everything had passed, she looked around again, for the second time in less than a minute amazed to still be alive.

"Was that Pepper?" Tony yelled.

"Ms. Potts was indeed in the vicinity recently," Jarvis replied.

"Tell me she's okay, Jarvis."

A salvo of heavy machine gun fire stitched its way across Tony's back and legs. Damage reports were minimal, but he wasn't going to stay lucky forever. The suit wasn't meant to be a target in a sustained firefight. It was designed to avoid sustained firefights by bringing overwhelming force to bear on its operator's chosen target—which in this case would be the War Machine suit were it not for the highly inconvenient fact that said suit contained a human occupant who, though traitorous and despicable, probably did not deserve to die.

"Certainly, sir," Jarvis said. "Would you like me to ascertain the truth of that statement first?"

"My display just zoomed in on her," Rhodey cut in. "She looks fine."

"Your display," Tony said. Why would—? Ah. That explained some things. If Ivan was controlling Rhodey's systems, he might also be the party responsible for checking on Pepper's status. Which meant that he viewed Pepper either as a target or as leverage.

It also probably meant that Vanko was sending Tony a message by choosing to put Pepper on Rhodey's heads-up.

What Ivan Vanko needed, in the parlance of the rural South, was a good killing. Tony resolved that this would be his good deed for the day, as soon as he got Rhodey back in control of his own suit.

Right now, though, he had problems with eight non-Rhodey bogeys on his tail. Tony plunged into a narrow passage between two of the Expo's on-site research labs, where local schoolkids could come and watch scientists at work from observation decks that looked down on the lab facilities the way a visitor to a zoo would look down on the alligator enclosure. Some of the white coats had complained that they felt objectified and dehumanized, but the way Tony saw it, why not put science out there where people could see it? Scientists were always feeling like nobody understood what they did. Now Tony was showing their working routines to the world, and they wanted to bellyache about it. People were never happy.

One of those labs blew up spectacularly as Tony jinked out of the way of a missile salvo. "Hope there was nothing toxic in there," he said. "Or nuclear."

"What!?"

"Kidding, Rhodey. Come on. That was where the kids went to see Science World." Tony ripped through a multi-g one-eighty and headed back across the Expo grounds. He was getting a sense of the drones as opponents now, and once he did that, Tony started to get a sense of how to defeat them. When you were talking about that kind of number imbalance—eight to one even if you didn't count Rhodey—any plan was complicated. So the first thing to do was bring those numbers down a little through creative use of evasionary tactics. Best defense being a good offense, or something like that.

Even over the blast of ten sets of repulsor-based thrusters, Tony heard the War Machine's super Gatling gun spin up again. The hail of bullets hit the Mark IV so fast that Tony nearly couldn't distinguish individual impacts; it was like the entire sky had turned into bullets, like the moment when it started raining so hard that you were soaked to the skin by the time you could register how hard it was raining. Something shorted out in Tony's combat sensors. "Quit shooting at me, Rhodey!" he said.

"I'm not!"

"I know, but quit it!" Figured, Tony thought. How many bullet impacts had the suit already absorbed? A few hundred? And this was the first real damage? That, Mr. Stark, is a pretty good suit, he congratulated himself. Thank you, Mr. Stark, he answered. But it won't matter too much if we die in it. True enough, Mr. Stark. So what we should do is stop running from these drones and start suckering them by pretending that we're running.

So true, Mr. Stark. So, so true.

It was Br'er Rabbit time again. Tony peeled into a high loop, slowing down ever so slightly. The Air Force drones closed and hammered away at him with small-arms fire. He wanted to keep them close and keep their fields of fire angled away from the evacuating crowds. Then he had a little surprise he was hoping to spring, when the time was right.

"Hey, Rhodey," he said to distract himself, keep his

mind from zeroing in too tightly on one problem and thereby ignoring others. "How long do you think Hammer's known about Vanko?"

"What? Known what about him?"

"You think Hammer broke Vanko out of jail?" Tony asked. "I mean, if he did, then he's no ordinary arms-dealing scumbag like I used to be. He's a genuine murderer in the sense that he knowingly did cause the deaths of other human beings without cause or justification."

"Quit trying to make me feel bad," Rhodey said.

"I'm not," Tony insisted. "I'm just trying to point out some uncomfortable truths here so we can both stop pretending they aren't true. Or uncomfortable."

"I associated with you when Stark was dealing under the table. I didn't know about that either," Rhodey pointed out.

"You need to choose your company more carefully," Tony said. "Lie down with dogs, get up with fleas. And hey, did I mention quit shooting at me?"

"I'm not!"

CHAPTER 32

Tony wasn't sure which feature of the Expo was his favorite: the Unisphere, reconstructed from the original built for the first Stark Expo, or the artificial lake Tony had added as a reflective pool. Two hundred feet tall, the Unisphere rotated on a solar-powered pedestal assembly, a globe whose longitude lines were I-beams and whose structural integrity was guaranteed by the stainless-steel continents and archipelagos that adorned it along with the massive STARK and accompanying arrowhead logo that stood out above the continents, angling across the Unisphere's equator from south to north. It was grand, over the top, redolent of turn-of-the-century ideas about Progress and the Destiny of Mankind. Tony loved it the way his father must have loved the original.

All of this went through his mind as he flew in a high arc over the lake. War Machine was hot on his trail. "Jarvis, we need to get a handle on that OS," Tony said.

"Displaying architecture," Jarvis said. A graphic rendering of the information architecture of the War Machine suit appeared on Tony's HUD.

Rhodey broke in. "What's going on up there, man?"

"Just bear with me," Tony said as the OS architecture flooded through his field of vision. He thought he must have been the only man in the history of the world who had ever found himself troubleshooting software while flying through the air at near-Mach speeds avoiding a group of homicidal robots.

He couldn't think. It was time to get rid of a couple of these drones so he had a minute to breathe. Tony dipped down close to the surface of the lake, letting the violent currents of his passage kick up rooster tails of water to confuse pursuers. At the same time he jinked and swerved through a series of tight loops and figure eights that were guaranteed to leave him with a headache in the morning. At the end of it all, he had lost a couple of the Air Force drones and gotten himself face-to-face with three others, with the length of the lake between them. They were steaming toward him at full thrust. The least he could do, Tony reasoned, was reciprocate the gesture.

Accelerating toward them, Tony felt the impacts of machine-gun fire on his shoulders. Nothing to worry about there. Pretty soon the drones would about have to run out of ammunition anyway.

Once Tony had found himself in a situation where to get away from three air-to-air missiles he had to fly straight into another one. At the moment of that impact, he had briefly been certain that he was dead. The noise had been so huge, the blast so powerful, that it had not only knocked out all of his sensors—leaving him for all intents and purposes deaf, dumb, and blind inside a suit that was magically transformed from an armored killing machine to an expensive alloy coffin—but momentarily convinced him that he was actually dead, and his spirit was experiencing the initial phases of whatever afterlife awaited him.

The impact with the center Air Force drone was not nearly that bad. A little shudder through the frame of the suit, a brief whiteout in the visual sensors as the drone's arc reactor went blooey, and then Tony was through the blossoming fireball with the Unisphere looming in his sights and the surviving Air Force drones—some of them, anyway, they were moving too fast for a reliable count— closing in on his tail again.

But none of them were as close as War Machine. Tony ran a targeting projection on the slowly rotating Unisphere while simultaneously poking at different corners of the War Machine suit's OS. Aha, he thought. Might be something there. At the same time he spotted a way to transect the Unisphere at a high rate of speed and in such a way that whoever tried to duplicate the maneuver behind him might run afoul of its mass.

Which was a fancy way of saying that he thought he could probably rub some of the drones off on either the longitudinal I-beams or the steel coastlines of the Unisphere's continents. Tony set his sights on the A in STARK and kicked up the repulsors.

"This might hurt," he said to Rhodey.

"What? No, you are not—"

"Yeah. I am." Tony stayed focused on the A.

Rhodey's voice beat on his eardrums. "No no no nonono NO!"

The way Tony had it figured, War Machine—and therefore Rhodey—were tight enough on his burners that whatever calculations worked for Tony would work for Rhodey too. The Unisphere didn't rotate that fast.

Further, he had observed the drones enough to have a pretty good sense of their processing speeds and battlefield reaction times. They were superb pieces of work, Tony had to admit. Ivan Vanko was a world-class weapons designer and roboticist. Credit where credit was due, et cetera; the more Tony learned about Vanko, the more he wished Vanko wasn't a psychopath with an inscrutable grudge against Tony for his father's death, and the more he wished that he would be able to conclude his interactions with Vanko on a non-murderous note. But that, given the way things had transpired so far, didn't seem likely.

The drones, at least the way Tony had it figured after watching them in operation these past couple of minutes, were plenty quick enough to acquire and hold a target through a number of complicated moves in open or partially confined spaces. That in itself was a huge leap in battlefield robotics. But he didn't think the drones had quite enough processing power to project a high-speed interaction with an object as complex as the Unisphere, which during the course of its motion presented different paths through it every fraction of a second. The upshot of Tony's assumptions here was that while he thought he could fly through the Unisphere and take that ingrateful and yammering Rhodey with him, he didn't think the Air Force drones were very likely to survive the same trip.

He was about to find out whether he was right about any or all of those assumptions.

The Mark VI Iron Man suit entered the A in STARK

moving approximately four hundred miles per hour. This was nowhere near the suit's maximum flight speed, but it was plenty for the scale of maneuverability desired within the confines of the Expo. At this speed, it took the Mark VI approximately one-third of a second to traverse the interior of the Unisphere and emerge between two longitudinal lines on the other side. His margin for error at the entry of the A was measurable in inches on either side of the suit.

Several of the Air Force drones tried the same operation. Their margins for error, like Tony's, were measurable in inches. But their processors, unlike Tony's, were not human brains augmented by full-on artificial-intelligence-guided real-time tracking and guidance systems. They were computers that could process incredibly fast but were not designed to tackle the kind of problem presented by the Unisphere's motion. One of them blew up against the K in STARK. Another deflected off the intersection of a longitudinal beam and the equator, tumbling through the interior of the Unisphere to explode against the interior surface of Australia. A third tried at the last moment to dip under the STARK logo but didn't quite make the move fast enough, fracturing the aerodynamic covering on its heavy machine gun. The resultant disruption of flow, combined with high-velocity flight, created turbulence that shook the drone apart before it had gotten to the other side. Some pieces of it shot out the Unisphere's other side to fall clanging into the Expo's central plaza.

That was three that Tony knew about. He took a quick glance through the Expo's security surveillance system and saw that there were five separate heat signatures on and around the Unisphere that could only be explosions. "See that, Rhodey?" he said. "Not bad."

"You didn't have to do that," Rhodey said accusingly. "You did that just to be mean."

"Mean?" Tony echoed. "You beat me up and steal my suit—on my *birthday*—and I'm the one who's mean? See if I fix your OS and get you out of there, buster. You just wait and see."

He turned back over the Unisphere, watching to see if it was going to fall over. He didn't want it to, but it had just absorbed a whole lot of impact energy that it wasn't designed to absorb. The structure of the I-beams would dissipate some of that energy, but the continental impacts were another story. That was a lot of angular momentum for the little pedestal to handle.

"Unisphere appears intact and rotationally stable," Jarvis reported.

"Who cares about the Unisphere?" Tony snapped, irritated that Jarvis had seen through him so easily. "Figure out Rhodey's OS. What do I pay you for?"

He might have gone on—it was more fun than it should have been to pick on Jarvis, since he had no physical body and couldn't do anything about it—but just then the surviving Air Force drones angled out of the sky, guns blazing. Tony kicked the Mark VI into a steep dive and made for the shadows at the edge of the Expo.

"So," Rhodey said. "Much as I'm enjoying this trip, I could sure live with a progress report that might tell me something about whether I'm going to live or die here."

"Quit being a baby," Tony said. The suit shuddered under bullet impacts. "Who's shooting at whom, here? I'm the one who should be worried about survival. Jarvis, come on. Make this happen."

"Making it, sir," Jarvis said. "You may be certain of that."

Pepper saw the explosions on the Unisphere and was nearly sick with dread. She got out her phone and called Tony, steeling herself for him not to answer because he was dead and in pieces of flaming wreckage in the bottom of the Unisphere. But no—he answered on the third ring. "Ms. Potts," he said. "I told you never to call me here."

"I just wanted to—"

Pepper heard impacts through the phone. "Ouch," Tony said. "Gotta go. Bye."

He clicked off. That's when she saw him reappear through the smoke billowing up from the Unisphere, with War Machine a few yards behind and what looked like the last two Air Force drones flanking the two of them. War Machine was firing with everything it had except the big missiles. Whatever the reason for not deploying those, Pepper was glad about it. She could only imagine what one of those would do in the middle of a crowd like the one currently trying to get out of the Expo.

She looked around, shoving her way across the main surge of the crowd. There was Coulson. He was waving to her and gesturing toward the main gate. Pepper angled through the crowd to meet him.

While everyone tried to get out of the Expo, Ivan Vanko walked in. As he had with the Grand Prix, he chose a rear entrance guarded by machines rather than humans. The chaos in the skies over the Expo had distracted all of the human security. This was just as well. Ivan had no desire to kill anyone who did not require killing. He hacked down a steel door and went down a short stairwell to a concrete maintenance corridor, part of a system that ran under the entire Expo grounds. The blueprint of the system, courtesy of Hammer's files, was clear in his head. Ivan walked confidently, loving the feel of this armor on his body and these whips that extended his arms and turned them into lightning. He felt invincible. He felt sure that the drones and the suborned War Machine would weaken Stark's suit to the point that when Ivan chose to confront him, the outcome would be a foregone conclusion. Part of him wished to prolong it, but Ivan knew this impulse to be foolish. No one kept an enemy alive any longer than necessary.

And no one had a more dangerous enemy than Tony Stark. Ivan would end him, avenge his father, and then . . .

And then. There was no "and then." It did not matter. What mattered was Stark.

Ivan stopped. He was standing at the base of a steel ladder that led up to a manhole cover. If he remembered the blueprints correctly—and he did—this cover would let him out near the perimeter of the Expo, not far from the main entrance.

He retracted the whips and began to climb.

CHAPTER 33

Before the limo had come to a complete stop outside the main access gate to Hammer Industries' New York regional research facility, Natalie already had the door open. "Wait here," she said.

"No way," Happy shot back. He turned the car off and got out himself. He was damned if he was going to be out-machoed by a girl, or ordered around by one. Even one who looked like Natalie Rushman did in form-fitting black. "You're not going in there alone."

She gave him a pitying look. "Please. Not now."

That look was the last straw. She could sandbag him in the ring. She could boss him around where Stark Industries was concerned. She could drag him out here well after working hours when he should have been back at the Expo where he might be needed.

But under no circumstances could she pity him.

Coming around the front of the car, Happy shook his head. " 'No' is not an answer I'll accept."

"Fine," she sighed. He thought he could see on her face that she knew she'd been out of line. He also thought he could see a little bit of the entitlement that beautiful girls gradually got to feel, where they never had to say they were sorry because people always wanted to be around them no matter how they acted. She turned and headed for the lab complex. "Stay on my six," Natalie said over her shoulder. "And out of my way."

Like most high-tech research buildings, the Hammer lab was closed at this hour but its parking lot was full of cars. Research never stopped, and researchers who wanted good jobs at a place like Hammer Industries soon learned that they never stopped either. Happy was about to ask how they were going to get in when Natalie cruised up to an electronic access pad next to the front door and tapped in a code like she owned the place. She glanced over at him, anticipating his question. "S.H.I.E.L.D.," she said. "We're like the government, except better."

Inside, they headed across a broad, multistory atrium before getting past the part of the building that was for show into the part of the building where the work happened. Here, the Hammer lab looked like any other lab or hospital in the world: sterile surfaces, neutral colors. Lots of signs telling you which way to go, lots of cameras detecting whether you went there or somewhere else. "How do you know—" Happy began.

"Where Vanko's lab is?" Natalie finished for him. "A little birdie told me."

He was starting to think that Miss Natalie Rushman, or whatever she called herself when she wasn't pretending to be a pretty young thing just out of law school, wasn't very trustworthy. She knew too much and was too casual about what she knew. She had gotten too close to the boss too easily. Plus, Ms. Potts didn't like her. If there was one barometer of people Happy went by, it was how Pepper Potts reacted to them. She was almost never wrong.

And Pepper Potts did not like Natalie at all. This, in addition to the incident in the gym, made Happy not like her very much either, and made him question her motives, and nearly made him suggest that she ought to call in some other S.H.I.E.L.D. people, whoever they would turn out to be, because he figured he could trust them more than her.

Still, when they came around a corner and ran smack into a Hammer security guard doing his rounds, Happy's twin instincts of chivalry and mission dedication kicked in before he knew it.

"You go ahead, I got this guy!" he said. "I'll be okay! Go."

She started to say something, but then she went, running down the hall deeper into the building before the guard could stop her.

The thing about boxing that distinguished it from real-life fighting was that in boxing you saw guys take lots of punches and keep on going. In real life, ninety percent of fights ended up on the ground, and once they ended up on the ground, they were usually over real fast. Happy knew this. This was one of the reasons he hated mixed martial arts. They took fighting and made it more like life, where boxing took the idea of the fight, the one-on-one confrontation, and through the application of artificial rules made the fight a thing of beauty. People could call it outdated, they could say that boxing was dead and that the coup de grâce had been administered by Kimbo Slice or any other of MMA's first generation of starts, they could say anything they wanted. Boxing was beautiful.

Happy squared off against the Hammer guard, who was a little bigger than he was but whose reach looked about the same. He'd fought guys like this before, who had lots of gym muscle and attitude but no real toughness. The guard came after him, all ferocity and no technique, swinging haymakers that Happy could have dodged in a rocking chair. Happy returned fire, snapping jabs and staying on his toes, spotting in a right when he had an easy opening. He didn't try to load up, didn't try to win the fight in a single punch. The trick was to know your plan, understand your opponent's weaknesses, and win by sticking to the plan. The Hammer guard was big and—as Happy found out after taking a couple of those wild punches on his arms and shoulders—brutally strong. But he wasn't in great shape, and it took a lot of energy to swing all that meat he had on his arms. Happy stayed with him, slipping his big punches and giving a few of them back, and it wasn't long before the guard delivered a huge roundhouse that missed Happy by feet. Happy stepped in, knowing now was the time. He hooked, he fired straight rights, he went high and low with combinations . . . and he realized that unlike a lot of big guys with gym muscles, the Hammer guard could take a punch. Happy nailed him with everything he had, and the guard stayed on his feet, every so often sending a little something by return mail that had Happy seeing stars.

It was a body punch that finally did it, the kind of liver shot you saw in the ring sometimes, that unstrings the opponent's knees and leaves him gasping on the canvas. Happy landed it, and landed a crusher of a right on the guard's jaw as the guard was on the way down. The guard hit the floor in front of a door marked QUIET and stayed down.

"I did it!" Hap said, breathing hard. His hands felt like he'd spend the afternoon sparring with a brick wall; fighting without gloves was for idiots. Time to find Natalie and make sure she hadn't gotten herself into more trouble. Happy turned to start after her.

The entire length of the hall floor between where he stood and where Natalie waited impatiently near a T-intersection was strewn with the battered and unconscious bodies of at least a dozen other Hammer security personnel. It looked like a team of infuriated gorillas armed with baseball bats had gone on a rampage. Happy looked from Natalie to her handiwork and back, just flat unable to believe that she had done all this in the time it had taken him to knock out one guard the old-fashioned way.

"Come on!" Natalie said. To her credit, she didn't comment about his boxing skills or complain that he had made her wait.

Coming in low and hot over the lake, Tony thought briefly that he'd lost the Air Force drones. Only War Machine showed up on the pursuit radar. Then the HUD started squealing about multiple target locks and he understood that he hadn't lost them; they had peeled off to stay out of the field of fire when the eight Army drones lined up on the Tent of Tomorrow's pavilion unloaded everything they had in the general direction of the Mark VI.

What hit him first was small arms. No sweat, just more noise pollution in the helmet and more promised headaches when he got up in the morning. But then came what the HUD had noticed: eight volleys of laser-guided forty-millimeter cannon shells, coming at him at three hundred rounds per minute. Tony was less than twenty feet off the ground, and approaching the ToT pavilion nearly head-on, which made him for all intents and purposes a stationary target. The volley lasted ten seconds, during which the eight Army drones fired off four hundred rounds. Maybe ten percent of them hit Tony directly. Another two or three strays hit War Machine, keeping Rhodey's attention on the here and now. The rest ripped through the Expo like a hurricane of shrapnel. Trees disintegrated. Streetlights exploded before the poles themselves were chopped to bits. The facades of buildings in the field of fire blew apart in clouds of concrete dust and blooming fire. It was the beginning of the end of the Stark Expo. It was also the end of the end for both of the remaining Air Force drones, which hadn't gotten far enough out of their service rivals' field of fire. They were falling in fiery pieces out of the sky amid fluttering leaves and—incongruously—cherry blossoms. Tony hadn't remembered calling for cherry trees out in this part of the Expo. He thought they were all in the dome on the other side of the Tent of Tomorrow. Hm.

As the first fusillade hammered into Tony's armor, he returned fire with a full-on raking sweep of repulsor bolts. The Army drones blew into pieces along with large parts of the pavilion, but he didn't think he'd gotten all of them. He fired again, from a little closer to the ground, focusing on the drones that still looked upright and functioning.

The next Stark Expo, Tony decided, was going to be different. A lot different.

If he lived to do another Stark Expo, that was. The forty-millimeter pounding he'd just taken had slowed Tony down and set off more status alerts and recorded-Jarvis alarm messages than Tony could keep track of. He let off another series of repulsor bolts in the general direction of the remaining Army drones, just to buy himself some time, and then War Machine crashed into him and drove him the rest of the way into the ground.

Tony had not spent much time working on close combat in the suit. His preferred method was to hit the other guy before the other guy knew he was there, or failing that to stay far enough away that he could hit the other guy and the other guy couldn't do anything about it. If this was cowardice, that was fine. It seemed to Tony like common sense. He had sparred quite a bit with Happy to get the basics of hand-to-hand combat in his head, but he'd never really had much of a chance to work out how that translated into suit-to-suit combat. After all, he'd only been in a suit-to-suit fight twice—once with Rhodey and once with Obadiah Stane. Pretty small sample size, he thought. No way to know what worked and what didn't.

But here was data point number three. Tony took off again, powering up into the air with War Machine grappling along his back. War Machine wrenched Tony off course and sent them both scraping along the side of a building, peeling off a floor's worth of windows and a long line of steel framing underneath them.

"Aaahhh!" Tony cried out. "I will remember you did that."

They shot clear of the building, out toward the edge of the Expo grounds. Tony braked hard, pivoting him and War Machine around their collective center of gravity. War Machine's grip on him loosened, and Tony took the opportunity to fling War Machine—with the unfortunate Rhodey inside yelling all kinds of unprintable things on the HUD-to-HUD frequency—into the base of a freeway overpass abutment. The force of the impact buried the War Machine suit halfway in the concrete. Cars on the freeway, some of which had stopped at seeing the unfolding carnage at the expo, started going again. For the vast majority of people, having a flying suit of armor crash into the bridge you were standing on brought the show a little too close for comfort.

Stay there for a while, Tony thought. At least until I can get your software problems fixed, get rid of all these drones, save the lives of these poor saps running around my Expo, find Pepper, and settle Ivan Vanko's hash once and for all.

That wasn't so much to ask, was it?

CHAPTER 34

Having left Rhodey more or less entombed in the bridge abutment while Jarvis tried to sort out what the hell was going on with the War Machine's stubbornly impossible-to-crack security, Tony decided to ping Natalie and find out what she had found. He was blasting over a canal that ran along one edge of the Expo property, using the kicked-up spray to hide out from the remaining drones while he assessed his systems and figured out how the rest of the world had been getting along in his absence.

"Hello?" Natalie—dammit, Natasha—said as her face appeared in a little square of Tony's HUD. It was a still photo. She wasn't linking with video.

"Natalie, what the hell is going on?" he asked.

He could tell she was moving. "We're getting close," she said, breathing a little hard.

"Well, get closer faster." Tony ran a three-dimensional radar sweep and detected no drones and no pursuit of any

other kinds. "We need some answers. We've got your pro-
verbial handbasket of hell here."

"That's not the proverb," Natashalie observed.

"From you I need information," Tony said. "Not cor-
rection. How close is close?"

"Close," she said.

"Call back when you know. Soon."

"Will do, Mr. Stark," she said, and clicked off.

Still not seeing any pursuit, Tony slowed and hooked
around the back side of one of the local subway ventila-
tion towers that also housed an electrical substation for
the Expo's utility needs. He'd had a couple of ideas about
how to attack the War Machine problem, and now that
there was a moment to breathe before he got answers from
Natalie, he thought he'd try them out. All of this would
be a lot easier if he had Rhodey on his side instead of just
sitting around while his suit along with a million drones
tried to mash and blast Tony into a gruesome organic-
mechanical slurry.

"Jarvis," he said. "Reroute Rhodey's base operating
system. Attack the kernel . . . "

"Displaying kernel contents."

Tony watched the kernel code, rendered as a graphic
on his HUD. He figured that's where the problem must be,
since the War Machine's hardware hadn't been touched
after installation and the control systems applications
were still functional. The kernel was the part of an operating system that let hardware and software talk to
each other. In the case of the War Machine suit, it was
the part of the operating systems that turned instructions
from, say, the fire control and flight navigation software
packages into real-time actions. It was also what reported

back to those software packages what the hardware was doing. It stood to reason that if you were going to commandeer an immensely sophisticated piece of equipment and couldn't either run the onboard systems or affect the hardware, you'd go for the interface between the two. Once you'd convinced both sides of the conversation that you knew what the other one was doing, you could tell them anything, pretend it was something else, and they'd do it. In vastly oversimplified terms, it was like the old game you played with a little kid. Why are you hitting yourself? Why are you hitting yourself?

If Tony was right, he—and Jarvis—were about to figure out a way for Rhodey's suit to stop hitting itself. Then it could start hitting the bad guys like it was supposed to, and things would sort themselves out pretty quickly. This was an outcome devoutly to be wished.

"How's that look, Jarvis?" he asked.

"Most promising, sir," Jarvis said. "I believe we will find this a fruitful line of inquiry."

"Outstanding. Nothing I love more than fruitful lines," Tony said. He was about to say something else, to see if he could get Jarvis flustered, but right then the War Machine suit walked through the wall of the substation and the whole fight was on again.

Rhodey's suit was damaged from the cannon fire and the impact with thousands of tons of concrete and rebar. The Gatling gun didn't fire right and some other smaller projectile systems that couldn't hurt Tony anyway were no longer functional. So now they were down to the old hand-to-hand again. "This makes me feel dirty," Tony said as he took a punch in the head and threw one back. "It's so intimate. I don't want to know you this well."

"Imagine how I feel," Rhodey said. "I know where you've been."

"You catty old woman," Tony said. "You need a boyfriend."

Rhodey yanked him into the building and started pounding on him. It seemed to Tony that either the War Machine suit was better designed for close combat or Rhodey was better trained, or both. The fact of the situation was that Tony was getting his ass kicked—in real time, as Rhodey had said a few weeks before about the first encounter with Ivan Vanko.

Tony struggled free, his head ringing, and slipped War Machine's next attempt at grappling by sidestepping it and delivering a roundhouse kick that would have powdered the skull and jellied the brain of an ordinary human. Rhodey's suit, unfazed, kept coming. "I'm watching all of this happen," Rhodey said, "and I still can't believe it."

"Pretty unbelievable, yeah," Tony said. "I mean, who would have thought that the military would do something unsavory with my design? That's really amazing. I still can't believe it's happening."

"Tell you what, when you can stay sober enough on your birthday that you're not about to blow some girl's head off playing William Tell with a watermelon, then you can lecture me about what's unsavory," Rhodey said. They were trading punches along with words. Tony got sick of the whole thing and blasted off, wanting distance from Rhodey at least until Rhodey had control of the War Machine. Then if he wanted to fight, that was fine. But he didn't want to listen to Rhodey complaining while Tony pounded on the suit Rhodey was wearing despite the fact that Rhodey wasn't trying to use the suit to attack Tony.

In addition to time for a War Machine operating system solution to present itself, Tony needed a little me time to figure out what was still working on the Mark VI and what wasn't. The next time he had to fight a drone army, he would be better off if he knew how the suit and its weapons systems were functioning.

He took off. To his surprise, War Machine grabbed his leg.

"Let go!" Tony shouted.

"I can't!" Rhodey shouted back. Tony's thrusters weren't quite at full capacity and the two of them started to tumble. War Machine—or whoever was controlling it—had decided to really pull out the stops. Bullets whined and spanged off Tony's armor, and one of Rhodey's fists, like a platinum pile driver, hammered dents in the Mark VI, damaging important circuitry every time. The Mark VI was stronger, faster, and better-looking than any of the other Iron Man suits, but its sleekness meant that it didn't have much space for systems backups. If this physical pounding kept up, more and more of Tony's systems were going to be out. He could imagine how that would end, either with War Machine or Whiplash. He didn't like either outcome.

They grappled across the landscape of the Expo, gyros whining and repulsor thrusters firing in all directions. "Jarvis?" Tony prompted. "Need some good news here."

"It would appear as if one of the kernel modules has been altered," Jarvis said. "It is the in the area of executable instructions."

"Aha," Tony said. "Any idea what it's supposed to look like?"

"One might suppose that it would resemble other

kernels from other advanced Defense Department projects," Jarvis said. "In any event, that is where one would begin, were one to desire a new kernel that operates as it was intended."

"Do I—oof—detect a hint that you have maybe already constructed such a kernel, Jarvis, you devil, you?"

"Perhaps, sir. If you are extremely vigilant and attuned to the idiosyncrasies of my programming, you will perhaps have noticed that an executable code module is currently resident in the Mark VI suit's download quarantine. At some point, should you wish to do something with it, that would of course be your prerogative."

"Outstanding," Tony said. He and War Machine, looking for all the world like one of the comical failed projects from the videos Tony had played at the Senate hearing, tumbled and spiraled across the Expo, punching a hole through the geodesic dome that stood at the other end of the lake from the still-rotating Unisphere.

Inside the dome, they fell to the ground, landing next to a quiet pool ringed by cherry trees. As outside, so inside, Tony thought. He wondered if he'd been subconsciously toying with that principle when he put the whole thing together. Odd how rampaging through your own creation while deranged robots blew it apart gave you a whole new perspective on it. Their impact shook blossoms loose and sent ripples across the face of the pool as pieces of glass and steel pinged and shattered on the floor.

Tony didn't waste any time. The minute he got the edge on War Machine, through a simple leg sweep takedown, he took advantage of it. One of the doodads he'd built into the Mark IV despite not being convinced he'd ever really have a use for it was a retractable stiletto spike made of tungsten and sitting on a spring that ejected it from its slot at velocities sufficient to punch it through the armor of an Abrams tank. It was also—and this was the part that Tony had built in even though it had seemed kind of frivolous at the time—cored with a high-powered wireless antenna capable of T3-plus upload and download speeds. You just never knew, Tony thought.

"Sorry about this," he said to Rhodey as the War Machine suit hit the deck on its back. Tony extruded the spike and Rhodey's eyes nearly popped out of his head. He started forming words, but nothing came out and Tony wouldn't have heard anyway because he had shut off the HUD-to-HUD channel so he could concentrate on getting the spike aimed . . . right . . .

Shling!

There. He buried it in the base of the suit's neck, missing Rhodey's own neck by maybe a centimeter and piping Jarvis' new kernel through the spike into the onboard network. War Machine went inert. Rhodey was talking—Tony could feel the vibrations through the spike—but no sound came through because the suit was down.

"Rebooting systems," Jarvis said smoothly.

About thirty seconds later, the War Machine suit came back online, system by system. Rhodey sat up, and Tony let him. They settled next to each other on the edge of the pool, enjoying the peace and quiet for a moment. It sure was nice inside this dome. Tony had wanted it to be a space where contemplation and reflection could be enshrined the way that innovation and the aggressive pursuit of progress were in the rest of the Expo. There were Western-style rock gardens interspersed with *karesansui*, Zen rock gardens complete with rakes for people who wanted to get away from the Expo for a little bit and create a bit of internal peace. There were something like a hundred cherry trees winding along the edges of the pool and the paths that circled the pool and wound through the gardens. It occurred to Tony that he might like it if some of the grounds of the Malibu house were like this. That was something to look into once everything had been settled here.

"Feeling better?" Tony asked after a bit.

"I'm so sorry," Rhodey said.

Tony thought for a minute about how easily some people could apologize. "We need to talk," he said.

CHAPTER 35

The trail of carnage she'd left in her wake on their way from front door to lab door was more than enough to make Happy nod instead of argue when Natasha said, "Wait here." He looked abashed as she headed into the lab, and she felt a little bad for him. It wasn't his fault that he was old-fashioned and that his way of fighting was a little bit like a zip gun in a roomful of Bofors L70 auto-cannons. But she didn't have time to coddle him, either, or to massage his wounded masculine ego. There were homicidal maniacs and threats to national security that required her immediate attention.

What she found in the lab was evidence of admirable creative energy and further evidence of two savage murders. The bodies of the two security guards lay in various locations around the floor and ceiling. Ivan had left them as a message to whoever might come looking for him. Each of their right hands sat on a small table next to the access touchscreen at the lab's security door. Clearly Ivan had removed the guards' hands and used them to get out. As for the rest, there were discarded prototype drones, bits and pieces of arc reactor models, a complete machine shop and tool-and-die works newly built in one corner, and an incredible mess. Unused or broken parts lay where they had fallen on the floor or on tables. Cables, conduits, and hoses ran from here to there all over the space, with no visible system or guiding principle. Computers were left on, their screens displaying information that in any reasonable security regime would have been hidden away immediately upon use.

The psychological implications of the space were clear to her. The man who worked in a space such as this was obsessive and brilliant, a determined loner with a pure hatred of standards and practices and traditional ways of doing things such as lab work. He did things his own way not only because he could—he was smart enough to re- member where everything had fallen and always find it again—but because he had to. He was the oppositional, tragic, doomed individual hero against how the entire ap- paratus of state and culture and capital stood arrayed.

How very Russian, Natasha thought. All that was miss- ing were vodka bottles scattered all over the floor and an inch-thick coating of cigarette ash on every surface.

She dialed Tony. "He's gone," she said.

With cherry blossoms drifting around him, Tony said, "Well, where is he?"

He missed whatever Natalie said in response because his attention was drawn to the entry—through the wall,

shattering the peace and quiet he and Rhodey had until
then been enjoying—of what was apparently the last remaining Army drone. It was slightly the worse for wear,
with obvious repulsor burns and scoring on its armor, but
it was moving on its own two feet, and it apparently had
not lost track of its mission.

Having hung up on Natasha, Tony opened a HUD-to-
HUD with Rhodey. "Well," he said. "You ready to make
it up to me?"

"I think we got this," Rhodey said. They stood facing
the lone drone.

Then they heard a rumble from outside the dome, and
more blossoms began to shake loose from the cherry
trees. The rumble grew louder, its vibrations coming up
through the soles of their boots, and out of the dimness at
the highest point of the dome's ceiling descended sixteen
more drones. The Marines had arrived. So had the Navy.
The reinforcements landed in a precise pattern, creating
a crossfire but keeping each other out of the planned field
of fire. Either they had learned from the demise of the
last two Air Force drones or they were executing routines
that the Army drones hadn't had time to execute. Whatever the cause, the odds were now seventeen to two. Tony
kind of felt like he'd just done his part, where he was in
the middle of a bunch of drones pointing guns at him.
The only difference from last time, when he'd been on the
stage at the Tent of Tomorrow, was that this time Rhodey was on his side instead of a captive of the bad guys.
Which was a substantial improvement.

"Or not," Tony said.

Where before there had been drifts of cherry blossoms,
now there was a blizzard; the pool looked like you could

walk across it on them. And the dome was filled with tons of hostile iron and electronics, with systems locked, loaded, and zeroed in on Iron Man and War Machine.

The Army drone had come in first and it took the initiative. With a ratcheting whine, a missile rack opened up out of its shoulders and snapped into position.

Tony didn't waste any time. He was closest. He stepped up and reached out, tearing the rack from the drone's torso while it was still executing the firing routine. Before it could abort, Tony had taken the launch tube and turned it around. The missile fired, annihilating the robot's upper half and temporarily whiting out Tony's heads-up.

He let it drop and said, "That's one."

Not that they were keeping score.

"Where are the rest of the drones going?" Coulson wondered.

"My guess is in Tony's direction," Pepper said. She tried Tony again. He didn't answer. "Hi, this is Tony Stark, and you're Pepper Potts," said his voicemail, which was run by an intelligent subroutine of Jarvis that deployed individualized messages for each person in Tony's inner circle who might call. "Right now you don't know where I am, and probably I want to keep it that way. So maybe you should leave me a message about why it's critically important that I call you, and how I'm failing both you and myself by not being here, and then once I get feeling good and guilty about it I'll give you a ring and we can work it out. Okay?"

Beeeeep.

Pepper hung up. There could be any number of reasons

why Tony might not answer the phone. Out of all those possible reasons, there was only one that involved him being dead. She made a firm decision to go with the odds and believe he was alive and otherwise engaged. Probably with all of those drones she and Coulson had just seen.

Back to the task at hand, then, which was making sure that Justin Hammer did not get out of the Expo unless it was in handcuffs. What a list of charges he was going to face, Pepper thought. Unless . . .

She cut a glance at Coulson. He looked like a middle-school history teacher. It was hard to believe that he was part of an organization that made people disappear, or faked reports of how they died, like they'd done with Obie Stane.

Would they do something like that with Hammer? And would she do anything about it if she found out they were about to?

Let's see, she thought. He was a mass-murdering, fugitive-harboring, research-stealing liar who was at the helm of the biggest defense contractor in the United States. Maybe he should just disappear. Maybe people like that shouldn't be allowed to exist.

But Pepper didn't want to live in a world where the good guys made decisions like that. She wanted him to stand trial before a jury of his peers, with the best lawyers his money could buy, and then she wanted him to spend the rest of his life in prison. Because that's how civilized people did things.

As if she had conjured him, there he was, skulking along the edges of the crowd that even now was pressing toward the front gate. There had been maybe fifty thousand people on the Expo grounds when all hell had broken loose. Maybe more. It took a while to get them all moving in the right direction and out the doors.

"There he is," Pepper said, pointing. Coulson was closer. He headed in Hammer's direction. Pepper started to follow, putting her phone away; then she froze still as a rabbit when with a flash of light and a crack that rang in her ears, Ivan Vanko appeared to snap his whips in front of her.

She looked past him, but Coulson was already gone into the milling crowds, working his way toward Hammer. Even if he'd heard Ivan, he was too far away to do anything. And this Ivan was different, not the half-naked invader of the Monaco race track. This Ivan was armored in a deranged parody of the Mark IV suit, gleaming like a gladiator, his hair loose and face obscured behind a triangular mask. This Ivan Vanko reminded her of Obadiah Stane. He loomed between her and Coulson, between her and safety.

"Congratulations on the new job," he said.

CHAPTER 36

The scene inside the dome, unfolding in the storm of cherry blossoms, was like an old samurai movie. Two men, old friends recently reconciled after a bitter quarrel, stand back to back, facing overwhelming odds. They survive because each relies unquestioningly on the other and because truth and justice and right are on their side— also because they are just better than the other guys. The rabble of enemies charge them and fall back, charge and fall back, and allow themselves to be picked off because they lack the discipline of our back-to-back heroes.

All you had to do was add suits of armor so technologically advanced they were nearly sentient, and change the enemy rabble to a double rank of implacably menacing robots packing heavy weapons, and you had exactly the situation in the contemplative, reflective space of the geodesic dome. Tony normally enjoyed this type of irony, but at the moment he was sick of the way everyone was wrecking his Expo. Particularly he had had it with the damage being done to the dome, which had felt like a minor personal triumph when he'd thought of it. He remembered saying to Pepper at the time that he normally didn't consider contemplation as a part of the innovative process, and that maybe he would try to do that in the future.

Since then, of course, he'd been nearly dying of palladium poisoning and he had become, in Pepper's phrase, the worst version of himself. But he was on the verge of changing that. It was marvelous how your outlook could change when you knew you weren't going to die any minute.

Well, except Tony didn't know that. But he did know that he wasn't going to keel over dead from palladium toxicity, and that was a good thing.

And if he was going to die today, he would at least take some drones with him. He could hardly stop himself from yelling Yippeekiyay . . .

Foom! One of the Navy drones went up in a small mushroom cloud that Tony recognized as the type produced by an overloaded RT. Usually they just shut down, but if there were impurities in the arc space at the heart of the RT, sometimes they went boom. One more Navy drone down. Rhodey was in the process of holding one of the Marine drones down while his various weapons chewed through its armor and ricocheted around inside through all of the vital electronics. It jerked and spasmed in a way so lifelike that for an unsettling moment Tony was certain that that particular drone must have had a human operator. Gross, he thought, and tore the arm from another one that had gotten its thumb stuck in one of the Mark IV's joints. He jerked the thumb free and cracked the drone with its own arm before dropping the mangled limb and clamping one hand over the empty socket. The drone set off grenades in his face, but Tony held on, unleashing a repulsor bolt straight into the empty socket. A muffled whump was the only sound that came out, but the drone fell limp as its internal electronics were vaporized or melted into silicon mush.

"Ahoy pal," Tony said HUD-to-HUD. "Taking bets on whether we get this done before Ivan shows up to take advantage of us in our weakness."

Rhodey was having his own brand of fun. The drones came thick and fast, but they were outclassed. As long as they stayed more or less back-to-back, keeping an eye on each other, neither letting the other get completely surrounded, they were going to be just fine. And man, was it fun to fight an enemy and not have to worry about its humanity, or about ethics of any kind. You could do anything to a drone. You could beat it to pieces with its own limbs, a la the old joke, and it didn't make you crazy. It made you efficient because you were saving ammunition. What could be better?

"Well, now, that would be just like him to take advantage, wouldn't it?" Rhodey said.

"Thing is," Tony said, and then paused briefly to put a Rhodey-crippled drone out of its mechanical misery. "Thing is, if he's not coming here, then where's he hiding? I mean, really. If you want to kill me, here I am."

"I don't want to kill you," Rhodey said. "Not right now, anyway."

They combined fire on a Marine drone that looked to be setting up some kind of heavy munitions that neither one of them wanted to know anything about. Rhodey pinned it down and chewed it up with the big machine gun and Tony finished it off. Whatever it had been setting up went off with an intense heat flash that melted the drone to a puddle. "What do you think, Rhodey?" Tony said. "Thermite, something like that?"

"Looked like it burned hotter than that. Tell you what, remember the spot and we'll figure it out later."

In the middle of all this, Pepper called. Again. Tony had ignored her last time because he and Rhodey were still having their moment, and you couldn't always just ignore guy time when the little woman called. Who in this case wasn't Tony's little woman and would probably have killed him on sight if she'd heard him call her that, or think of her like that . . . but the point, he was certain, still held. Bro's before ho's, was the pithiest expression of it.

Anyway, he and Rhodey were not enjoying a moment of a different sort, less intimate and more free-wheeling, so Tony didn't feel bad about answering the phone to let her know that there were lots of parts of drones flying in lots of directions, and no, she didn't have to worry about anything because as soon as he was done here he was going to go find Vanko and tie up that last troublesome loose end . . .

His lighthearted attitude evaporated the second he saw her face. She was mortally terrified, he could tell that even at the lousy resolution he got in heads-up images. "Pepper?" Tony said.

"Tony . . . " she said. And that's when the view shifted a little and he saw who else was there, and understood both her terror and why she had made the call.

Sometimes it seemed to Tony that the suit responded to

the intensity of his emotion, amping up just a little more when his fight-or-flight instincts were in full flower—in either direction. This time he felt it again, as he unloaded a repulsor bolt into the already-damaged grille of the nearest Marine drone, splattering slag and bits of electronic hardware across the nearest rock garden. Now why didn't that happen every time, he thought as he wound the pre-flight repulsor thrust modulators up to Warp 8, Save the Girl speed. Jarvis had already pinned down the location of Pepper's phone when she made the call.

"Where the hell are you going?" Rhodey shouted HUD-to-HUD, over the shriek of his Gatling gun and the answering thunder of various explosive projectiles from the diminishing number of drones. Tony counted two Marines and four Navy left. From seventeen to two, the odds had improved to six to one. Tony felt like he had done his part.

"Keep them contained. Don't let them into the fairgrounds," Tony said, and thundered away.

CHAPTER 37

Fifteen seconds later, Tony landed in front of Ivan and Pepper hard enough to shake the ground and cause a momentary swirl of interference across his heads-up. Vanko held Pepper in one hand, lazily flicking the tip of a whip around her feet. She was clearly terrified, but Pepper Potts was also one tough customer. She stood straight, didn't beg, didn't give him anything. Tony loved her in that moment like he'd never loved anyone else.

"Let her go," Tony said.

"If you take her place, maybe I will let her go," Vanko answered with a smirk and a flick of the whip.

"That what you want?" Tony said.

"No, Tony," Pepper said. "Don't do it."

In his HUD, Rhodey said, "Don't do what?"

"None of your business," Tony said. "Take care of the drones."

"They're about to be taken care of. Then I'm headed your way. Think I'll bring the ex-wife."

"Ex-wife? Reconciliation is good, I guess," Tony said.

Vanko, watching Tony but unable to hear his HUD-to-HUD conversation with War Machine suit, prompted him a little. "Fine woman you have here, Stark. She doesn't want you to be a fine man." Vanko winked. "Or maybe she knows you too well."

"Hope you're picking up the ex-wife soon, Rhodey," he said.

"Keep an eye out. I'll be coming in low and hot."

Tony triggered the armor's automatic-eject protocol. "No, Tony, no," Pepper was saying, but the suit fell away from Tony piece by piece, deconstructing itself from the helmet right down to the boots before folding itself into a scarlet and chrome rectangle not too much bigger than a bathroom scale.

"Okay, Ivan," he said. To Pepper he added, "Chivalry, Ms. Potts, is not dead."

"Easy, wasn't it?" Ivan said. He spread his arms, for all the world like the host of a party welcoming a long-awaited guest. "You think I want to kill your woman? No." *Snap!* went one of the whips. "I only want to kill you."

"We have a problem, then," Tony said. Never in his life had he hated anyone the way he hated Ivan Vanko right then. His hands were shaking with it. "Because what I want to do is kill you."

"On this we agree, Stark. So let's get on with the swap. You for her. Then you can play hero. In your head. While I kill you slowly for what you did to my father." Vanko let Pepper take a step away from him, but kept one of his whips curling near her feet. "Slowly, Pepper Potts," he said. "You wouldn't want to surprise me so I make sudden moves."

Tony walked toward him, measuring his pace so he got one step closer for every step she took away from Vanko. "It's not my fault your dad thought he could turn the arc reactor into an ATM," he said. "It was never meant as a way to get rich. And it's not my fault that you had to grow up in Siberia because your dad couldn't follow through on the promises he made to the Kremlin."

Snap!

Miscalculation, was the first thought that went thought Tony's head.

Amazement that he was still alive followed right on the heels of that thought. If the whip that Ivan Vanko had just flicked out to curl around Tony's neck had been charged, it would have melted through skin, muscle, tendon, and bone, decapitating Tony before he had ever seen Ivan make a move.

The whip wasn't charged, though, and instead of severing Tony's head, the whip looped around his neck and jerked him off balance, pulling him toward Vanko as Vanko's other whip sparked out. "Tony!" Pepper screamed. Her hesitation cost her, as Vanko flicked his recently deactivated whip out to capture her as well.

"Chivalry," Vanko said, "is dead."

The last time Tony had tangled with Vanko, he'd been wearing the previous version of the portable suit from the football and Vanko had been using an experimental prototype of his whips and the armored frame that supported them. Now Tony had no armor and Vanko had taken a cue from Tony and armored up as well. The odds were substantially altered, he had to admit.

Plus, Tony had to admit, he had handled the hostage-swap like an amateur.

Emotion had clouded his judgment. He'd left Rhodey in the middle of a crowd of drones so he could come zooming over here, get out of his armor, and hand himself over to Vanko like a willing sacrifice. A dumb, dumb, willing sacrifice.

"How do you like being the powerless one, Stark?" Vanko crooned. He flicked his wrist and the whip coiled a little tighter around Tony's neck. "I told you I was going to destroy in forty seconds what it took your family forty years to build. But perhaps it will take a little longer."

"Let him go," Pepper said.

Ivan chuckled, the same chilling low noise Tony had heard in the French jail cell. "Miss Potts," he said. "I've waited too long to get him. And now I don't think I will let you go either."

The whips slithered a little tighter around Tony's neck. "Please," Pepper said. "Tony."

Another slight contraction of the whip brought sparkles to the edge of Tony's field of vision. He looked at her and tried to speak, but the whip was too tight. "A little tighter, a little tighter," Vanko said softly.

"Tony," Pepper said.

He rolled his eyes in her direction, figuring that if Ivan Vanko was going to strangle him to death in front of her, at least he could try to maintain eye contact. Where, he wondered distantly as the blood supply to his head was slowly exhausted, was Rhodey? And his ex-wife?

Then he managed to focus his eyes, just for a moment, and saw that Pepper was trying to show him something—in her purse of all places. The Tech-Ball.

Stay with it, Tony demanded of himself. Stay with it. He tried to nod at her, but knew he couldn't because he was the sole focus of Vanko's attention. Vanko was even letting his whip fall from around Pepper's waist as his long-sought goal—the death of Tony Stark—came finally within his grasp. So he let his eyes stay a little unfocused and gave his best impression of someone slowly strangling to death. It wasn't a difficult performance to bring off.

"Think fast," Pepper said.

Tony looked over at her as she tossed the Tech-Ball to him, low and flat, the way a pitcher makes the toss to first on a sacrifice bunt down the first-base line. He got a hand up, more out of reflex than anything else, and watched as the Tech-Ball snapped itself into the glove shape he'd surprised Pepper with a couple of weeks before.

Things happened a lot faster after that. Tony got the glove up and caught the whip around his throat. Pulling himself to his feet, he snapped the whip off with a jerk and a twist of the glove. As it loosened up and oxygen flooded his brain, the world flooded into focus around Tony.

And he remembered Rhodey and his ex-wife.

"Pepper," he said. "Get out of here!"

But she wouldn't. Damn her, she was loyal and a little in love with him, and if that didn't get both of them killed, Tony thought, he was going to have to have words with her about it. His train of thought was derailed by a whip cracking through the air right in front of his face.

"Are we really doing this because of something you think my dad did to your dad?" Tony asked, dancing around in front of Vanko. "And what was that thing, exactly? You think my dad stole the arc reactor idea, right? That explains all of the mimicry and your whole shtick about me being a thief and a murderer? Because I don't think I'm a thief and a murderer. You, on the other hand, are a murderer for sure. Thief I don't know about. But you have killed a bunch of race car drivers, and I think a couple of Hammer's security guards, although maybe we can write those off to self-defense. What's your excuse for the drivers, though? Or for the people who died here today because of your drones? Is it their fault that your dad didn't get credit for the arc reactor?" Tony shook his head. "You're just nuts, is all. Your dad is a convenient excuse, but you're nuts. It's nobody's fault but your own."

He was trying to provoke Ivan, and it worked. But the reason he was trying to provoke Ivan was to get Ivan to ignore the fact that Tony was working around close to the new football containing the Mark VI, and simultaneously getting Ivan to forget about Pepper. It was working, it was working . . . Ivan came at him like a hundred buzz saws, and before Tony knew it he was dodging the whip as he stepped onto the football and bent backward from a last flick of the whip as the suit built itself around him. The next thing he knew, a whip snapped around his ankles and his feet were jerked out from under him. As he hit the ground, he was already starting to get up again, but then Ivan changed tactics.

He turned to look for Pepper again.

"No, no no," Tony said. He toggled the HUD. "Rhodey, now's a good time."

"Thank the Lord," Rhodey said. "I cannot wait to be rid of this here ex-wife."

If things had happened fast before then, they all

happened at once now. Tony took advantage of Vanko being distracted to hammer him to the pavement. He caught Pepper around the waist, hearing the rumble of Rhodey's thrusters and—thanks to the hypersensitive electronics in the Mark VI—the slightly lower thrum of the Ex-Wife's smart guidance jet.

And then he blasted away up into the air over the Stark Expo as below them, the entire front of the Tent of Tomorrow disappeared in a huge blooming sphere of fire and debris.

"Pretty good throw," he said to Pepper. "For a girl."

CHAPTER 38

They landed on the roof of a ten- or twelve-story building just on the other side of the Expo grounds, not far from one of the ramps onto the Grand Central Parkway. Tony set Pepper down and took a step back. He breathed in and out, slowly, feeling the bruises Ivan Vanko's whip had left both on his skin and inside, on his trachea.

"What were you thinking?" Pepper yelled at him. "Why did you take off your suit?"

He triggered the protocol to deconstruct the suit and stood there in front of her. "I was trying to be selfless," he said.

"Selfless!?" she repeated.

"Yeah, selfless. Is that so weird?"

Pepper boggled at him.

"Don't answer that," Tony said.

For a minute he watched the fires burn. It was kind of like watching the shadow of his father burn away. The steps on the front of the Tent of Tomorrow, destroyed by the Ex-Wife, were now Ivan Vanko's funeral pyre. Fathers, Tony thought. The things they lead you to do. Part of him rebelled against the idea that he and Vanko had anything in common.

But part of him had to admit that if he'd grown up with a father fueled by frustration and rage in Siberia, he might well have turned out more along the lines of Ivan Vanko than Tony Stark.

"Selfless," Pepper said again. "Tony, you've never played the hero because you were selfless."

There were maybe a hundred different things he could have said then. His choices included bluster, bravado, self-pity . . . he could have played the *don't you know I was dying?* card or the *my drinking problem affected my behavior* card. He could have talked about how he needed to live up to his father's example, or how he never felt good enough and so he had to drive himself in all kinds of unhealthy directions to compensate. He'd said all of those things before, and meant at least some of them. But right now, looking out over the wreckage of his father's dream as the remains of the crowd made it to their cars and as helicopters started to arrive from local TV and national cable stations, he couldn't say any of them.

Instead Tony took a breath and said, simply, "I'm sorry."

"Wow," Pepper said. She took a moment to savor the moment. "For a first apology, that was decent. Apology accepted." Something out in the Expo blew up, possibly drone ammunition cooking off beneath the burning geodesic dome. She reached out and and took his hand. "I missed you."

"I missed you, too," he said, taking her other hand. Sirens rose in the distance.

Then Pepper said, "I quit."

"What?"

"I can't be CEO," she explained. "It's too stressful, it . . . I just can't do it."

"So you don't want to quit," Tony said. "You want a different job. Less responsibility. But I bet you want the same salary."

"Actually, after this I think you owe me a raise."

"A raise? After I nearly get strangled by a crazy Russian who had a grudge against my father, you have the nerve to ask for a raise?"

"Imagine how Stark Industries stock is going to take off now that Iron Man has shown up and taken care of business," she said.

"Spoken like a true CEO," he said, half-hoping that she would admit that she really didn't want to step down. He didn't want to step up again; he liked being the profligate boy genius down in the lab. But maybe Tony had finally reached the day when he started dealing with things like a grown-up instead of the brilliant, lonely, eccentric inheritor of a great industrial empire.

Pepper shook her head. "No, sir. I am your subordinate again."

"Hm," he said. "I'm not sure how I should respond to that."

"Carefully," Pepper warned.

"I'm not so good at careful," Tony said, and before he could convince himself not to, he leaned in and kissed her. It was a long kiss, slow and sensuous, and it lit both of them on fire. In that kiss were all the times that they had ever wanted to kiss but hadn't. Tony couldn't remember another kiss like it, with any woman at any time. Pepper was one of a kind.

When at last it broke, he wasn't sure what to say. As she usually did, Pepper stepped in. "Was that weird?" she asked.

Tony thought about it. Of course it was weird . . . wasn't it? They'd been avoiding it for years, coming close to it without ever doing it, feeling strange and upset about the possibility, letting the tension sublimate itself into banter and flirtation . . . so of course it was weird.

Except . . .

"No," he said. "I liked it."

"You liked it? Just liked it?"

"I really liked it. It was . . . it felt good. You know?"

Pepper shook her head and cut her eyes away from him. "You sure know how to romance a girl, Mr. Stark."

"Well, I tell you what," came Rhodey's voice. Startled, both of them looked at him. He was sitting on the edge of the roof, still suited up, with the face shield open. "I think it was weird," he said.

"Good thing you didn't have to do it, then," Tony said.

"In fact, it was so weird that I'm feeling a little traumatized," Rhodey went on. "I might have to keep this suit just to make myself feel better. So I can make the bad memories go away."

"Keep my suit?" Tony said.

"It's not your suit. This here suit is the property of the United States Air Force." Rhodey thumped his chest and then saluted the skyline.

"It's Stark technology," Pepper said. "I was just arguing with a general about that this morning."

"Well, whoever the tech belongs to, I'm keeping this suit. Maybe when Iron Man takes a day off, I'll step in." Rhodey was getting a bit more serious. Tony wasn't sure how he felt about this. A day off for Iron Man? What would that mean, especially now that Pepper wasn't CEO anymore?

I might have to work for a living, Tony thought. At least until I can figure a way to get out of it.

He walked over to Rhodey and stuck out his hand. Rhodey stuck out a gauntlet and they shook. "Thanks for dropping by with the ex-wife," Tony said.

Rhodey acknowledged the thanks with a little dip of his head. "It was time for her to go," he said. "I'd been carrying her long enough. She needed to earn her keep."

"There is just nothing that the two of you can't turn into frat-boy humor," Pepper said. "Is there?"

Tony and Rhodey thought about it. They looked at her. "Probably not," Tony said. "But you can keep trying if you want to."

He walked back over to her and put an arm around her waist. They looked out over the ruined Expo. Anton Vanko's funeral pyre had spread, and now burned all along the front of the Tent of Tomorrow. Smaller fires burned all across the grounds of the Expo where drone missiles had ignited or where drones themselves had crashed. The air was full of sirens, as every fire department in the tri-state area responded to the chaos.

"Later," Rhodey said. "I've got a suit to hide and all kinds of superior officers I should tell lies to."

War Machine's face shield snapped down and he blasted away from the roof, riding a bright blue spark into the sky and trailing an arc of condensation like a jet's contrail as he vanished quickly over and beyond the Manhattan skyline.

"Huh," Tony said.

"Huh what?"

"I never saw the suit fly away before." Tony turned and winked at her. "Wicked cool."

ABOUT THE AUTHOR

Alexander Irvine's most recent novels are *Buyout* and *The Narrows*. He is the author of nonfiction books including *The Vertigo Encyclopedia* and *John Winchester's Journal*, as well as comic series *Daredevil Noir* and *Hellstorm, Son of Satan: Equinox*. He teaches at the University of Maine. Find out more at http://alexanderirvine.net.